THE CUILLIN DEAD

A D.I. DUNCAN MCADAM MYSTERY

THE MISTY ISLE
BOOK 4

J M DALGLIESH

First published by Hamilton Press in 2024

ISBN (Trade Paperback) 978-1-80080-310-7
ISBN (Hardback) 978-1-80080-420-3
ISBN (Large Print) 978-1-80080-552-1

Look out for the link at the end of this book or visit my website at **www.jmdalgliesh.com** to sign up to my no-spam VIP Club and receive a FREE novella from my Hidden Norfolk series plus news and previews of forthcoming works.

Never miss a new release.

No spam, ever, guaranteed. You can unsubscribe at any time.

SCOTTISH NAMES

Places

Uist - (Ooist)

Portree - (Por-tree)

Strathaird - (Strath- air-ed)

Sgùrr Alasdair - (Sgur Alasdair)

Eynort - (Eye Nort)

Sgùrr nan Eag - (Sgur nan e-ch)

Sligachan - (Slee-gak-an)

Scavaig - (Scar-vaig)

Cuillin - (Cue-illin)

Maelrubha - (May-all-Roo-ar)

Elgol - (El-gol)

Coruisk - (Cur-ishk)

Ullinish - (Oo-lin-ish)

SCOTTISH PHRASES AND SLANG

Slang
   Wee - (Small)
   Cannae - (Cannot / can't)
   Dinnae - (Did not / didn't)
   Disnae - (Does not)
   Nae - (No)
   Bam - (Someone who is daft or misbehaving)
   Ned - (Young troublemaker or criminal)

THE CUILLIN DEAD

PROLOGUE

THERE IS a gentle breeze tonight which I am thankful for. My skin is still clammy to the touch and I've got this headache that I've been unable to shift for the last two days. It's this damn heat. There are two to three weeks a year where we have weather like this and every time it feels like a personal torture. I'm not prepared for it. It's something to do with the genes, I reckon. Fair enough if I'm deployed in Afghanistan or Iraq because you expect it there, but not here.

I'm grateful that we're not out on exercise somewhere but, then again, having something useful to be doing would help focus the mind as well as help pass the time. Instead, I'm standing here in this little box on the main gate, alone. At least during the daytime there would be someone else to speak to along with the comings and goings of daily activity as people pass in and out. No one comes through here in the wee small hours though, unless it's after the pubs have kicked out on the weekend. No, this night is going to drag. I know it.

I can feel the sweat inside my shirt running down my back. I'm hot and sticky, my skin is crawling. What wouldn't I give for a cool shower just now? This is my third rotation where

I've pulled guard duty overnight and I know full well why that is. I'm not going to give him the satisfaction of showing my displeasure though. He'll be looking for it, looking for that chink in the armour that he can exploit.

However, I'm not confident I'll win through when all is said and done. I'm stubborn, certainly, but I'm not stupid. One thing I do know is that I'll go down fighting. I've been up against the likes of him before and I'll stand my ground even if I have to take a kicking every once in a while. My old man taught me that. It's arguably one of the few things he did teach me, that and not to accept drinks from strangers in foreign climes, although that also works when you're back home too. I've learned that the hard way.

No one gives you anything for nothing. There's always a cost... and the payback can be painful.

Stepping out of the gatehouse, I look up at the stars. They're dimmed by the light pollution from the nearby town and the base lights along the road don't help either, but I can still make out the familiar families of the constellations. They are the same here as they were in the night sky back home, but they are more plentiful and vivid once the sun goes down. Here, they're muted.

In Afghan, once out beyond the wire, the sky was wondrous to behold. The patterns above us were different obviously, and I'd love to go back one day and take the time to view them properly. Out on patrol was not the time, but when we laid up for a bit and I wasn't on watch, I used to take in what I could.

Being out there, so far from home, and seeing the vastness of the universe made me realise just how insignificant we are. *How insignificant he is.* He can do his worst, but he'll not beat me down. Pulling in a deep breath of warm air, I feel the skin on my arms prickle as I stare out into the darkness, along the fence line and into the trees beyond. *What is it that's caught my eye?* Tensing ever so slightly, I narrow my eyes as I peer into the gloom wishing I had a set of NODs to help. I've learned to trust my instincts over the years, instincts honed in several conflict zones in faraway lands I never knew existed let alone could point to on a map.

A flash of light from deep within the trees followed by a familiar crack splits the peace of the humid night and I'm diving for cover, hitting the ground hard and scurrying to get my back up against the wall of the gatehouse. There was no whistle though... no fizz of a round passing overhead.

Now, there is only silence. Was I mistaken? No... I know what I heard, and it was unmistakable. A second crack. Another round discharged, but not towards me. Keeping low, I crawl back inside the gatehouse and reach blindly for the telephone receiver on the desk above me whilst gathering my service rifle in my hands. I'm breathing heavily, but muscle memory takes over, phone clamped between my shoulder and the side of my head. I don't have to think as I check the magazine is in place, the safety catch is to the right, and I pull the cocking handle back and release it, chambering a round.

Just in case.

But I know what this is. When I saw them earlier, I had a thought that something was wrong. I hope, for their sake, I'm wrong this time too...

CHAPTER ONE

THE SOUND of the waves crashing against the cliff face far below carries up on the breeze. The oystercatchers, whirling overhead, are calling out their warnings about the incomers before descending to the giant outcrop, weather-beaten and hewn from the basalt by repetitive Atlantic storms. Duncan stands back, away from the edge of the clifftop, gently buffeted by the wind coming at him from the direction of the Western Isles.

Looking towards Uist, feeling the warmth of the sunshine on his face, the fact he can no longer see the islands is ominous. The path used to be much further back from the new fence that kept the grazing sheep from venturing too close to the edge. On this side of the boundary, the path narrowed at the far edge of the croft, bringing the path to less than two feet in width, and precariously close to the cliff edge that'd been gradually collapsing into the water below for some years.

Come away from there," Duncan said. "Psst! Come away."

The dog ignored him, far more interested as it was in the birds whirling and diving to the outcrop barely twenty feet from them. Twenty feet as the crow flies, but it may as well be twenty miles when it came to the dog. He wouldn't make it. The leap was far too great but something told Duncan that in its mind, the dog fancied its chances.

"Hey, Derek!" Duncan shouted at Grace's golden doodle - what he considered to be an expensive mongrel - stepping forward and reaching for the animal's collar, bringing him closer to the edge than he'd like and catching a glimpse of the frothing water below. Feeling an almost overwhelming urge to jump, Duncan recoiled from the edge, leaving the dog to choose its own fate. "Stupid animal," he muttered beneath his breath.

"That's not how you talk to dogs, Duncan."

Duncan turned to see Grace clambering over the stile, camera hanging from a strap around her neck, approaching him with a smile. "Oh, is that right?"

"Aye," Grace said. "He'll not listen to you unless he respects you anyway."

"Sounds just like your mum then," Duncan said with a wry grin. Inclining his head towards the dog, he nodded at it. "I think your wee dog there has a death wish."

Grace smiled and looked at Derek, still inching ever closer to the cliff edge, his tail erect and twitching excitedly. Grace whistled and the dog glanced her way before momentarily looking back at the potential prey before throwing in the towel and coming back to Grace's side, and sitting down obediently.

"You've got it well trained."

"I have him well trained," Grace said.

"He, it... whatever," Duncan said, glancing out to sea. "We'd better get back to the house. I reckon we have fifteen to twenty minutes before the heavens open."

"Aye, right enough," Grace said, following Duncan's gaze towards the weather front moving towards them. Walking past Duncan, she set off descending the slope back to the shore. The descent would take them around five minutes and then they'd have to climb over the rocks to access the road. Then it would be another five to ten minutes to walk back to Duncan's croft house.

"Did you get what you needed?" Duncan asked.

"More or less," Grace said, referring to the photographs she's just taken of a nesting site on the cliff face. "Although, to my mind, there's never a bad set when it comes to wildlife photography."

It was something of a passion of Grace's: wildlife photography. A hobby that encouraged them to be outdoors. It was one that Duncan himself didn't really have any interest in, but he enjoyed being outside, irrespective of what weather they faced. That was one aspect of living on Skye you had to love; changeable weather, often without much notice.

If you didn't care for four seasons in one day - perhaps in one hour at times - then you were definitely in the wrong place.

The wind was picking up and the first few spots of rain could be felt on their faces as they reached the shoreline. Lined with giant boulders and shelves of basalt, jutting out above the water, they clambered up and over the rocks, taking care on the treacherous surface as the sea water had pooled in places and the tide was already washing over their route back.

Derek had no such problems, leaping up and scampering ahead of them, disappearing from view only to reappear off to the left or right, keeping an eye on them to make sure they were following.

"I think your mutt doesn't trust me," Duncan said as the floppy ears of the dog pricked up, staring at them before running off again.

"He's a good judge of character, that's all," Grace said.

"Thank you very much," Duncan said, using both hands to

lever himself up atop a particularly large outcrop before turning and offering Grace a hand. He pulled her up along-side him and the ocean spray struck both of them, Duncan tasting the salt on his lips. They'd been spending a lot more time together as spring drifted through to summer. Their casual relationship was becoming something a bit deeper, although neither of them had, so far, broached the subject.

"Derek just has to get to know you a bit better," Grace said as her dog rejoined them briefly, sniffing Grace's leg and then bounding away. "Same for my mum."

Duncan scoffed. "It'll take a bit more than that with her."

"Don't be daft. She'll no' bite."

"That's not what I heard," he said, allowing Grace to take the lead over the last section of rock before they'd reach the thin strip of machair between the shoreline and the road.

"Heard from whom?" Grace asked, curious.

"I had it on good authority from someone who was bitten by your mother."

Grace sent a backhanded swipe in his direction which he deftly avoided, smiling. "Seriously though, what's her problem?"

"With you?"

"Aye, with me."

Grace smiled ruefully, breaking eye contact and picking up the pace. It was raining now, only lightly, but would steadily increase from here. They wouldn't make it back before the weather front struck.

"Seriously," Duncan said again, hurrying to catch up with her. "What is it about me she doesn't like? I remember getting on well enough with her back in the day."

"Aye, but you weren't dating her daughter then."

"So, she doesn't like you dating... or is it me specifically?"

Grace didn't look back, ignoring the question and setting quite a pace now they were back on relative dry land. "Hey!" Duncan said, catching up and moving alongside, sensing she was avoiding answering the question. "What is it?"

Grace pulled up abruptly, Duncan stopping a half step later, caught by surprise. She looked pained. "It's... difficult."

"Try me."

Grace took a breath, gathering her thoughts. Both of them ignoring the steadily falling rain. "My dad was in the forces."

"Aye, the Black Watch. I remember."

Grace inclined her head. "Well... he saw some things."

Duncan tried to read her expression but couldn't. "Such as?"

She shook her head. "I don't know the details, but... Mum said it changed him, you know?"

"Aye, I guess. So what?"

"I think... it made things hard for her... having to cope with him after he left the army."

"Did he have PTSD or something?"

Grace exhaled heavily. "Maybe, I don't know. They didn't really do mental health back then. You just... sort of got on with it."

"I didn't realise he had a problem," Duncan said.

"You didn't?"

"No. I just thought he was a moody old sod, you know?" Grace's brow furrowed and Duncan held up his hands in supplication. "No offence."

She smiled. "I think... Mum just doesn't want me to go through the same sort of things, I reckon."

"Right," Duncan said, unsure of what his response should be. They'd only been dating for six months and seriously for less than a third of that in his mind. He hadn't really considered the rest of his life. Grace, with her hidden talent, appeared to read his mind.

"Don't worry, I'm not expecting you to propose anytime soon."

"Thank God for that!" he said, immediately regretting it as her expression soured. "I mean… you know… we're not going there, are we?"

"Apparently not," Grace said, turning away and setting off. Duncan sighed, casting his eyes heavenward and hurried after her.

"I mean, we're not at that stage," he said, trying to limit the damage.

"No," Grace replied, whistling for Derek to come back from the road. He appeared a moment later. "But it's good to know where you are."

Duncan could hear the undertones. He didn't think for a second that Grace was expecting a proposal, but he had answered a little too swiftly and no one in a relationship, male or female, wanted to feel like they were wasting their time.

"I didn't mean for you to—"

"I know," Grace said, glancing at him as he caught up with her, "it's fine." They were at the fence line now, and Grace was negotiating the stile. The fence was damaged beneath it and Derek slipped through the gap with ease, waiting patiently on the other side for them. Duncan climbed over, jumping down to stand beside her as Grace attached the lead to the dog's collar for the walk back to the croft house. She set off again without another look. Clearly, it wasn't *fine* at all.

The next stretch took them along the tarmac road winding its way along the shore before cutting inland. Here, it formed the sea loch upon which the McAdam family croft was located. They made that walk in an awkward silence. Duncan wanted to break that before they got back to the house or it would create an atmosphere for the coming evening.

"Listen," he said, trying to arrange his thoughts. Grace glanced sideways expectantly. "I know... I think... that—"

"I'll save you the trouble, Duncan. You're not thinking about the future."

"That's it... exactly," he said. Her expression didn't alter and he wondered whether she wanted him to be making plans. "I didn't think you were either," he asked, hoping he wasn't digging himself his own grave. "Am I wrong?"

Grace didn't respond immediately, reaching down and patting Derek affectionately as they continued on. "No... I don't have us walking down the aisle, Duncan." He was relieved but thought better of saying so. "It's just..."

"Just what?"

Grace stopped, turning to face him, her lips pursed. "Mum has me thinking, that's all."

"About us?"

"About life."

Duncan thought that was a conversation with an awful lot of scope. Far too much for them to cover adequately just now. Part of Grace's appeal for him was her vivacious approach to life, carefree – to an extent – and looking for fun. She never seemed to take life too seriously. Duncan could get on board with that, but this was different. He couldn't help wondering what had sparked it. All parents have plans for their children, aside from Duncan's father that is. All that man ever cared about was where his next bottle was coming from, and it usually meant Duncan and his sister, Roslyn, would be going without as a result.

"Life?" he asked, tentatively. "As in future plans?"

"Aye," she said, fixing him with a stern look. "It might surprise you Duncan McAdam, but some of us do like to think ahead."

"I... I just didn't have you down as a..."

"As a what?"

"I don't know… a planner."

"Why not?" she asked, sounding hurt. Duncan couldn't fathom what he'd said wrong but, clearly, he had erred somewhere.

"I don't know. It's just… you've never seemed like someone who thought much about the future, that's all. I mean, you're in your late twenties and you're still just a barmaid—"

"*Just?*"

Duncan winced. "I didn't mean that as it sounded."

It was too late, Grace was stalking away from him. Derek looked back at Duncan, and he could swear the dog shot him a withering look.

"Aye, dropped a clanger there, didn't I?" he whispered before setting off after her. He didn't manage to catch up before they rounded the next turn, bringing them back in sight of the croft. The croft house was set back from the loch and rather than follow the winding road, it was a short cut across the grazing land back to the house.

Duncan was surprised to see Alistair's pick-up parked in front of the house. Grace was about five metres ahead of him by the time they reached the house and Alistair, Duncan's detective sergeant, got out to greet them.

"Oh, hi there, Grace," Alistair said, smiling at her.

"Hey, Al," Grace said, greeting him warmly. "How are you keeping?"

"All the better for seeing you," he replied. Grace's smile broadened, but she didn't stop, heading straight towards the side door. Duncan was breathing hard when he came to stand before Alistair. Grace really hadn't wanted him to catch up with her. Alistair raised an eyebrow. "Everything all right?"

"Aye, fine," Duncan said, but he didn't sound convincing.

Alistair's smile turned to a grin. "It's fine. Honest. What are you doing here?"

"You're not answering your mobile."

Duncan cocked his head. "Aye, lack of signal."

Alistair raised his hand, clutching a mobile phone. He pressed the green tab on the screen and moments later they could both hear a mobile ringing from inside Duncan's car. Alistair winked at him.

"It would help if you took your phone with you," he said.

"Aye, and if I did that it would negate the opportunity to have an afternoon with—"

A door slammed, drawing the attention of both men. Grace rounded the corner of the house, her overnight bag in one hand and Derek's lead in the other.

"Aye, aye," Alistair said jovially. Leaning in towards Duncan, he lowered his voice. "Am I interrupting something, by any chance?"

Duncan ignored him, hurrying over to Grace, joining her just as she threw her bag onto the back seat of the car. The boot of her hatchback was already open, and Derek leapt in, well aware of the drill. "Hey!" Duncan said, trying to sound upbeat. Grace closed the door and pressed the button on the fob, lowering the boot lid. Derek ducked, lying down, as the boot closed on him but it didn't stop him from woofing which he always did at the same point every time he got into the car.

"Hey yourself," Grace said calmly, rounding on him.

"I... I..." Duncan stammered. Grace arched her eyebrows.

"Is that it?"

"Well... what did I—"

Grace laughed but without genuine humour, rolled her eyes, and turned away, yanking open the driver's door. Duncan moved to intercept, gently taking hold of her forearm. She didn't protest but met his eye. "You don't get it, do you?"

He didn't. He really didn't get it at all. His brow furrowed and Grace sighed. "What did I say wrong?"

"Well, Duncan," she said. "I think I'm a little old to be your relationship guide, okay?"

Duncan frowned, catching sight of Alistair behind him, mock grimacing. Fortunately, Grace had her back to him. Somehow, Alistair witnessing this exchange was unlikely to help matters.

"I... thought you were staying—"

Grace looked around at Alistair. "Something tells me, you'll be working tonight. Am I right, Alistair?"

"What's that?" Alistair called, but Duncan was sure he could hear every word.

"You're needing Duncan for something, right?"

"Aye. I'm afraid so."

Duncan frowned, lowering his voice. "Can I... can I call you later?"

"Of course," Grace said and Duncan smiled. "Whether I'll answer is another matter entirely," she said, getting into the car. Duncan closed his eyes and felt a jolt as Grace pulled the door closed, hitting him because he was in the way. Duncan stepped aside without being asked and Grace closed the door, firing up the engine. She pulled away. Alistair smiled and waved as she passed him, and she returned the gesture.

Duncan watched her go for a moment, Derek lifting his head and looking back at him, before he rejoined Alistair. His DS was grinning broadly.

"I'd ask you if you were enjoying your rest day... but I think I know the answer to that already."

Duncan sighed. "No need to enjoy it so much, Alistair."

"I just like seeing you youngsters travel the same path as I did, many years ago."

"Any advice?"

"Aye, sure," Alistair said, looking thoughtful. "When you're in the wrong, apologise."

"A real pearl of wisdom there," Duncan said. "Thanks. Are there any more where that gem came from?"

"When you're in the right... apologise."

Duncan laughed. "What about when you're not sure what the hell is going on?"

Alistair raised his eyebrows, smiling, and both men said in unison, "*Apologise.*"

Duncan shook his head. "I knew there was a reason I didn't get married."

"Aye, that plus you've no' found anyone who'll put up with you."

"Thanks for that. Is there a particular reason you've come out here, or is witnessing my personal suffering a source of entertainment for you?"

Alistair smiled. "It could be worse, sir."

"How's that?" Duncan said, looking down the road to where he'd last seen Grace's car before it disappeared from view, feeling the rain getting heavier, and wondering how he'd make this right. Whatever *this* turns out to be.

"You could've been found lying dead at the foot of the Cuillins?"

CHAPTER TWO

ARRIVING IN ELGOL, Duncan looked over to the jetty as Alistair parked his pick-up. They had two choices to reach the scene. Either they took a short ride on one of the charter boats providing ferry trips across Loch Scavaig and into the foothills of the Cuillin range or it was an eight-mile hike in from the other side, starting at Sligachan.

The small wooden charter boat was moored, and Duncan could see the skipper at the helm. He sighed. "You couldn't get another boat?"

Alistair scoffed. "At this time of the year?" He glanced at Duncan. "We're lucky they'd fit us in now. They've been booked solid for weeks."

"I know," Duncan said, "but..."

"Come on, man," Alistair said, getting out. "Time's a wasting."

Duncan opened his door and was immediately struck by the stiff breeze coming at them across the loch. Coming straight at them across from the small island of Soay in the distance, from the south west, it felt warm. True, it was summertime now but even in June the monthly average high for the island was still only fifteen degrees. In the sunshine, with a light wind, that could feel positively balmy for the Isle of Skye. It was ideal weather for exploring the Cuillin ridge.

Today though, the breeze was unsettling the waters of Loch Scavaig, a sea loch off the west coast of the Strathaird peninsula. The peaks of the Black Cuillin range were shrouded in cloud and it looked like the weather around them might be closing in.

In this light, the Black Cuillins appeared dark and foreboding. In sunlight they could look anything from grey to brown. Formed by the ejection of magma from deep underground chambers, the Black Cuillin ridge formed a narrow crest over fourteen kilometres long, a mix of steep ridges and scree slopes that could, and often did, catch out even the most experienced and adventurous of climbers.

The two men made their way across the car park towards the boat. The highest point on the Isle of Skye, the peak of Sgùrr Alasdair, standing well over three thousand feet tall, was hidden by the cloud. "You can't see much of your namesake," Duncan said, looking into the distance. Alasdair was the ancient Gaelic for Alexander, Alistair being one of the Anglicised variants of the name.

"Aye, towering over all around it," Alistair said. "Like the guardian of the island. Much like its namesake, I might add."

Duncan smiled but it faded as the skipper of the boat turned to greet them. "Mr McAdam," he said, nodding a curt greeting, his voice clipped.

"Hey, Roddy. How have you been?"

"Better than ever," Roddy replied, turning away and making ready to cast off. "You ought to get on board. I've got to pick up a party and waiting for you has already made me late."

Alistair and Duncan both climbed aboard and Roddy's

fellow crew member cast off the bow line as Roddy returned to the helm and started the engines. Roddy Mcintyre's family had run boat trips across Loch Scavaig for as far back as anyone could remember, Roddy's father spending his entire working life at sea in one capacity or another. Roddy chose not to leave the island and stayed to help run the family business, Duncan having come across him as a person of interest in the investigation that brought him home to Skye.

Seeing Duncan again, in an official capacity, probably didn't bring back fond memories for the young skipper. He may state he was doing well, but that didn't stretch to welcoming the sight of Duncan again.

Once out on the water for the short trip, around half an hour, Duncan sensed Roddy was pushing it far more than he would with tourists aboard. They'd likely arrive sooner than that and Duncan could feel the air temperature dropping as they moved out into deeper water. The seawater around Skye was barely into double figures at this time of the year, likely to peak around August following the warming period through spring and summer. The sea breeze was also cooled by its passage over the water. It was noticeable.

Alistair looked uncomfortable almost as soon as they'd boarded, but he was now pale and sporting a tense expression. He wasn't keen on being out on the water with an aversion to boats that Duncan found amusing seeing as he lived on an island. "You okay?" Duncan asked, sitting down in the stern near him, but not too near, just in case.

"Aye, grand. Once I'm back on the old terra firma, I'll be grand."

Duncan nodded, leaving his DS to cope with the choppy ride and made his way to the helm where Roddy Mcintyre was looking out ahead of them. He was reticent to talk as

Duncan came to stand beside him, but he did acknowledge Duncan's presence.

"You found the body, I understand?"

Roddy shook his head. "No, one of our groups did. When we came back to pick them up around midday, they told us what they'd found, and I went to see." He turned the wheel, guiding the boat along a route he clearly knew like the back of his hand. The steep slopes of the Cuillins were looming large now as Roddy steered them towards the river mouth. *River Scavaig* was known as one of the shortest rivers in the UK, being all that separated Loch Coruisk from the sea.

The Black Cuillin ridge curved in an irregular semi-circle around Loch Coruisk, which lay at the heart of the range, with steep slopes rising up all around it. Roddy steered towards the landing pier, little more than a staircase bolted to the side of the cliff face. The Coruisk memorial hut, a white-painted squat building, was in the background. Duncan spied several groups of people on land. One group was close to the landing point and watching the boat's approach. Another group was further away, taking up a position on higher ground, and all were looking inward towards Loch Coruisk.

"Did you notice anything odd?" Duncan asked Roddy, who shrugged.

"Odd? Like what?"

"Anything that stood out to you?"

"I spoke to your colleagues earlier," Roddy said without sounding offhand. "Like I said to them, I've no idea what I'm looking at. The man... was clearly dead. What more is there to say?"

"Nothing, I guess," Duncan said. Roddy was focused on his approach. The swell was likely making this harder than it might be on days where *Loch Scavaig* could be reminiscent of a mill pond. There was no further conversation and Roddy expertly brought them within distance of the landing point. His crew mate stepped over onto the stairs and tied the boat off swiftly.

Alistair was first off, climbing the stairs which were damp underfoot and needed to be negotiated with care. Duncan followed, thanking Roddy for the ride. The skipper begrudgingly accepted the appreciation.

"We'll be back to collect you around six o'clock. After that, you'll be needing to stay the night in the hut," Roddy said, pointing towards the memorial building that they'd seen from their approach. Duncan hoped it wouldn't come to that. If this was a crime scene then the forensic guys could have a late one, but he had no intention of staying out here for the night.

"We'll be waiting," Duncan said. "Thanks again."

"Aye, no bother," Roddy said, waiting with the boat for the tourists who would descend once the policemen were clear.

The body was the topic of conversation amongst the waiting visitors which was not a surprise. After all, they'd come for the sightseeing, magnificent scenery and wildlife, but had stumbled across something more like a movie scene. However, this wasn't fiction, it was real life.

They found PC Ronnie Macdonald waiting for them as they made the last turn of the stairs and climbed to the top. The constable greeted both men and led them away from the group who began making their way down to the boat.

"Sir," he said to Duncan.

"What do you think?" Duncan asked. "Accident or something else?"

Ronnie frowned. "Could be either, but there are things that don't ring true, if you know what I mean?"

"Not really, no."

Ronnie smiled. "You'll see." He turned and led them along the path towards the loch. From this point there were multiple options which is what drove tourists here in such high numbers. If you wanted to, you could walk around the loch itself which was an easy-going route and popular among visitors, or you could venture up into the mountains themselves.

The scree slopes of the range were quite a challenge but the views from the high points of the ridge were breathtaking. Then there was also the coastal path which wound its way back to Elgol. This in and of itself required a degree of local knowledge to negotiate and wasn't for the faint-hearted. There is a notorious chunk of rock, an outcrop nicknamed *Bad Step*, that required some courage to negotiate.

Ronnie took them around the loch and rounding a bend in the path they came upon a small group of officers who'd roped off an area blocking anyone from using the path. Above them, looking down, was the group of onlookers Duncan had spied from the boat. There were eight or nine of them, dressed for the weather in hiking kit. Duncan glanced up at them. Ronnie noticed.

"They've been here much of the day. Ghouls," he muttered.

"Has anyone spoken to them yet?" Duncan asked.

"No."

"Right," Duncan said, turning to Alistair. "Have someone get up there. They might have seen someone or something untoward. You never know."

Alistair nodded. The colour had returned to his cheeks now, and he was paying attention. He looked at Ronnie. "Who's here with you?"

"I've got Fraser and wee Robbie."

"Right. Those two can go up there and interview that lot," he said, jabbing his thumb in the air for emphasis. "But make sure Robbie keeps his head in the game. You know what he's like when he gets to talking about climbing."

Ronnie chuckled. "Aye, right enough. Hopefully, none of that lot has made it to base camp."

Duncan smiled. Robbie had made two unsuccessful trips out to climb Everest, but had only made it to base camp, no mean feat in and of itself, on both occasions. From base camp they needed to charter a helicopter to get them out to the point where they could begin their ascent only to have their transport hijacked at the last moment by those with deeper pockets. It was a frustrating experience for the constable.

Duncan knew though, as they all did, that Robbie would make that climb one day. He was that driven. Approaching the scene, they were met by DC Angus Ross, the first member of CID to make it out to Coruisk.

"Hello, sir," he said to Duncan, then smiled and nodded to Alistair.

"Angus," Duncan said, looking past him to see a figure lying face down at the foot of a steep scree slope. "What can you tell us?"

"Not a lot, sir, if I'm honest," the DC said glumly. "The body was found this morning around ten o'clock by the first group who arrived by boat from Elgol."

"What time did they make it off the boat?"

"They landed around half-past nine. Some of the party set off up into the mountains, keen to make headway before the weather closed in. The others were only planning to stay on the island for around ninety minutes and they eventually made their way down this path to have a closer look at the loch. It was then that they came across him." Angus looked around, gesturing towards the body.

"All right. Let's see what you have for us then."

CHAPTER THREE

ANGUS LED them over to the body. Duncan was immediately struck by the immense physical size of the man. He was comfortably six feet tall, and despite being kitted out extensively in all-weather gear shrouding the lines of his body, Duncan could tell he was in good physical shape. His shoulders were broad, and his neck was thick with muscle.

Duncan didn't want to get too close for fear of disturbing any evidence should they conclude that this was indeed a crime scene. Dropping to his haunches and angling his head, he took in the man's features. He was lying face down, but his face was angled slightly to one side, looking towards the scree slope. His eyes were open, staring, lifeless. Duncan guessed he was in his forties, perhaps older, although it was hard to tell. Dried blood streaked the side of his face, long since having ceased flowing from a wound just above his hairline.

The blood had soaked into the ground around where he lay, and mud was mixed in with the dried blood on his face, indicative of a fall from height, gathering mud and detritus from the ground during his descent. Duncan looked up, as did Alistair, standing slightly behind him. The slope extended up from them. The surface was loose rock, known as scree, and was notorious a surface to traverse. Especially bad if the conditions were damp or snow covered.

"Any climbers reported overdue in the last twenty-four to forty-eight hours?" Duncan asked.

"Climbers, no," Angus said. Duncan looked at him. "But someone was reported missing from one of the local estates."

"Which estate?" Alistair asked.

"*Maelrubha*," Angus said. Alistair arched his eyebrows.

"What?" Duncan asked.

Alistair shook his head. "No matter."

"He matches the description of the missing man," Angus said. "But it doesn't shed any light on how he made his way out here. We're on the wrong side of the mountains for *Maelrubha*."

Duncan took the information in, turning his focus back to the landscape. There was no snow at this time of the year. Occasionally, it could still be found on the peaks if the conditions were right. Snow could fall under certain circumstances as late as July, but that wasn't common. The warm air currently being drawn across the island was Mediterranean in origin, coming up on a strong wind from the Sahara. Even so, in good conditions it was possible to have an accident if you weren't paying attention.

"That's quite a tumble," Duncan said quietly.

"He wouldn't be the first," Alistair said.

"No, true enough."

Duncan cast his eye over the body. His gear was in good condition. He was wearing breathable, but waterproof outer gear. His jacket had several tears and rips in it but that was certainly consistent with falling in this terrain. The loose rock was unforgiving if you hit it at the best of times, let alone doing so at pace. His boots were also in good condition and the right choice for navigating this landscape.

Duncan moved and took up a position a metre to his left, eyeing the soles of the deceased man's boots. They were obviously well worn, but with plenty of life left in them. There was mud and detritus gathered in the treads, consistent with having hiked through the boggy ground that could be found across the island.

"Have you clocked the laces?" Alistair asked. Duncan checked, glancing at his detective sergeant with a quizzical look. He didn't see it, whatever it was. "The method of tying. It's army lacing."

Duncan looked again. "Say again?"

"The way they're laced; the horizontal and diagonal crossovers are on the insides and the vertical sections are on the outside, do you see?"

"Meaning?"

"It's the inside-out version of the Bow Tie method. Tactical boots are made from strong leather, it's sturdy and durable. That offers a lot of support but they're a pig to wear until they're broken in, and even then, they're not particularly comfortable. This method of tying them increases flexibility, by loosening the leather to either side." Alistair cocked his head. "Once you learn that, you'll never change."

"You think he's military?" Duncan asked, sceptical.

"Or he reads survival guides," Alistair said. "Judging by his size, I wouldn't be surprised though. I mean, check out the haircut as well."

The man's hair was close cut on the top, back and sides. It certainly was what you might find from a serviceman. Duncan was struck by something else, and he scanned the nearby ground. "Did you find anything else?"

"Such as?" Angus asked.

"A backpack, equipment... anything he might have been carrying?"

Angus shook his head. "No. All we've got is what you see here. But we'll need to scout the higher ground. We don't know from where he actually fell yet."

Duncan found it odd that he wasn't sporting some kind of backpack or rucksack. If he was on the move, which is likely if he fell whilst traversing a difficult patch of scree above, then it would stand to reason he'd have his kit upon him. No one hikes this terrain with a bag over one shoulder. Therefore, it was unlikely to have fallen from his grasp on the way down.

Duncan looked at the deceased. Besides the obvious head injury, his face, and the exposed skin of his hands showed multiple cuts and abrasions consistent with a fall. He must have tumbled from quite a height. "If he fell," Duncan whispered.

"Sir?"

Duncan glanced at Angus. "Just thinking out loud. The people who found him..."

"We have their details, sir. We know who they are and where they're staying."

"Good. This guy definitely wasn't with them on the boat?"

Angus shook his head. "No, they were adamant they'd never seen him before."

"Right."

"Should I go higher?" Angus asked. "See if I can find where he was when he... you know?" Angus was clearly keen not to describe it as an accident, since Duncan didn't seem too sure. Duncan looked up into the cloud line which seemed lower than it had only a quarter of an hour ago. The temperature had also fallen since they'd got off the boat.

"Do you have mobile signal?" Angus nodded. "Now, get onto Willie Mac and his mountain rescue team. Get them out here and then go exploring. I don't want you or anyone else winding up besides our man here."

"Understood, sir," Angus said, taking out his mobile and stepping away. Duncan rolled his tongue along the inside of his cheek.

"Ronnie's right," Alistair said, drawing Duncan's attention. "A curious one, for sure."

"Aye, isn't it?" Duncan agreed. "How long do you think he's been here?"

Alistair inclined his head. "Hard to say, with the conditions."

"Take a guess?"

Alistair wrinkled his nose. "Overnight, a few hours before he was found at the absolute least. You?"

"Same," Duncan said. "If he came across on the later trips yesterday, then someone in his party would have missed him."

"Maybe he was alone… and planning a lengthy hike."

"Through the night?" Duncan said, arching an eyebrow quizzically. "In this terrain… with no kit—"

"That we know of," Alistair said, looking up into the descending cloud line. "It could be up there."

"Aye, it could. And he could have put his kit down before falling but…"

"You don't tend to fall unless you're on the move."

"Yes. As you say, a curious one," Duncan repeated the earlier sentiment. Duncan inspected the man's fingernails. They were trimmed close but there was still mud beneath them. The skin of his fingertips although rough, indicating he was a man used to physical labour in some fashion, also showed signs of wear. It was like he'd been scrambling, which was necessary when negotiating the landscape of the Black Cuillins.

The gabbro, the igneous rock that made up much of the

Black Cuillins, along with basalt, was rough, jagged, and hard on both unprotected hands and feet, making it something of a surprise for this man to be traversing it barehanded. He seemed well equipped for the conditions in the main, but then lacking some of the basics: gloves, a head covering and some way of carrying equipment and provisions. This was an unforgiving environment, and this man seemed like someone Duncan figured would know that.

This was a curious accident indeed. If it was an accident. Duncan looked at Alistair. "Have a scenes of crime team come out here." He glanced at the clouds again, feeling spots of rain on his face. "As soon as you can."

"I'll make the call."

"And get a proper description of this guy who is missing from the *Maelrubha Estate*. If it matches, then…"

"Then?" Alistair asked.

"Maybe someone from there will be able to tell us what he was doing out here by himself."

Alistair nodded. "If he was by himself."

CHAPTER FOUR

"WHAT CAN you tell me about the *Maelrubha Estate*?" Duncan asked as Alistair negotiated a stretch of road which narrowed just as he met a long line of traffic backed up behind a mobile home. The driver was struggling to avoid moving onto the soft verge beside the road.

"Tourists," Alistair said under his breath. He wasn't being disparaging, merely observing the higher-than-normal volume of traffic on the local roads at this time of the year. They were passing close to the Fairy Pools, one of the most visited sites on the entire island, and there was one road in and out.

After this turn off where much of the traffic was coming from or going to, they would drive further along the peninsula towards *Glenbrittle* on the west side of the Cuillin range. Once back in Elgol, they had no choice but to make the drive around the entire mountain range to bring them down to the *Maelrubha Estate*. It was a forty-five-mile trip and should only have taken them an hour and a quarter but with the number of vehicles on the road, it had added another fifteen minutes to that already.

"The estate?" Duncan reminded Alistair once they were back underway. "I've not heard of it."

"Oh aye... right. You won't have heard of it," Alistair said. "It didn't exist until about five years ago. It's made up of a number of different landholdings that were all acquired in quick succession by an overseas owner. There was a bit of a stink about it all."

"Really? Sounds interesting."

"Aye, well... it was a company which agreed the sale, throwing quite a bit of money around as I recall. There were a few petitions to the Crofting Commission, but they managed to get around all of that, but it left a sour taste in a few mouths, if you know what I mean?"

"Aye, I do." There was a real passion among the islanders to maintain the history and unique culture of the island. There were others though, who were less bothered about that, and it was quite a balance to keep the equilibrium between the two factions. Many others, however, just wanted to get on with their lives and could do without all the fuss. "So, how big is this estate we're going to?"

Alistair thought about it. "About sixteen thousand acres... all in, I reckon."

"And the name?"

"Taken from the name of a ruined chapel over in *Eynort*," Alistair said. "Quaint."

"I'll bet that annoyed a few people as well?"

"Aye, didn't it just," Alistair said, with a wry smile. "The new owners wanted to branch out into reenactments and accommodation, servicing the influx of tourists and depriving them of their hard-earned pennies."

"Doesn't sound so bad," Duncan said, watching the landscape roll by as the windscreen wipers squeaked in front of him.

"I think people saw the owners as trying to be something like a themed holiday park, half expecting gnarled old power-lifters tossing cabers in Day-Glo tartan outfits and the like."

"Ah... I get it. Didn't happen?"

Alistair shook his head. "No. Thankfully, someone had some sense in the council and kyboshed it."

"So, what do they do now?"

"Marketing it as a traditional hunting estate in the main. Shooting parties... stalking... all that sort of thing."

"Popular?"

"Seems to be," Alistair said, taking a turn off the main road through a set of brick pillars; two sea eagles, cast in iron, adorning them. *The Maelrubha Estate*, the sign said in gold lettering on a glossy black background.

The estate office buildings were converted from an old steading, single storey with a broken slate-lined parking area to the rear. Parking the pick-up, they were directed to the main reception by a young woman who was leading a horse back to the nearby stables from a manège where riders were practising their show jumping. The estate was a hive of activity and they had to wait in the reception for a few minutes before they were spoken to.

Duncan showed his warrant card to the lady on reception and if she was surprised, she didn't show it. "Please take a seat and I'll call someone through to see you," she said, instructing a groom to head out to find the right person. Neither Duncan nor Alistair sat down, but instead they stood by the floor-to-ceiling glass elevation of the gable end, watching the riders being put through their paces a short distance away. Duncan had never been one for horses. He didn't trust them. He was also quite sure the feeling was mutual.

"Detective Inspector?"

Duncan, lost in thought for a moment, turned to find a

man in his forties smiling at them. He smiled, accepting the man's hand. "DI McAdam," he said.

"Alex Brennan," the man replied.

"This is my DS—"

"Aye, Alistair," Brennan said, glancing at Alistair who smiled. "I know." Duncan noted he didn't return Alistair's warm greeting, but he didn't feel the need to ask why. "What can I do for you?"

"You reported someone missing from here two days ago," Duncan said. "Steven Phelps?"

"Aye," Brennan said. "Steven is staying with us. He's one of a small party here for the week."

"What is he doing here?"

Brennan shrugged. "Well, the party are here for a bit of a holiday, but while they're with us, we're doing a bit of shooting... and we took them out stalking as well."

"Stalking?" Duncan asked, pretending to be ignorant. "What do you stalk?"

"Red deer mostly," Brennan said. "The estate stretches to the mountains... and it's a real mix of terrain. Easy going in places, but it can get tougher. Then we have the woodland as well. Visitors get to see the landscape, wildlife—"

"And get to kill it, too," Alistair said drily. Brennan cocked his head.

"Aye, if that's their pleasure they can, yes."

"Do you get many people through here?" Duncan asked.

"Oh aye, we do. We see a lot of Europeans coming this way, Germans in particular. Americans too."

"They don't have deer in Germany?" Duncan asked.

"Different kinds. To a hunter, each species is viewed like a climber sees a different Munro. The climber wants to bag another mountain over 3000 feet, and a hunter wants to kill something they've never shot before, you know?"

Duncan nodded. "What about Steven Phelps? What can you tell us about him?"

Brennan thought about it. "Not much really. His party arrived five days ago, booked into site accommodation for the week. It's a stag party. The groom is getting married week after next, I believe. A bit of a lads' trip, from what I can gather."

"How many in the party?"

"Six in total."

"Are they still here?"

"Aye, they are. They dinnae want to leave without their pal like, you know?"

"And he went missing two nights ago?"

Brennan nodded. "The party reported him missing to the office the following morning. We turned the staff out... did a bit of a search just in case..."

"In case of what?" Duncan asked.

Brennan shrugged. "It's a stag do. He could have just been sleeping it off somewhere. We didn't want to go to the trouble of bothering you lot if he was just sleeping off a bender or..."

"Or?"

Brennan shrugged. "Hooked up with someone for the night. I mean, they're not stuck here on the estate. These parties often head off into the town for a bit of a ceilidh or something."

"But not Phelps?"

"No, he didn't show up and we couldn't find any sign of him, so we... called you guys and reported him missing. Has something happened to him then?"

"What makes you ask that?" Alistair said.

"Well, a DI and a DS are here asking questions... so it disnae take the brain of Britain to think something's up."

"Fair enough," Alistair said. "Good job, bearing in mind it's you we're dealing with, after all." Brennan glared at Alistair, Duncan shot him a dark look as well, Alistair averting his eyes.

"What do you do here, Mr Brennan?" Duncan asked.

"Estate's manager," he said. "Why?"

Duncan ignored the question. "How much have you had to do with this party, Phelps's group I mean?"

Brennan's forehead creased. "I led them on the stalking party three nights back, along with two of my guys."

"Did you take them over to the Cuillins?"

"No, not the mountains themselves. They're off limits, and we don't cross the line." Alistair scoffed, but Brennan continued. "We took them through the woods and then up into the foothills, within our boundary, and then brought them back."

"How long were you out?"

"It's a full-day package," Brennan said. "It's pretty intense if you're new to it but these guys had done similar before. Well, some of them. The others just sort of tagged along."

"Do you know where the party are now?" Duncan asked. Brennan nodded. "We'd like to see them if possible."

"I'll send word and have them gather at the lodge."

"The lodge?"

"Aye, it's an old laird's property that we've converted into a traditional hunting lodge. We serve meals there, hire it out for wedding receptions and the like.

"Great, thank you," Duncan said. Brennan excused himself and Duncan took a step closer to Alistair. "What's the history between the two of you?"

Alistair chuckled. "All I'll say is take everything he tells you with a massive pinch of salt."

"Like that is it?"

"Aye, he's pretty special is our Alex."

"Thanks for the tip."

Alex Brennan reappeared a few minutes later, ushering them out of the reception and leading them out of the front door and onto the open ground between the estate office and another building a hundred metres away.

Surrounded by a walled garden, the restored laird's house was quite imposing. The landscaping around the building was impressive with gravelled pathways leading through a well-tended garden that was enclosed on three sides by mature trees giving the property both seclusion and protection from the high winds coming in off the nearby sea.

"You mind talking a bit of shop?" Duncan asked as they covered the ground.

"Sure," Brennan said.

"How much does a day's stalking set you back?"

"Depends... on how many are in your party and how many hunters you want with you."

"How about this group?"

"Eight hundred a head," Brennan said.

"Sounds steep," Duncan said.

"That doesn't include ammunition, trophy prepping, venison butchery... or gratuities."

Duncan exhaled heavily. "I'm in the wrong business."

"Do you shoot?" Brennan asked.

Duncan shook his head. "No, guns... hunting... aren't really my thing."

"It's not everyone's that's true."

"Is it yours?"

The estate manager inclined his head. "Some of us are used to firearms and miss it when we're not around them anymore." Duncan caught Alistair shooting a withering look towards Brennan, but he didn't see it, so Duncan didn't comment. He'd ask later.

"You served in the forces?" Duncan asked.

"Aye. British Army, man and boy." Brennan sighed. "I left on a medical discharge... but I tell you, I miss it every now and then."

They were approaching the building now and Duncan could see a small group of men coming towards them from another direction. Behind them were some cabins which he presumed were the accommodation they'd hired.

"Tell me, Alex, if I can call you Alex?" Duncan asked. Brennan nodded. "Was there any issue within the party in the first couple of days. Any tension?"

Brennan exhaled, rubbing the back of his neck. "Not really. Not that I'm aware of... I mean, there was some banter going between them. But they're all friends, and lads on a trip... it's to be expected, isn't it?"

"Nothing that you found odd?"

He shrugged. "No, I can't say there was. They were a top group, to be fair to them."

"Well, if anything comes to mind, do let me know, yes?"

"Of course," Brennan said, nodding furiously. "Anything I can do to help."

Brennan showed them into the laird's house where they waited in a magnificently decorated drawing room. The room was double height, with a galleried mezzanine level wrapping around above them. Hunting trophies and paintings hung from dark panelled walls. Around them was an array of oxblood chesterfield chairs and sofas; set out before a huge fireplace.

It wasn't quite right though, but Duncan couldn't quite put his finger on what was wrong with it. Perhaps the locals who'd protested were right all along, because the room had the feel of a themed chain pub, rather than a traditional hunting lodge.

The door opened and the group were escorted into the room by another of Alex Brennan's staff. Duncan observed them as they quietly filed in.

CHAPTER FIVE

DUNCAN ALLOWED Alistair to make the introductions. He was keener to analyse the group. There were two of them, in particular, he could see were more confident than the others. One was very reserved, hanging at the back and almost looking to blend into the background, eyes flitting around the room. None of this was indicative of anything, but Duncan found human nature intriguing. After all, so much of his job was involved with the skill of reading people.

His mind drifted back to his time with Grace earlier, and he realised he wasn't as skilled at it as he might believe. Lastly, Alistair introduced Duncan who stepped forward and all eyes fell on him.

"Thank you for allowing us to speak with you all, gentlemen. I'm afraid there's no easy way to tell you, so I'm just going to say that we have, this morning, found a male body. From the description, Alex," Duncan said, gesturing to Brennan, "provided when your friend was reported missing, we believe it to be that of your friend, Steven Phelps."

With the confirmation, there was an audible gasp and some of the men began talking amongst themselves, several cursing.

One man though stepped forward, tight-lipped. Duncan met his eye. "My name is Tony... Tony Sinclair, and..." he glanced around at the others and conversation ceased, "I'm the groom. This... all of us being here together, has all been for my benefit."

Duncan nodded to him. "I'm sorry for your loss." Tony acknowledged the gesture glumly with a tilt of his head.

"Can you tell us what happened to him, please?"

"I'm afraid I don't have any answers for you at this time," Duncan said. Several made to protest, and Duncan held up a hand to quieten them. "Your friend's body was found around ten o'clock this morning. It's still very early in the investigation, so I'll please ask you to give us time to—"

"Time?" Another man stepped forward, scowling. "Steve has been missing for two days, and I think you've had enough time to find him. Where has he been?"

"I'm sorry, but you are?" Duncan asked.

"Ryan... Masters. I'm... Steve's pal."

Duncan assessed him. Of the assembled group, Ryan was the closest in physical size to Steven Phelps, athletic with a muscular frame. Duncan spied a tattoo poking out from the man's collar and his bulk was visible beneath his shirt.

"I can appreciate your frustration, Mr Masters," Duncan said. "I really can, but we need space to do our job."

"Where was he?" Ryan repeated.

"He was found just above Loch Coruisk, on the eastern side of the Black Cuillins."

"What the hell was he doing out there?" Ryan asked.

"I was hoping one of you might have some idea about that," Duncan said flatly. Ryan ignored the question, running his hand through his close-cropped hair. Duncan caught the eye of another man, one of the quieter ones.

"I'm Neil, Neil Banister," he said, forcing a smile. "I was at school with Steve..." he gestured towards Tony and another man who Duncan hadn't heard speak yet, "and Ollie here." Duncan nodded to the two men, focusing on Neil. "Can you tell us how he died?"

Duncan thought about that momentarily, exchanging a quick glance with Alistair who nodded his agreement. They could share some information, and maybe it might tease something useful from the group. "We're not sure yet, but it would appear as if Steven fell from height. It's possible he was making his way across the slope and lost his footing."

Neil looked down, frowning, disconsolate but Ryan shook his head, dismissively. "No way! Steve was a great climber. We've scaled mountains together, ones far higher than anything Skye has to offer."

"As I say," Duncan said, "we're still investigating. Did you have plans to do any climbing while you were up here? I assume you live..."

"All over," the man named Ollie said, his arms folded across his chest. He nodded towards the groom. "Tony and I live down in London, Neil is based in Birmingham these days and Nathan," he pointed to the last man who so far hadn't uttered a word, "he lives in the Midlands."

"What about you?" Duncan asked Ryan. "Where are you from?"

"All over," he said. When Duncan maintained the eye contact, insisting on a proper answer, Ryan relented. "I work abroad a lot, with Steve. I guess my base is in Glasgow, but only because I have a flat there. And my daughter lives in Pollokshields with my ex, so I tend to stay there when I'm in the country and not working."

"What work is it you do, Mr Masters?" Alistair asked.

"Security."

Alistair nodded. "And Steven?"

"Aye, we worked together a fair bit. He got me a way in when I left the army."

"I thought so," Alistair said. "You've got the look."

"What look is that then?" Ryan asked, turning to face Alistair and lifting his chin.

"The same one I see when I look in the mirror," Alistair said and something passed between them, some form of communication only veterans could understand maybe, Duncan didn't know, but it worked on Ryan. He bobbed his head towards Alistair and let the matter drop. "When we have more information about what happened to your pal, we'll be sure to brief you."

Ryan acknowledged the comment, taking a step back. His aggressive stance dissipated.

"What is it you do, Nathan?" Duncan asked.

"I'm a builder... a main contractor," Nathan said. "It's my own business."

"Right, and three of you were at school together," Duncan said, looking around. "And how do the rest of you know each other?"

"I served with Steve," Ryan said. "We go back a way... and I was in town, so he said I should come along."

Nathan met Duncan's eye. "I did some work for Tony over the years—"

"You've renovated and built two of my properties," Tony said. Nathan nodded, forcing a brief smile.

"And you're getting married next week, Tony, is that right?" Duncan asked.

Tony nodded. "Yes, I'm supposed to be."

"Right, well we need a favour from one of you," Duncan said. "As soon as we've finished processing the scene, we'll need one of you to carry out an identification of the body. Usually, we do that with the next of kin, but Mr Phelps is not from around here—"

"He disnae have any," Ryan said quietly. Duncan looked at him. "Steve isn't married... disnae have any kids and his folks passed away years back. It's just him."

"Well, in that case, we definitely need to ask for one of you—"

"I'll do it," Ollie said, stepping forward. Ryan looked ready to object but Ollie cut him off. "He's here – we're all here – because I arranged it, so I'll take the responsibility."

"Thank you," Duncan said. "I didn't catch your full name."

"Oliver Caistor," he said glumly. "Or just Ollie."

"Thank you. It will be either later tonight or tomorrow, depending on how things progress out there," Duncan said. "Are you okay with that?"

"Yes, of course. Whatever you need."

Duncan smiled gratefully, and then noticed Ryan's right hand had an abrasion along the knuckle. His gaze lingered a moment too long because it was noted by Ryan who withdrew his hand, slipping it casually into his pocket.

Duncan subtly cast his eye over the others. Only Ollie appeared to have any injury of note, an abrasion – or it could have been a rash – around the left side of his neck, stretching around almost to where the V cut of his undershirt met his chest.

"When was the last time any of you recall seeing Steve?" Duncan asked. The group exchanged looks but no one seemed able to put a time on it.

"We had a few drinks," Ollie said at last. "We didn't fancy going out. We'd hired a minibus to take us up to Portree the night before and it was a bit of a late one. None of us is quite as good on the pop as we used to be."

"Speak for yourself," Ryan said.

"Anyway," Ollie continued, looking between his friends. "We had food… a few beers and were planning on an evening of cards but… er… Steve never came through."

"Yeah," Neil said. "We figured he was getting an early one."

"Any of you sharing accommodation?" Duncan asked and no one answered. Neil did look towards Ryan though. The former soldier sneered ever so slightly.

"I'm sharing a cabin with Steve."

"And you didn't notice he was missing?"

Ryan shook his head. "Nah. We're sharing a cabin, not a bedroom. If he wants to sleep off a session, then that's up to him, isn't it?"

"Of course." Duncan looked at them, finding it peculiar that no one could pinpoint when Steve was last in their company. "So, you raised the alarm the next day?"

"Yes, when he didn't show for breakfast," Ryan said. "I went back to the cabin and found his bed hadn't been slept in."

"Did he say anything to any of you about wanting to go out on the mountains?" They all shook their heads. "What about collectively? Were you planning to?"

"No," Tony said. "We're all up for a bit of a hike but the stalking was about as much as I wanted to do. I don't fancy hiking up into the clouds."

"And how did you get on?" Duncan asked. "With the stalking?"

"We bagged a couple," Tony said.

Ryan laughed. "Steve and I did. You lot can't shoot to save your lives."

"Well, we haven't all honed our skills on shooting civilians in Basra, have we?" Ollie said with a vague hint at dark humour. If Ryan found it funny, his face didn't crack, but he stared Ollie down.

All in all, Duncan found the men's behaviour to be strange. Not strange enough to set alarm bells ringing, but something was off. He just didn't know what that meant. Of course, it was quite conceivable that the plans they'd made had been scuppered in the most bizarre way, and now none of them knew quite how they were supposed to react to one another or to the police. Even so, it struck Duncan as odd. He could read Alistair's expression too. Although his DS didn't give a lot away, once you got to know him you could interpret quite a lot from his micro expressions.

Alistair wasn't impressed with this lot either.

"Please can I ask for all of you to provide us with your contact details, how to get in touch with you, as well as where you will be heading when you leave here." Duncan looked around the group, ensuring he made eye contact with each and every one of them. "We will also have officers come and take statements from you in due course, so please don't head off anywhere just yet."

"Statements?" Ryan asked.

Duncan nodded. "Aye."

"What for?"

"We will want to know everything you remember about your time here, together as a group and with Steven in particular."

"Yes, but why?"

"Just routine," Duncan said. Ryan nodded, turning and walking slowly away. Tony Sinclair, the groom, came over to Duncan as the others began filtering out of the room or forming their own conversations.

"What did you mean before?" Tony asked.

"When?"

They were joined by Ollie as well, who sported a

concerned expression. "When you said you were... how did you phrase it, *processing the scene?*"

"We have to examine Mr Phelps, assess what could have happened, and how he wound up where he did." Tony nodded and Duncan made to move away, keen to speak to Alistair. Ollie grasped Duncan's forearm with a grip he found surprisingly strong. Ollie lowered his voice.

"Am I mistaken in thinking that you suspect something untoward?"

Duncan met his eye and then glanced at the restraining hand. Ollie released him, smiling apologetically. "It is too early to say with any certainty." Duncan looked between them, seeing both Neil and Nathan watching them from across the room. The only person who'd already left was Ryan. Alistair had gone too.

"That's not a denial," Ollie said firmly.

"No, it's not," Duncan replied evenly. "Tell me, has anything happened between you all this week?"

"Like what?" Tony asked defensively.

"Anyone fallen out?"

"With Steve?" Ollie asked. Duncan inclined his head. "No, not at all."

"You're sure?" Duncan asked. "A stag trip... a lot of alcohol, men being men." He shrugged. "It happens."

"This is ridiculous," Tony said, shaking his head and striding away. Duncan watched him go. He didn't speak to anyone, blanking his school friend, Neil, who tried to speak to him as he passed. Neil looked crestfallen.

"You'll have to forgive him, Detective Inspector," Ollie said, standing beside Duncan and also watching his friend leave. "This isn't the trip he was hoping it would be."

"I can imagine."

"He'll come around. It's just all been a bit of a shock."

Duncan agreed, taking a deep breath. "Why here?"

Ollie looked at him and Duncan glanced sideways with a quizzical look. "Excuse me?"

"Why come on a stag trip all the way up here? I mean, most lads' trips are to Amsterdam or Prague. Why here?"

Ollie shrugged. "Why not?"

"Not a great deal to do, the night life isn't exactly stellar… no real night clubs or dancing girls…" Duncan shrugged. "So… why Skye?"

Ollie inhaled deeply. "We're a bit long in the tooth for strippers and all-night drinking sessions, Detective Inspector. Besides, that's all a bit naff, isn't it?"

Duncan nodded. "I suppose so. Tell me, what do you make of Ryan?"

Ollie blew out his cheeks. "Not a lot. A bit of a neanderthal, if you ask me."

"You're not a fan then?"

Ollie smiled briefly. "No, not really, but Tony doesn't have many friends, so Steve was just trying to make up the numbers. You know how it is."

"Not really, no."

"Where did you have yours?" Ollie asked.

"My what?"

"Stag do. Did you go trawling through the red lights of Amsterdam?"

"Not married, never have been," Duncan said, "so I've never really thought about it."

"Well, when you do," Ollie said, "maybe give Skye a miss. It's turned out to be a bit of a killjoy." With that, he made to leave without another word.

"I'll send a car to pick you up," Duncan said, calling after him. Ollie looked back quizzically. "To take you to the identification." Ollie nodded, turned his head and resumed his course. Neil and Nathan fell into step alongside him, and Duncan could see the two men were leaning into him, firing questions at him as they walked. "All very odd indeed," he said to himself.

CHAPTER SIX

"TELL ME ABOUT STEVEN PHELPS." Duncan threw his jacket across the nearest desk, staring at the information board set out at the front of the ops room. So far, the board wasn't populated with a great deal of information, but it was still early. Russell finished munching the last of his ever-present packet of crisps, screwing up the bag and tossing it into the waste bin beneath his desk, brushing the remnants of oily residue from his hands.

"Angus says the forensic guys have finished up and the body is being moved to Craig Dunbar's office for the postmortem."

"Is that tonight?" Duncan asked, checking his watch. It was gone 9 pm and he figured the pathologist would begin the next day.

"Aye, it will be there tonight," Russell confirmed.

"No issue with the boat?" Duncan asked, remembering his conversation with Roddy earlier that day.

"No, no bother at all. Old man Mcintyre will see us right." Duncan recalled Roddy's father wasn't too keen on the police but was pleased he was willing to help.

"Make sure they know we appreciate the assistance," Duncan said. Alistair agreed.

"I'll give him a call after we're through here."

Duncan nodded, looking back to Russell. "Phelps?"

Russell cleared his throat, took a sip from a can of coke and scanned his notes. "Steven Phelps, forty-six years old, born in Airdrie – poor sod – a few notes on his record as a teenager, expelled from school aged fifteen—"

"Any trouble with us?" Duncan asked.

Russell eyed his notes. "No... he joined the army at sixteen—"

"Paras?" Alistair asked.

"Aye, second battalion," Russell said. "Two combat tours of Iraq," Russell peered over the rim of his reading glasses, "the second one, and then served in Afghanistan... three tours, earned a military cross in that period too. He left the army ten years ago."

Duncan considered the information. "That's a lot of detail. The Ministry of Defence feeling generous today, were they?"

Russell laughed. "No, I'm still waiting to hear back from them, unsurprisingly. I got all of this from his website."

"Website?" Alistair asked.

"Aye, Phelps has his own business and I got all of this from the *About Me* section."

"Doing what?" Duncan asked.

"All manner of things. After he left the parachute regiment, it looks like he went out contracting—"

"Mercenary?" Alistair asked.

"No, I don't think so," Russell said. "From what I can gather, he took on positions in private security firms in trouble zones around the world. Primarily in the Middle East and Africa."

"So... a mercenary," Alistair said drily.

"I suppose you wouldn't put that on the web, would you?" Russell argued. "It might cut off corporate clients. Anyway, he did that for three years or so and then set up a business called *Gold Star*, which he still runs today. Well..." Russell said, rocking his head from side to side, "until he wound up dead anyway."

"And what do they do?"

Russell checked his notes again. "Private security..." he glanced at Alistair, seemingly expecting him to interrupt but the DS was silent, arms folded across his chest. "Although on the company page it cites CQP as its primary business, working for corporate clients with overseas interests."

"CQP?" Duncan asked.

Alistair answered. "Close Quarter Protection. Bodyguards effectively. If they are working for corporations then you're looking at oil industry executives, perhaps IT companies with contracts in post-war or conflict zones."

"How much is that worth, do you think?" Duncan asked.

Alistair cocked his head. "Danger money... for the guys on the ground it pays incredibly well, thousands per week depending on where you are, I guess. If you are the company and get the contract... a small fortune. You only have to see the amount of money governments are throwing at private contractors to offset the need for official assets to be on the ground to see how profitable that would be."

Duncan exhaled. "Good work if you can get it."

"And if you can stay alive," Alistair said. "Not for me." Duncan shot him a quizzical look. "When you have a flag on your arm, then people are going to look out for you if it all goes pear-shaped. Politicians have the media backlash to contend with if they put you in harm's way. Take that flag off your kit..." He sucked air through his teeth, "then you're expendable. If the proverbial hits the fan, you're more than likely on your own."

"Sounds scary," Duncan said. "Why would you want to do that?

"Aye, not for me at any money," Alistair said. "But… some of these guys… the military is all they know. In the army they're the best they can be at what they do. They're trained to be the best, equipped, part of something larger than themselves. Warriors."

"You make them sound ten feet tall, sarge," Russell said. Alistair stared him down and Russell looked away.

"Don't underestimate it," Alistair said. "Then, one day, you leave and all that training, that experience… can get you a job driving a taxi – no offence to cabbies – or a uniform on the door in a supermarket, minimum wage and all because you're not qualified for anything else. Or…"

"You can get paid thousands of pounds to drive around a suit in a foreign country," Duncan said. "If you put it like that… I can see the appeal."

Alistair tilted his head to one side. "But you know that your card can get stamped at any moment. It's a tough life, one that's hard to merge with a civilian life back home. Much like when you're in the forces, period."

"Probably why Phelps is single then?" Duncan asked.

Russell continued. "Yes, he was married but that was back when he was serving. No next of kin on file, his mother passed away a few years back… no father listed."

"Does he own this business outright?" Duncan asked.

"No, there are three directors listed on the Companies House database. They each have an equal share in the business."

"Names?" Duncan asked.

Russell checked a window he had open on his computer,

scrolling down momentarily. "Ryan Masters..." Duncan and Alistair exchanged a glance. "And Anthony—"

"Sinclair," Duncan said. Russell looked up at him.

"Aye, do you know him?"

"Phelps is up here for Sinclair's stag party. Masters is too."

"Right, I'll have a root around and see what I can find out about them too." Russell made a note. "Are we... thinking something isn't right about this lot then, sir?"

Duncan took a breath. "There's something off about them, that's true. Today..." He glanced at Alistair, "they all acted... I don't know."

"Like they've got something to hide," Alistair said. "I had that idea as well."

"Where did you go, after we'd finished talking to them?" Duncan asked him. Once they'd finished out at the estate, Duncan found himself busy with briefing the hierarchy and he hadn't had a chance to speak to Alistair about it.

"Oh, I figured I'd have a wee chat with Ryan Masters."

"Thought so. What did he have to say?"

"Not a lot," Alistair said. "He's a bit... annoyed, is probably too light a word for it, but he's aggravated by all of this."

"Did you pitch him with the whole *comrades-in-arms* thing, soldier to soldier?"

Alistair laughed. "No, not yet. I figured I'd keep my powder dry on that one and use it when it might really help us."

"Fair enough," Duncan said. "What did you make of the others?"

"That Ollie is an insipid little shite, isn't he?"

Duncan smiled wryly. "No, tell me what you really think of him. Don't hold back."

"I am holding back," Alistair said. "Something about him... makes my skin crawl. He's too calm... too polished."

"And Tony?"

"Same... although my reaction is slightly less visceral. Masters is... a tough one to read. I'd hate to play a hand of poker with him. He'd take the shirt off my back, unless he gets a bit jumpy when the pressure's on but somehow, I doubt it."

"Aye, he was aggravated today, wasn't he? Is that a veteran thing? A dislike of authority?"

"No, I wouldn't say so. Most people I know who served quite like the discipline. Not being shouted at, we all bloody hated that, but there's something to be said for knowing where you are and what's expected of you, and when."

"What do you mean?" Duncan asked, perching himself on the edge of a desk.

"Think about it," Alistair said. "You don't have to worry about where you're going to sleep, when you're going to eat... where you have to be... it's all taken care of."

"Sounds awful," Russell said.

"That's because you like to be able to graze on crisps whenever you like!" Alistair said. "And don't get me wrong, everyone would be moaning when hanging around the barracks or about being on parade, so the point is, you don't have to think about it. A lot of these lads, when they get back into civvy street, they're suddenly cut adrift and no one is there to tell them what to do, where to be... or cooking their meals for them. Once they fall out of this routine... for some, it's too much and they go off the rails. Don't bother shaving, eating properly... and when you have to make yourself go to work..."

"You make them sound like idiots," Russell said, shaking his head.

"No, not idiots," Alistair corrected him. "Just conditioned to live a certain way. Why do you think our prisons are stuffed full of veterans, because they damn well are? These guys aren't prepared for civilian life and for some, they just can't do it. Throw in the stresses of combat service and you get an added dimension of poor mental health and it's a recipe for disaster."

"They just need to get married," Russell said. "Then they'll have someone to tell them what to do every day for the rest of their lives."

"The pay's not very good though, is it?" Alistair said with a smile. "And I bet you don't say that in front of your missus."

"No way," Russell said. "I probably wouldn't stay married for long…"

"What about the other two?" Duncan asked. "The IT guy, Neil Banister, and what's his name, the builder?"

"Nathan," Alistair said. "Hard to judge. Neither of them was particularly vocal. I reckon Tony and Ollie call the shots in that little fraternity. I'll bet not a lot happens without their approval."

"Where do you think Steven Phelps fits into all of this?"

Alistair was thoughtful. "If his website isn't a pack of lies, then I reckon he'd be on a par with his business partners, wouldn't you say?"

"Agreed." Duncan sat in silence for a moment, contemplating. None of this brought them any closer to knowing how or why Phelps came to be where they found him. "Where's Caitlyn?"

"She's helping Angus get the body back, and earlier on she was dealing with the tourists, taking statements from them," Russell said.

"Okay, when she's back in the office, I want her to help you with getting backgrounds on all of these guys who are together on this stag trip. I want to know if there's any needle between them. Old friends they may well be, but in longstanding relationships there's always tension. Maybe something came together this week and boiled over."

I'm on it, sir," Russell said, turning back to his screen and reaching for another packet of crisps. Duncan got up from the desk, coming to stand before the photograph of Steven Phelps pinned to the information board. Alistair came to join him.

"So, you're leaning towards a friend-on-friend scenario?" he asked. "He will have made enemies abroad in his line of work."

Duncan wrinkled his nose. "I'm not necessarily disregarding a work-related motive, but before I start looking into his globetrotting exploits, I think it's prudent to stay closer to home. After all, the simplest explanations are usually the most accurate. Besides, if someone meant him harm, then there are far easier places to kill someone..."

"And Phelps spent a lot of time in those."

"Exactly," Duncan said. "Let's get into his life, starting with his friends, and then work from there. There's something about that lot... they seemed surprised we'd found him."

"That could be because they didn't think he'd been harmed."

"True... or was it that we found him so quickly."

"What do you mean?"

Duncan was pensive. After all, it was purely conjecture at this point. "Well... he's evidently a proficient soldier and what are soldiers good at when it comes to operations, putting themselves in harm's way?"

Alistair was thoughtful. "British soldiers? Preparation... planning. It might not go as it should, but we'll be prepared for it either way."

"I agree. So... put that mindset into Phelps's life, both business and personal. He's going out on the mountains, either that day or night, we don't know which. You saw him today...

and you've got a military background. What do you make of it?"

"He wasn't prepared for a climb…"

"Or even a hike," Duncan said. "Not really. Coat, trousers… boots, sure." He shrugged. "But…"

"No provisions… hadn't let anyone know where he was going – as far as we know – in case he got into trouble and needed help."

"That's what I'm thinking," Duncan said. "If he was planning to go out there, surely a man like him with his experience would know all of that, right?"

"I'd expect so, yes."

"So, that presents another set of questions," Duncan said.

"Did he feel like he was taking a risk, at all? Alistair suggested.

"And did he go there of his own free will?"

Alistair grimaced. "How would someone get a guy the size of Phelps out there if he didn't want to go?"

Duncan knew Alistair had a point. "Maybe he didn't know he was in danger."

"Or there is no mystery, and he just cocked up?"

"Or he just cocked up," Duncan said, nodding. "We'll have a better idea tomorrow, once Craig Dunbar's carried out the postmortem.

Duncan stepped away, checking the time. Taking out his mobile, he called Grace. She didn't answer and the call cut to voicemail. Sighing, Duncan didn't leave a message.

CHAPTER SEVEN

DUNCAN FOUND sleep difficult that night, waking before dawn to the sound of a strong wind buffeting his house and waves crashing against the rocks on the nearby shoreline. Finding Grace wasn't beside him when his eyes opened came as a surprise until he remembered their parting the previous day. Scooping up his mobile from the bedside table, he glanced at the screen, scanning the notifications that came through overnight but there was no message or missed call from her.

Getting out of bed, he took a quick shower, made himself a cup of coffee, and sat down before the picture window overlooking the water this side of the headland. From his bedroom on the first floor, he had quite a view across to the Western Isles, weather permitting, but he liked this spot to have his morning coffee as the sun rose behind the house.

His mobile beeped twice in quick succession and he looked, hopeful it was Grace, but he was disappointed to see one was from his sister Roslyn, asking if he'd be able to call in to see their mum in the nursing home later on and the other was from Dr Dunbar. He'd made an early start and expected to have a cause of death before eight o'clock. The pathologist must have risen even before Duncan. But Craig was a little odd, and Duncan wasn't surprised.

Craig Dunbar was an experienced pathologist, and Duncan knew colleagues working in Glasgow who could be taught a thing or two by him. He was wasted here on the island, and Duncan figured he could have made a real impact if he ever wanted to move to the mainland. Craig was happy here though and wouldn't have his head turned by the bright lights of a big city.

Duncan messaged Alistair, suggesting they meet at Dr Dunbar's office. The team had their assignments, and with a cause of death, they'd know which direction to take the investigation. Sending Roslyn a quick text to say he'd stop by later, after lunch, he considered sending Grace a message as well, but decided against it. Clearly, she was upset with him, but it must be more than simply what he said about her job. Until he figured out what the issue was, he didn't know what he was supposed to do.

"WELL, DUNCAN," Dr Dunbar said, removing his glasses and cleaning the lenses with a microfibre cloth before putting them back on and fixing him with a stern look, "you've given me quite a puzzle to solve."

Duncan and Alistair exchanged a quick look. "I have?"

"Indeed. Fortunately, most of what I found puzzling falls into your sphere of influence rather than mine."

"Sounds ominous," Alistair said.

"I'll start with the basics, if that's all right with you, gentlemen, and then we can explore the fun stuff?" Duncan nodded, unclear on what the *fun stuff* could be referring to. "Mr Phelps was in fine physical condition in the run-up to his death. I can find no ailments or health concerns that would have manifested in inhibiting in any way that could cause injury, or even death."

"He was healthy?" Duncan clarified.

"Tip top!" Dr Dunbar said. "Oh, to be in such fine fettle as this man was. Evidently, he managed a fitness regime, a decent diet, strong cardio and resistance training, no doubt. He was athletic, but not overly muscular, with a body on the lean side of the fat to muscle ratio. As I say, good condition."

"So, is that your long-winded way of ruling out death by natural causes, doc?" Alistair asked with a half-smile.

"Yes, but why waste the opportunity to use one's vocabulary, Detective Sergeant?"

"You live alone, don't you, Craig?" Alistair replied.

"Yes, I do. And, quite frankly, I'm amazed that *you* do not, Alistair."

"Me too," Alistair said with a grin.

"Do you have a cause of death for me, Craig?" Duncan asked.

"I do, yes. Along with several other factors which no doubt had a hand in contributing to it."

"The fun stuff, you mentioned?"

"Oh no, but please be patient." Duncan smiled, gesturing for the pathologist to continue at his own pace. Dr Dunbar gathered his notes, holding the sheets away from him despite wearing his reading glasses. "I really must have my prescription checked. The print is getting smaller, I swear. Anyway, I digress," he said, lifting his eyes to meet Duncan's. "The short version is that Mr Phelps died from exposure."

"Time of death?"

"He was found around ten o'clock in the morning, wasn't he?" Duncan nodded. "I should imagine he passed away during the previous night, between midnight and 3 am. It is hard to be more precise because of the weather conditions, but that's about as accurate as I can be, I'm afraid."

"We can work with that, Craig, thank you," Duncan said. "You said there were contributing factors?"

"Ah, yes. I believe he was unconscious when he passed away, but that wasn't a result of hypothermia but down to a head injury," he said, beckoning them over to the mortuary table where Steven Phelps's body lay, covered by a sheet. Dr Dunbar pulled the sheet down to the shoulders, and he leaned in towards the head, which had been cleaned for the post-mortem procedure. "You see this wound here?"

Duncan inspected it. This side of the head had been hidden from view at the scene, but it was clear this was where much of the blood around the head had originated from. It was a large wound, and damage to the skull beneath was visible.

"You see the depth of the laceration and then the depression in the skull?" Dunbar asked. Duncan nodded. "Well, that was certainly a large enough blow that would render him unconscious. It also caused a subdural haematoma, here on the side of the brain, which would have been very nasty for him… had he survived the night obviously."

"That's a bleed on the brain, isn't it?" Duncan asked.

"Yes, more or less. It occurs when blood collects under the dura mater, one of the layers of tissue that protect your brain and builds up. It comes from a head injury and can prove fatal if untreated. Now, there isn't a lot of space in that area of our heads. We have the brain," Dunbar said, holding his hand above his head, fingers extended, "and then there is what we call the dura mater, the layers of tissue surrounding the brain which cushion and protect it. I won't delve into the venous drainage of the scalp, the superficial and deep layouts of the arterial components… because that's not necessary here—"

"Thank you!" Alistair said.

Dr Dunbar sighed, looking at Alistair. "Of course, some of us have much smaller brains, and therefore more space within our skulls, than others." Alistair laughed at that. "The point I am trying to make is that Mr Phelps would have been in significant trouble if he hadn't reached a hospital within a few hours after receiving this injury. In any event, it's academic because the elements got to him first."

"Did the injury happen from a fall or can't you say?" Duncan asked.

"It would be quite conceivable for him to have such an injury from striking his head, yes. However, I don't believe that's the case here."

"You sound confident," Duncan said.

"I am," Dr Dunbar said, crossing to his desk and taking out two prints of X-rays depicting Phelps's skull. One was from the side and the second from above the head, looking down. The depression was clear to see in both, but from the side there was a very clear impact point. "I think it is self-explanatory, don't you?" he said, passing the sheets to Duncan. Alistair came to stand beside him, and they both examined the images. The impact point was circular, and almost perfectly round.

"That's not from any piece of rock I've ever seen," Alistair said.

"Quite correct, Alistair," Dunbar said. "Unless you find a piece of polished rock, smoothed over, and an inch in diameter... pretty much to the millimetre."

"What is it, a hammer?" Duncan asked.

"That would be my guess, yes. Or something similar. In any event, it punched a hole through the skull on the side of his head there, you can see the fissures emanating out from the impact point across the skull. The depression is spherical, so I would be looking for a ball hammer... as I say, the head would be an inch in diameter, perhaps slightly smaller. The hole could be enlarged by the velocity of the strike."

Duncan exhaled heavily, passing the image in his hand to Alistair for closer inspection. "So, we're definitely talking about manslaughter if not murder."

"Indeed, Detective Inspector. Now, we can progress to the more curious elements to the puzzle you've handed me."

"The *fun stuff?*"

"That's right," Dr Dunbar said. "Now, obviously I found the cause of death fairly quickly, and this head injury didn't exactly test my capabilities, but I have been thorough with the remainder of the postmortem. There are several soft tissue injuries I found on his body, bruising and abrasions, but they occurred thirty-six to forty-eight hours prior to his death. What had he been up to in the days prior to his demise, do we know?"

"Hanging out with friends, deer stalking... that kind of thing."

"Hmm... I suppose he could have got these injuries from bumping and bashing around in the wilds of Skye... but he does have some tissue damage to his hands." The doctor returned to the body, lifting the sheet to reveal his left hand. "You see here, abrasions to the backs of his hand here, both hands show similar, and there is also soft tissue damage to the fingers."

"Yes, we saw that at the scene. We thought he might have been scrambling," Duncan said.

Dunbar agreed, nodding sagely. "Yes, that would be consistent. That will do substantial damage to one's extremities to do so without gloves, but I agree, I think that is how his hands were damaged. That, and trying to stop the descent when he fell."

"Ah..." Alistair said, "but you said he was unconscious from the blow?"

"I did, but I don't think that was his only fall," Dunbar said. "If you examine his clothing – I'm sure your lab boys and girls will know better than me – you'll see dust, dirt and grime, tears in the fabric... the same with his boots... all indicative of moving at pace through our unique terrain. Quite a challenge at night."

"That makes it sound more like he was... running—"

"Incredibly risky to do so at night," Dunbar said. "I took the liberty of checking the weather on the night in question and he wouldn't have had any help from moonlight."

"No, it was very overcast," Duncan said.

"A night climb... and at the pace I imagine he was moving at is foolhardy in the extreme."

Alistair exhaled heavily. "Foolhardy... unless you're more frightened of what you're running from."

"Which brings me to the next piece in this seemingly endless puzzle," Dunbar said, gesturing for them to come closer. He lifted Phelps's left hand, pointing at the wrist. "You can see these circular marks? They can be found on the other hand as well."

Duncan frowned. "He was restrained."

"Definitely," Dunbar said. "You see here, where the skin has broken. The edges to these cuts are straight. He struggled to free himself from them. The line of the cuts... I think imply the use of cable ties, plastic... perhaps five-millimetre width."

"They aren't as strong as people think," Alistair countered. "They're perfect for tidying the cables at the back of your desk or in your workshop at home, but they won't restrain a man as strong as Phelps. Not for long anyway."

"You're quite right, hence the breaking of the skin and the

abrasions around it. As I say, the wounds are the same on both wrists—"

"He broke free?" Duncan asked.

"Or... was trying very hard to break free before he was released. I can't say for sure, but he was certainly bound wrists and ankles."

"Any sign of him being dragged?" Duncan asked.

Dunbar shook his head. "No, he walked onto the mountainside, but..." he was thoughtful, "tell me, when was he reported missing?"

"Two days ago," Duncan said. "So, he was missing for two nights."

"Hmm... that is interesting," Dr Dunbar said, pondering what that might mean. "The abrasions and the cuts to his wrist... they were fresh."

"How fresh?"

"Yesterday, perhaps the skin was broken a matter of hours before he passed away."

"What's the significance of that?" Duncan asked.

"Well... Alistair is correct, a man like this could have broken free of these restraints in short time, so I imagine he was in the process of doing so shortly before he died."

"Could he have been cut free after his death, to make it look more like an accident?" Duncan asked.

"Perhaps, but I'd argue the hammer blow puts a large hole in that theory, no pun intended. And the way his arms, forearms and upper arms have impact injuries, suggests they were free to flap about, so to speak, on his descent. I dare say his wrists were not restrained when he tumbled down the mountain. It also looks like the blood supply to both hands and feet was restricted for some time, prior to death, as well."

"Are you suggesting he was bound up... and left somewhere before being taken out to the Cuillins?" Duncan asked.

Dr Dunbar arched his eyebrows, lips pursed. "Mine is not to reason why... purely just to see who died." He smiled at his rewording of the Tennyson poem. His smile faded as neither Duncan nor Alistair responded. "Anyway... I carried out a blood toxicology test."

"And?"

Dr Dunbar shook his head. "Traces of alcohol, which fits with the theme of the week but not enough to incapacitate him."

"Drugs?"

"No, nothing." Dunbar frowned. "It's all a bit cryptic, isn't it, Duncan?"

"It certainly is, Craig. As you say, lots to think about."

"Good luck!" the pathologist said, smiling warmly.

Duncan thanked him and they left the mortuary. They didn't speak as they made their way back to the car. Once inside, Duncan glanced at Alistair. "Does what we know about Steven Phelps make you think he's the type of guy who would allow himself to be held captive before being led out onto a mountain in the dead of night?"

Alistair stared straight ahead. "No. Quite the opposite, if anything."

"That's my thinking, too."

"So, what do you think is going on?"

Duncan sighed. "Someone's not telling us the truth, that's for certain."

Alistair chuckled. "Life would be dull if everyone did though, wouldn't it?"

CHAPTER EIGHT

THEY FOUND the ops room a hive of activity when they returned to the station. Duncan gathered everyone together for a briefing. He began by outlining the results of the postmortem. "So, this has now been confirmed as a murder investigation, but we need to keep that within these four walls for the time being," he explained. "I don't want wild conjecture doing the rounds in the media, putting pressure on us and diverting resources away from where we want them to be focused. That means no leaks, understood."

Everyone murmured their agreement, but Duncan knew that with the best will in the world, they'd not be able to keep a lid on this for very long. The press were already interested; the death of a climber on Skye wasn't necessarily unusual but under these circumstances, it was far from normal.

"Right, let's summarise who we have here," Duncan said once the conversation had died down. "There are six members in this stag party. We have the deceased, Steven Phelps, his army pal, Ryan Masters. Phelp's school friends, Neil Banister, Tony Sinclair and Oliver Caistor. Lastly, the builder, Nathan

Aldred. Oliver Caistor is the organiser and Tony Sinclair is the prospective groom. There is also our islander, Alex Brennan, the estate manager, who took the group out stalking. Now, the lines of inquiry for us," Duncan said, "I want to know everything about Steven Phelps; where he lived, worked, friends, acquaintances... bank accounts... everything. Secondly, the same goes for all of these people." Duncan crossed to the information board where all of those in attendance for Tony Sinclair's stag week were listed. "If anyone is going to know what has been going on in Phelps's life, it's going to be them. So far, they've not been particularly forthcoming. That might not be due to anything suspicious, or one of them might have killed him."

"They all might have killed him for all we know," Alistair said.

"Treat them all," Duncan continued, undeterred, "as suspects for the time being. I want to know where they've been since they arrived on the island. Who they've spoken to... everything. Take statements from them all and then cross check for irregularities and or omissions but keep it relatively informal. I don't want them going to ground and offering us nothing. Let's turn Steven Phelps's life upside down and see what falls out." Duncan looked at DC Caitlyn Stewart and Russell McLean. "What do we have so far?"

"Anthony Sinclair is an interesting associate of Phelps's, sir," Caitlyn said. Duncan encouraged her with a nod. "He's the third son of Rhodry Sinclair—"

"Of the Edinburgh Sinclairs?" Duncan asked.

"The very same."

"Who are they?" Alistair asked.

"Rhodry Sinclair is an old school Scottish gangster," Duncan said. "They were pretty big in the extortion and money laundering game until about a decade ago when they lost ground to the next generation of low-life neds coming up the way. Is old Rhodry still alive?"

Caitlyn nodded. "Aye, but as you say he's gone a bit quiet. I spoke to one of our colleagues in Edinburgh and, in his words, the Sinclairs have been gentrified."

Duncan scoffed. "I doubt that very much."

"I think it was a euphemism, sir."

"What about Tony specifically?"

Caitlyn read from her notes. "He hasn't come up on our radar, but I've dug up as much as I could on him. He was educated at Gordonstoun until he turned fourteen and then he went to board down in London."

"Get him away from Scotland I expect," Duncan said.

"He's a businessman now. He has a property development company, commercial stuff based in and around London. Then he has an investment company and the one you already know about, the partnership with Steven Phelps and Ryan Masters."

"Any of his interests overseas by any chance?" Duncan asked. "Say... in conflict zones?"

"No, not as far as I can see. He's purely based here in the UK."

"You said he was the third brother. What about his siblings?"

"William... he's doing a stretch for fraud, and the eldest brother, Connor—"

"Was shot dead in an organised killing two years ago," Duncan said.

"You know him?"

"Of him, aye," Duncan said. "The Sinclairs tried to move out of Edinburgh a while back. I suspect that was because of pressure coming their way in their patch, so they tried to move to pastures new. The locals didn't like it much and things got a bit hairy for a time. Connor was on point, trying to establish a new order. They took him down."

"Did you catch who did it?"

Duncan shrugged. "There were some names in the frame but as far as I know it's still an open investigation."

"You think it's related to our case?"

"I doubt it, seeing as we've no connection between Tony Sinclair and his family business, but let's keep an open mind. Where the Sinclairs are involved, I wouldn't rule anything out. Where are you with the others?"

"Oliver Caistor is a well-connected man. Eton educated, I found his profile on multiple social media accounts linked to the school. Another businessman with a varied portfolio of interests but his main role is working in his father's business, manufacturing equipment for medical and pharmaceutical companies."

Alistair grunted. "I told you he was a little shite."

Duncan smiled. "Not all privately educated children grow up to be horrible human beings, DS MacEachran."

"No, I know that... just a large percentage of them."

"Any criminal record?"

Caitlyn shook her head. "No, he's clean. Nathan Aldred, on the other hand, has controversy swirling around him."

"Why, what's he been up to?"

"Nothing that's been deemed illegal, yet. He is the director of six separate building and property development businesses. He's a busy man, seeing as he is the sole owner of all of them."

"Why does a man need six businesses all operating in the same field?" Duncan asked.

"That's it exactly," Caitlyn said. "Four years ago, one of his businesses, the only one he operated at the time, got into financial difficulties. Long story short, he folded the firm with debts of several million, but not before setting up another business with a similar name, and trading in the same field, as a parent company. He folded his troubled business while the ink was still drying on the paperwork of his new one."

Alistair arched his eyebrows. "Isn't that called phoenixing?"

"Yes, it is, sarge."

"And it's illegal, the last time I looked."

"Aye, but only if HMRC bother to investigate it properly and prosecute. That's where the controversy comes in. If you do an internet search on Nathan Aldred then you find it all over social media and in the papers, fury at him not paying up or completing projects but," Caitlyn shrugged, "he wasn't prosecuted, so that's the end of it. There's no tie in with any of the businesses with Steven Phelps though, that I can see, or any of the others for that matter."

"Scammer," Alistair said. "That's why he'll have multiple companies... muddies the waters in case anyone comes looking and asking questions."

Duncan laughed. "You're a cynical man, Alistair."

"Aye, but that doesn't mean I'm wrong though, does it?"

"Neil Banister?" Duncan asked, reading the last name on the list.

"Aye, that's me. I had him," Russell said.

"Good, I'm pleased you managed to do some work while we were out policing," Alistair said.

Russell frowned but ignored the jibe at his expense. "Neil Banister works as an IT consultant for a business in Birmingham. They specialise in cyber security provision, maintaining corporate sites all around the country."

"What does he do?"

"Sales," Russell said. "He goes around to businesses touting for work and securing contract extensions with existing clients. It must be one of the most sinfully boring jobs you can have, to my mind."

"Any criminal background with him?"

"Despite being the dullest of all the characters, yes, he does. He was charged with aggravated assault three years ago. He received a two-year custodial sentence, suspended for two years."

"Who did he assault?"

"His wife, apparently. She decided not to press charges, but the Crown Prosecution Service threw the book at him anyway."

Duncan thought about it. Neil Banister's conviction proved he had the capacity to be violent, but Duncan couldn't see him taking on someone like Steven Phelps.

"Right... an interesting group of people. Now we need to know what issue they might have had with Phelps."

"I was also looking into Ryan Masters, sir," Russell said. Duncan had managed to forget him. Russell glanced at Alistair. "That's why I was a little behind on the others, I spent most of the day getting the runaround from the MOD."

"What did you find out?"

"We know he served in the second battalion of the Parachute Regiment, where he met Phelps. They served together in Iraq. The MOD sent his service file over to me, eventually, but I had to really push for it."

"Give us the highlights," Duncan said.

"Multiple combat tours where his performance was exemplary, but he also has quite a disciplinary record which he shouldn't be proud of. He faced multiple charges for breach of discipline, not that they'll tell me what he did, mind you. He was discharged in 2016 but, again, the reason why is not in his file. Curiously, his last five years of service state he was in the Paras but didn't detail where he was, which unit he served in... or anything. It's like..." Russell frowned, "like he wasn't there at all."

"SFO," Alistair said.

"What's that?" Duncan asked, and everyone else was waiting for an answer too.

"Special Forces. He'll have been off somewhere, doing who knows what. Those guys are professional, but they don't stick to discipline very well. At least, not day-to-day army discipline. They are great in theatre, but it wouldn't surprise me to hear he didn't care for the mundane side of things." Alistair cocked his head. "That'll be why his file had chunks missing out of it. They'll never tell you what he was up to."

"Well, that makes him a lethal figure in all of this, doesn't it?" Duncan said. He looked at Alistair. "Did you see the abrasions on his knuckles?"

"Aye, looks like he'd been fighting to me."

"Let's find out who with," Duncan said.

CHAPTER NINE

DUNCAN HEARD someone entering the ops room, calling his name. He turned to see Fraser Macdonald ambling across the room towards him. "Hey, Fraser, what can I do for you?"

"Sorry to interrupt, sir," Fraser said, nodding a greeting to Alistair. "But... am I right in thinking you've been out having dealings with the lads from the Maelrubha Estate today?"

"Aye, that's right. The deceased man we have out at Loch Coruisk has been staying on the estate with his pals."

"Ah... right. I see." Fraser said, frowning. "Okay, nae bother."

"What is it, Fraser?" Duncan asked just as the constable made to turn away from him.

"Oh... probably nothing like. I thought you were actually investigating something to do with the estate itself, is all."

"Why?"

"Well, it's probably nothing but..." he glanced at Alistair. "You remember Charlie Lumsden, from over in—"

"Aye, of course. What's he done?"

Fraser laughed. "The usual. Anyway, the other night I stumbled across him doing some sort of back-street deal...

you know what Charlie's like, always looking for an angle to make a few quid."

"What was he doing?" Duncan asked.

"Dealing, I imagine," Fraser said. "Not that it went through, you know, because I happened across it and the car Charlie had his head stuck through the window of, took off as soon as they clocked me. Nearly decapitated the wee fella."

"Aye, you wouldn't notice much difference in his behaviour if they had," Alistair said with a half-smile.

"Right. Anyway, the car sped away and I sidled up to Charlie. He was bricking it... hands in his pockets, best behaviour kind of thing. I let him be, I mean, it's Charlie... and he's harmless, isn't he?"

"And you were getting ready to clock off," Alistair said.

"Aye, I was, right enough." Fraser frowned. "But if I was to bring Charlie in every time he was caught up to no good, then I'd do nothing else, would I?"

"And you thought this would be of interest to me, why?" Duncan asked. Not that petty dealing wasn't something to take seriously, but Charlie Lumsden wasn't Al Capone.

"The car. I clocked the licence plate, and I ran it when I got back to the station, out of curiosity, you know? I wondered who Charlie was mixing with now."

"And?"

"The vehicle was registered to the Maelrubha Estate." Fraser shrugged. "I thought it might be relevant, but maybe not."

"I don't suppose you saw who was driving?"

"No, I can't say I did. They were heading away from me, you know? Sorry."

"That's all right, Fraser. We'll keep it in mind," Duncan said.

Alistair nodded. "And if you fancy doing some proper

policing at any point, feel free to feel Charlie Lumsden's collar every once in a while."

"That's unfair, Keck," Fraser said, referring to Alistair by the nickname reserved for those he went way back with. "I mean, it's Charlie." Duncan knew Alistair was only teasing the big man. "Oh, I tell you what mind," Fraser said, turning back. "It all happened just out the back of the wee Co-op, in Portree, the rear entrance is off *Cnoc na Gaoithe*."

"Aye, so?" Alistair asked.

"The car pulled away and took a right onto Bank Street, passing the front of the shop. They have cameras out front. They probably caught a look at the driver." Fraser shrugged, seeing both senior officer's lack of interest. "Aye, well... thought I'd mention it."

Fraser made to leave and was almost out of the room when Alistair called after him. "Fraser! What was the vehicle?"

Fraser turned, and excitedly hurried back to them. "It was a Toyota Land Cruiser. One of those big four-by-four things, dark blue. Only a year old as well."

"Right, and what time was it that you saw Charlie and... whoever he was talking to?"

"Just before eight o'clock in the evening."

"Thanks, Fraser," Alistair said. The constable smiled, pleased to be of assistance and left. Duncan fixed Alistair with a quizzical look. The detective sergeant smiled. "When we were leaving, I saw Alex Brennan get something out of his vehicle. It caught my attention."

"Why?"

"I'm thinking about trading mine in, and I liked the look of his."

"What was it?"

"A nearly new Toyota pick-up," Alistair said. "Dark blue. Nice." Duncan checked the time. He planned to duck out to see his mum today, and he'd have to pass the Co-op on his way to see her. It couldn't hurt to take a look.

DUNCAN MADE his way up the stairs along the well-trodden route to his mum's bedroom. Suffering from Alzheimer's, her condition hadn't improved in the last few months like he'd hoped. He'd barely spent time with her after leaving Skye, choosing to find excuses rather than come home to visit her. Duncan carried some guilt, not least because his sister would still point it out on occasion, especially if she thought he wasn't pulling his weight.

He'd been making an effort though, since he came home, and he'd hoped that seeing another familiar face, his, and stirring up old memories might help their mum. That wasn't the case though. If anything, he felt she was slipping further away from him every day. Those lucid memories, recalling fonder moments, were coming to mind less and less.

Knocking gently on the door, he entered. His mum was alone, sitting in her seat by the window. She liked to look out over the gardens, and she had a nice view across the water towards Raasay too.

"Hi mum," he said, coming to her and leaning in, kissing her forehead. She didn't acknowledge his presence, but that didn't matter. He sat down in the chair opposite her and began telling her about all the things he'd been up to. He hadn't been up to much, if he was honest, and found himself talking about the days he spent with Grace, how they were exploring the coastline, and she was photographing the wildlife.

It was weird, talking about Grace. She'd become an integral part of his life, but he hadn't realised it until now.

"Nice girl."

Duncan was snapped out of his thoughts. He looked at his mum. "Sorry?" She was looking at him, her eyes gleaming like they always used to when she was speaking fondly about something or someone. "Who, Grace?"

"Yes. A pretty little thing. Much better looking than her older sister."

Duncan smiled. She must be remembering when Grace and her sister were children and Duncan used to babysit for their parents on occasion. "Aye, she's all grown up now, Mum."

"A lovely red dress."

"Say again?"

"The dress she wore when you brought her to visit. It was red... and quite lovely."

Duncan thought about it. He'd stopped by the week before, with Grace, on their way out for the evening. Grace had spoken to her, but his mum had been away in her own world the entire time, he was almost certain. "Yes, she looked lovely, didn't she?"

His mum met his eye, smiling at him. "You should take care of that one. Feisty... but the type of girl you need in your life, wee Duncan." Duncan smiled. She hadn't called him *wee Duncan* in quite some time. His father had always been *big Duncan*, and the attachment stuck for years, even after his father's passing.

"Aye, well... Grace is a bit upset with me at the moment, Mum. I'm... er... not sure how much of her I'll be seeing in the future."

His mum scoffed. "Typical of you!"

"What's that, Mum?" Duncan asked, mildly hurt by her tone. She was just as he remembered her now, fierce.

"You, taking the easy route. Make it right. Whatever it takes."

"Ah... well, I don't actually know what I did. You see..." He looked at her, but the smile was gone, and she was back to staring out of the window again. Duncan felt a pang of loss in his chest, but desperately tried to hold onto that moment of connection, brief as it was. He smiled. "I'll see what I can do, Mum. Just for you."

"I was wondering when you'd stop by again," Roslyn said, entering the room. She was still in her overalls, likely having come straight from working on the old family croft. Duncan got up and kissed his sister hello. "How has she been?"

Duncan smiled, looking at their mother. "She's been grand."

"Really?"

"Aye, she was with me long enough to tell me off for messing things up with Grace."

"Did she now? Well... shouldn't come as a shock, should it? I mean, it is you!"

"Thanks very much, sis."

"Well, I know you, Duncan. You cannae keep it together for very long. So..." she said, hands on her hips, "what did you do wrong?"

Duncan laughed. "Another time. Now you're here, I have to go back to work."

"Likely story."

"I do. It's a big case."

"That ex-army guy they found dead out Coruisk way?"

Duncan sighed. "Does everyone know what's going on in my police station?"

She nodded. "Probably as much as you do, at any rate. So, who did him in?"

"No comment," Duncan said. His sister gave him a hug and he kissed her again.

"You'll come by the house later in the week?"

"Aye."

"Promise?"

"Aye, for crying out loud, I said I would, all right?"

Roslyn waved him off, taking his seat opposite their mum. Duncan lingered in the doorway, Grace coming to mind. He'd make it right, somehow.

Walking out to his car, he decided it would be quicker to walk across to the Co-op. Parking around there was a nightmare at the best of times and it was almost peak season. The little Co-op was the junior to the larger supermarket on the outskirts of town and sought to catch the footfall of visitors to Portree.

It was only a five-minute walk and he entered the cramped premises, seeing three members of staff behind the counter. Everyone was serving, and the shop was rammed. Despite this, he approached the nearest member of staff and presented his warrant card. Finishing up with the customer she had, she then turned to Duncan.

"Your camera outside, is it working?"

"Yes, why?"

"I need to see your footage from a couple of days ago, from about a quarter to eight in the evening."

"Sure, come with me to the office."

She led him through the shop and unlocked a secure door at the rear. The corridor was narrow but soon they were in a little office. There was a small monitor on the desk, the picture split into quarters showing the scene from cameras around the shop. She went into the history and within a couple of minutes, Duncan was watching the feed from the evening in question.

"Can you speed it up a bit," Duncan asked and he found himself watching at double the speed. The Toyota came into view but sadly, it didn't catch an image of the driver, only the rear of the car once it progressed along Bank Street. "Damn," he said softly.

"What were you looking for?"

"Oh... I was hoping to see who was driving the car," Duncan said. "It was behind you here, and then turned onto Bank Street—"

"Let's check the rear camera then."

Duncan looked at her. "You have one at the back too?"

She smiled, leaning past him and with a couple of clicks of her mouse, the feed changed. "Same time?"

"Please."

Duncan waited, unsure if this would be worth his time. It was probably unrelated, but it was coincidental, and coincidences rarely happened in his experience.

"There you are," she said merrily. "Look, it's really busy. Do you mind if I head back out to the shop floor before the customers riot?"

"No, not at all. I'll not be long," Duncan said.

"If you need a copy, just click on the three dots in the corner, download the link and then you can email it wherever you like."

"Thanks," Duncan said. He immediately saw the blue Toyota, but again, he couldn't see the driver. Charlie Lumsden was leaning against the car and the driver's window was down. He saw Charlie hand the occupant something and whatever was given him in exchange, he tucked into his pocket. At that moment, Fraser's car came into view at the far end of the street, Charlie stood bolt upright, and the Toyota sped away.

Still, Duncan couldn't make out the driver. "Was that you, Alex?" Duncan said, clicking on the three dots and selecting download.

CHAPTER TEN

CHARLIE LUMSDEN LIVED on one of the estates located on the outskirts of Portree, close to the large industrial estate that served as a base for much of the businesses working in construction or supplying those that did. Alistair took a right turn into a cul-de-sac of mixed properties, terraced houses, maisonettes and apartments, all wrapped around the access roads.

Pulling into a parking space, Alistair ducked so he could see one of the upper apartments, pointing up to their right. "That's Charlie's place, the second to last one, upper floor flat." Alistair was adamant Duncan had come across Charlie already, but it wasn't a name that he recognised, and he was usually pretty good with that sort of thing.

The weather had shifted today, the strong breeze moving the cold and wet conditions that had plagued them the last couple of days, now replaced by blue skies and sunshine. It felt warm now, and Duncan felt himself sweating having dressed for the wind-chill factor.

They walked across the road, mounting the exterior steps up to Charlie's maisonette. No one was about and, aside from the nearby traffic noise, all Duncan could hear were the birds and the wind passing through the branches of the trees flanking the estate.

Alistair approached the door, ringing the bell. They heard it sound indoors and they waited. The net curtains, hanging across the window to the left of the door twitched and they both looked. As soon as they did the curtains moved again as someone let go. Alistair sighed, pressed the doorbell twice more in quick succession and rapped his knuckles on the door window for good measure.

"Come on, Charlie, it's the polis!" he shouted. There was movement behind the obscured glass and a figure came close, unlocking the door but when it cracked open the security chain was still in place.

"What do you want?" a female voice said. Duncan looked past Alistair, peering through the gap at the woman's face. What he could see of it anyway. She had shoulder-length brown hair, with red highlights and he could see the roots were an inch deep since she'd coloured it. She sported a nose ring, and she had dark shadows around her eyes, a mixture of make-up and poor sleep, he figured.

"Come on, Lorna, open up," Alistair said. "You know who we are."

She closed the door and they heard the security chain slide across before she pulled the door open, drawing her dressing gown about her as she eyed both of them warily. "I didn't know it was you, Mr MacEachran." He smiled. She knew full well, because she'd looked through the window at them. "What are you after?" Lorna asked, looking at Duncan. "Who's your wee friend?"

"DI McAdam," Duncan said, reaching for his warrant card but Lorna had no interest in seeing it. Her eyes went back to Alistair.

"A DI? What's he gone and done now?"

"Charlie?" Alistair asked.

"Aye... my Charlie, I'm sure you're no' here for the bonny prince himself, are you?"

"Is he here?"

"Aye, he's in his bed," she said, folding her arms defiantly across her chest. "You got a warrant?"

Alistair laughed. "I don't need a warrant. I just want to speak to him." He inclined his head. "Is that all right with the gatekeeper?"

"Aye, but wipe your feet on your way in," she said, opening the door wider and stepping back to let them enter. "I've just cleaned."

Duncan doubted that very much, casting an eye around the entrance hall as he passed through the door, but he did as was requested, wiping his feet on the mat. The maisonette smelled of stale smoke and takeaway food. A baby buggy was folded up, leaning against the wall behind the door beneath a row of hooks bulging with coats. As if on cue, a baby started crying and Lorna rolled her eyes, pointing to the stairs.

"If it's not one, then it's the school phoning about the other," Lorna muttered. She looked at Alistair, her eyes shifting to the stairs. "Up there, first door past the bathroom. Get him out of his pit for me, will you? There's stuff to do!"

She left them in the hall, disappearing into a room at the back of the maisonette where Duncan caught sight of a mesh pen. Alistair took the lead, climbing the stairs, Duncan behind him. The stairs were narrow, hemmed in by walls on both sides and the landing above wasn't much better. There was a small bathroom at the top of the stairs and two bedrooms. It was a cramped space but serviceable for a couple with one child, perhaps two, but once they got a little older, then the family would soon outgrow this place.

The door was ajar, and Alistair didn't hang about, pushing it open with enough force to make it thud as it struck the wall behind it. A strong odour of stale air and sweat greeted them. Alistair wrinkled his nose. "Into the abyss with the great unwashed," he said, entering. The bedroom was in quite a state with clothes scattered all around the room, on the floor or hanging from wardrobe doors. It was difficult to see what, if any, were clean or waiting to be put through the machine.

The curtains were drawn across the one window and there was a lump lying beneath a thick duvet, far too thick for this time of the year in Duncan's mind, regardless of how cool the nights still were. He walked around the bed, doing his best not to tread on clothing but it was nigh on impossible, and threw open the curtains allowing sunlight to stream into the room. The rings shrieked on the metal rail and Charlie stirred but didn't wake.

A half-empty pint glass stood on the bedside table next to an ash tray, almost overflowing with cigarette butts and what Duncan guessed were smoked joints. The pack of rolling papers, the flap ripped in several places to form a roach, being the telltale sign. Alistair reached out, grasping Charlie's feet beneath the duvet and gave them a firm shake.

"Wakey, wakey, rise and shine, Charlie," he said, checking his watch, "it's your mid-morning wakeup call from your friendly neighbourhood policeman!"

Still, Charlie didn't surface and Alistair glanced at Duncan. He took the corner of the duvet and hauled it up and away, revealing Charlie in a foetal pose, wearing boxer shorts and a white vest.

"For crying out loud!" Charlie barked, glaring at Alistair who smiled wryly.

"I knew you were awake, Charlie... now get with the programme, time's a wasting!"

Charlie Lumsden, squinting against the brightness of the morning sunshine and holding a hand up to shield his eyes, cursed softly. "Geez... Keck! What's go' int' you?"

"Familiar little scrote, isn't he?" Alistair said to Duncan. "It's DS MacEachran to you, Charlie. Only my friends get to call me Keck, and only then if I'm in a good mood."

"You're never in a good mood, man!" Charlie said bitterly.

"Aye, well don't make it worse, then eh?" Alistair said as Charlie swung his legs off the bed, sitting up. He reached for a packet of cigarettes, taking one out and lighting up. He took a steep draw and then rubbed the back of his neck, blinking in the daylight and shaking his head as he exhaled.

"Whatever it is, I didn't have nothing to do with it, okay?"

"Use of a double negative, Charlie," Alistair said, standing in front of Charlie, his back to the window, almost silhouetting himself. "I don't think you meant that, did you?"

"What?" Charlie said, grimacing as if he was in pain. He coughed then, a deep chesty affair, bringing up phlegm. He looked around and then at Alistair, perhaps hoping he'd clear a path to the window to allow him to spit but Alistair didn't move. Charlie looked disgusted as he had no choice but to swallow it. "What do you want, Mr MacEachran." Alistair pointed to Duncan. Charlie turned his head, eyeing Duncan.

"Two nights ago you were seen dealing behind the Co-op on Bank Street—"

"I wasna dealing—"

"By one of my officers," Duncan continued. Charlie shook his head. "Now, we have it on CCTV, so let's not mess about. Just now, I'm not interested in what you get up to. We're not here to turn your place over, but I can if you choose not to be cooperative. Understand?"

"Aye, I get it," Charlie said, begrudgingly. "But I'm no' grass—"

Alistair laughed. "You'd sell your own mother into slavery if it got you off the hook, Charlie. Don't give me that nonsense."

"Aye, well," Charlie said, taking another drag. "She's a right old cow... so she'd deserve it."

"Two nights ago, Charlie," Duncan said.

"What about it?"

"Blue Toyota, behind the Co-op. Remember?"

"It's all a bit hazy, to be honest..."

Alistair kicked the bed frame next to him, startling Charlie who jumped. "All right! Bloody hell, man! I've just woken up, you know?"

"Two nights ago," Duncan repeated.

"Aye, aye... blue Toyota... what about it like?"

"What did you sell?"

Charlie's eyes flickered between Duncan and Alistair, possibly considering whether to lie again or if not, how little could he get away with saying. Alistair glared at him, inclining his head and Charlie relented, looking resigned. "Nothing major... there were some people in town and... it was just a bit of gear, you know? People looking for a good time. Nothing heavy," he said, looking at Alistair. "You know me, Mr MacEachran. I'm... just a..."

"A wee gobshite, aye," Alistair said. Charlie looked offended.

"I just sell a bit of personal... just to cover my costs, you know how it is?" He seemed apologetic, perhaps hopeful that the detectives would keep their word and leave him if he gave them what they wanted.

"And who did you sell it to?" Duncan asked. Charlie exhaled, shaking his head. "Come on, Charlie. You know how this works. We can have half a dozen officers here within ten minutes turning this place upside down."

"You included," Alistair added, fixing him with an uncompromising look.

"Ah... all right."

"Who was driving the Toyota?" Duncan asked.

"Brennan," Charlie said, "from down the way, on the Maelrubha Estate."

Alistair leaned over Charlie and smiled. "You see. That wasn't so difficult, was it?"

Charlie looked between them. "So... is that it?"

"That'll do for now, Charlie, aye," Alistair said, making his way to the bedroom door. He stopped as Duncan left the room, turning back to Charlie, who was still sitting on his bed, looking confused. "Oh... Lorna has a list of jobs for you, so up and at 'em, eh?"

Duncan waited for Alistair at the foot of the stairs. Lorna came out of the living room, a baby in her arms.

"Did you get what you were looking for?" she asked.

"We did, thanks," Duncan said, opening the front door. Lorna looked past Alistair, up the stairs.

"Are you no' taking him with you then?" she asked.

"No, not this time," Alistair said.

"Shame. I was hoping for a bit of peace and quiet today," Lorna said, bobbing the baby up and down in her arms. The baby smiled at Alistair and he tickled his cheek, making him laugh.

"Take care, Lorna," Alistair said, joining Duncan on the small landing outside. Lorna closed the door behind them. Alistair looked at Duncan. "Shall we go and have a word with Alex Brennan?"

"Aye, why not?"

CHAPTER ELEVEN

ALEX BRENNAN LIVED in a stone cottage on the Maelrubha Estate, not far from the estate offices they'd visited the previous day. Parking the pick-up, Alistair got out and pointed to the blue Toyota Landcruiser parked alongside the property. Duncan checked the registration plate against the footage he'd downloaded from the Co-op and it was the same vehicle.

Their arrival hadn't gone unnoticed, excited barking could be heard the moment they approached the house, coming from the rear. No one answered the knock at the front door, but they made their way around to the back where the barking intensified.

Behind the cottage was a small courtyard, on the far side of which were half a dozen kennels. The dogs inside, working spaniels, were leaping up against the wire cage to greet them. They didn't seem aggressive, just hyperactive which was common with the breed.

The back door to the cottage was open and Duncan peered through into the gloomy interior. Even though the sun was high in the sky, the cottage interior, with its low ceilings and small windows, still appeared very dark.

"Hello!" Duncan shouted, poking his head through the door. A woman appeared from another room and, at first, she seemed surprised to find a stranger at her door but she smiled and approached. Another dog came from between her legs, rushing over to check out the newcomers. Duncan didn't know the breed, but it looked like a miniature black Labrador crossed with some kind of terrier, he figured, and for a moment he wondered if it was a puppy.

Duncan held out the back of his hand and the dog tentatively sniffed it before deciding it liked what he'd found, leaning in against Duncan's leg and allowing him to pet it. Duncan dropped to his haunches, stroking the dog, and looking up at his owner. "What is he?"

"A German Hunting Terrier," she said. "Sorry, he likes everyone."

"He's no bother," Duncan said, rising. He took out his warrant card, displaying it for her. "I'm DI McAdam." He glanced over his shoulder at Alistair. "This is—"

"Aye... I know," she said, glumly, nodding at Alistair. "How are you keeping, Alistair?"

"All good, Niamh. Yourself?"

She nodded, biting her bottom lip momentarily. "Same."

"Is Alex around?" Duncan asked.

"Aye, I'm here," Alex Brennan said, entering the kitchen and nodding to the two detectives. "What can I do for you?"

Duncan smiled. "We just have a couple of questions for you, if you can spare us a moment?"

"Sure," he said, beckoning them to enter. "Come on, Alfie..." he said to the dog, shooing him away from them with the toe of his boot. "Away with you."

"Can I get you boys something to drink?" Niamh asked. "A cup of tea or coffee?"

"No, thank you," Duncan said. Alistair also declined. The kitchen was cluttered with barely any free surface space but it was relatively clean. They were clearly not bothered about minimalism, but looking at how Niamh was dressed, she likely spent a lot of time outdoors the same as her husband. The dogs were still barking outside, and Alex stepped across to the door.

"Quiet!" he yelled and much of the barking ceased immediately. "Sorry about that," he said, turning back to them. "You can't hear yourself think a lot of the time." He gestured for them to go through into the adjoining room, which they did. Alex Brennan followed. The drawing room was even darker than the kitchen, probably having the windows on the north side of the house didn't help, even in summer. "Take a seat if you like," he said but they both preferred to stand.

Duncan cast an eye around the room. You could tell Brennan worked outdoors, the interior of his home was geared up around that, functional and hard wearing. Pictures of himself and his wife, outdoor shots, with rifles and gun dogs as well as selfies taken out hiking in the Scottish Highlands were everywhere. Duncan clocked one particular image of Brennan with a toddler in a carrier on his back. Brennan noticed.

"I'll bet you've bagged a lot of the Munros?" Duncan asked, nodding towards the photographs. He pointed out one of the three of them, Alex, his wife Niamh and the child, standing beside a cairn with a glittering blue sea behind them. "No finer place in the world, is there?"

"Aye, if you catch the weather right," Brennan agreed. "More often than not, all you see is grey cloud and it's pishing rain."

Duncan cocked his head. "True."

"So, how can I help?"

"A couple of nights ago... where were you?" Duncan asked.

Brennan's forehead creased and he thought hard. "In a number of places, why?"

"Can you elaborate?"

He shrugged. "Sure. I... had a fair bit to do on the estate... there was a new fence going in on the northern boundary. I had to drive out and check up on it before it could be signed off." He took a breath. "Then there was the stag group... we'd taken them out stalking the day before. We had to get their trophies arranged."

"Trophies?"

"Aye, they'd done some shooting. A couple of the guys bagged a deer each, you know? They can pay to have a memento to take home."

"And later, in the evening?" Duncan asked.

Brennan shook his head. "Look, this'll go quicker if you tell me what you want me to say, because I've no idea what you're after? I had my dinner around seven..." He met Duncan's eye, who remained stoic, and then he glanced at Alistair. "Took a dump at half past..." Alistair rolled his eyes. "Well, tell me what you're after and I'll see if I can help."

Duncan's eye caught on a photo, framed and on the mantelpiece, behind Brennan. It was a shot of him in a military-style camouflage overcoat, posing with a rifle. Was he ex-army? "Were you in Portree, around 8 pm?" Duncan asked, turning his focus back to Brennan.

Alex Brennan's eyes narrowed and he held Duncan's gaze. "What's that?"

"Portree, just before eight o'clock," Alistair said. "Near the Co-op, to be exact."

"I..." he glanced between them, "don't know. Maybe. What if I was? Not illegal is it."

"No," Duncan said, producing his mobile and opening the file containing the video from the shop's rear-facing camera. He took a step closer, pressed play and turned the screen to face Brennan, holding it aloft. "Care to tell me what you were doing here?"

Brennan watched the video, his left eye involuntarily twitching. "All right... stop playing silly beggars."

"What were you buying from Charlie Lumsden?"

"That's an estate vehicle... any one of a dozen people has access to the keys."

"And yet, it's parked outside your cottage," Duncan said.

Brennan shrugged. "You've got all the answers, it seems, so what do you want me to say?" He glared at Alistair. "You've always had it in for me."

Alistair snorted. "Give it a rest, Alex."

"Why are you here on at me?" Brennan said. "Haven't you got bigger things going on than... than..."

"Than what?"

"Than lifting me for scoring a bit of gear?" He shook his head. "You want to see me lose my job... for that?"

"We're not interested in causing you problems, Alex," Duncan said, "but we do want to know if it was for use among the stag party." Brennan looked at Duncan, his lips pursed but he averted his eye from Duncan's. "We're trying to build a picture of the events around the time of Steven's disappearance."

Brennan exhaled, and was about to speak when his wife, Niamh, entered the room behind him. He glanced at her and smiled nervously. A partner knows when something untoward is afoot. "What is it?" she asked. Her husband shook his head. "Alex?"

"It's nothing love... just... something to do with this group we have visiting the estate just now, and... the guy, you know?"

"The poor man who died in the Cuillins?" she asked, looking at Duncan.

"Aye," Brennan said. "A bad business."

"Well, help them as much as you can," Niamh said, glancing at Alistair, she added, "a bunch of hoorah Henrys that lot."

"Are they? In what way?" Alistair asked.

"Just... men behaving like spoiled little boys once they're free of their wives and partners, is all," she said. "Did you tell them about that little escapade on the weekend?"

"Ah, none of my business really," Brennan said.

"What happened?" Duncan asked.

"You haven't said, have you?" Niamh admonished her husband. He smiled awkwardly.

"Look... these guys know my boss." He raised his hands in supplication. "What do you expect me to do?"

She shook her head. "Grow a spine to start with."

Brennan rolled his eyes as Niamh left the room. "Women," he said sheepishly.

"What happened?" Duncan repeated.

"Oh, just the lads... they wanted to go out on the town. I gather things got a bit... boisterous and maybe a little out of hand. Lads' stag do and all that. I don't think it was very serious."

"Let us be the judge of that," Duncan said flatly.

"Just a dust up with some of the local lads, that's all. It was the weekend, Saturday night. You know what it gets like sometimes, yeah?"

"Any idea who they got into it with on the weekend?"

"No, I don't. I only dropped them off and arranged for

them to be collected and brought back to their digs." He shrugged. "Everything I know was all second hand but... some of them had been scrapping, that was obvious."

Alistair shook his head. "And you didn't think to mention this before?"

"Ah, not my place—"

"This is a murder inquiry, Alex, for crying out loud," Alistair said. Brennan looked away. "Don't hold anything back from us, all right?"

"Okay... I'm sorry."

"What about the drugs?" Duncan asked.

"I want to help, but you think I want you sticking me on for – what do you call it? – intent to supply, as well? You'll get me sacked and banged up all in one day." He shook his head. "No, sorry. I've done as much as I can."

Alistair looked at Duncan, but there was no need to antagonise Alex Brennan any further by arresting him on a petty recreational drugs charge. Besides, without a confession under caution, he would never be convicted anyway. Brennan was right about one thing; they were working a much bigger case. Holding Alistair's eye, he almost imperceptibly shook his head. His DS seemed disappointed with the decision.

"Answer me one more question, Alex," Duncan said. "Where were you the night Steven Phelps went missing?"

"Easy, I was here, at home watching the telly. Then I went to bed."

"Anyone who can confirm this?"

"Aye, the missus," Brennan said, arching his back and leaning out of the room. "Niamh!" His wife came to join them. "Can you tell these two where I was two nights ago?"

"What?" she asked, her brow furrowing.

"They want to know where I was the night the Phelps guy

went missing. I said I was here with you, but my word isn't good enough." Alistair laughed. "I was here, Alistair."

"Yes, you were with me," Niamh said. She looked at Alistair and then Duncan. "All night. Why do you want to know?"

"Just routine," Duncan said. "And your husband wasn't taking any drugs?"

Niamh laughed, then her expression turned serious when no one else joined in. She glanced at her husband and then scowled at Duncan. "Alex doesn't take drugs. What kind of stupid question is that?"

"Sorry, I had to ask," Duncan replied.

Niamh shook her head. "If that's all, I have things to do?" Duncan smiled, nodding. Niamh met her husband's eye, shook her head, and left the room.

"She's no' too pleased with you, is she?" Alistair said.

"It doesn't help with the pair of you coming round here and stirring the pot, does it? Are we finished?"

"For now," Duncan said and Brennan escorted them to the front door. He had to block the terrier from heading outside when he opened the door, but it seemed obedient when he told it to stay by his side.

The front door was closed on them before they reached the pick-up. They got in and Duncan looked back at the cottage. The interior was shrouded in darkness, but he thought he could see a figure watching them through the window.

"What do you reckon?"

Alistair followed Duncan's gaze towards the house. "I think Alex is a dubious character, but he's harmless enough."

"Is he ex-army?"

"Hah! Brennan?"

"Aye," Duncan said. "I saw a photo of him in combat fatigues." He glanced at Alistair, who was bristling. "Is he or not?"

"Aye, he is… but he's not what he seems."

"You've got a real problem with him, haven't you?"

"Not just me," Alistair said. "A lot of people have… he's a bloody *Walt*."

"A what?"

"A Walter," Alistair said. Duncan shrugged. "A *Walter Mitty*. In military circles, we call them *Walts*. They bang on about their career… making it up as they go along. Stolen valour, we call it. I hate it. Anyone who served knows what I'm talking about."

"So, he wasn't in the army…"

"Oh… he was," Alistair said, "for a few months blanket stacking before he got himself out on a medical discharge." He shook his head. "Seriously, if you heard the way he talks about it, you'd think he won the war all by himself."

"Which war?"

"*All of them*," Alistair said. "It boils my… well, anyway… like I said before, take everything that comes out of that man's mouth with a pinch of salt. He's full of it." He started the pick-up, glancing sideways at Duncan as he selected drive. "And that's why I don't trust him and why I hate him."

CHAPTER TWELVE

THEY MADE their way down the winding access road towards the estate's gated entrance, coming upon the accommodation where Phelps and his friends were staying. Spotting Tony Sinclair and his best man, Ollie, sitting outside at a picnic table drinking coffee, Duncan had Alistair pull over. He got out of the pick-up and approached the pair.

"Good afternoon," he said. Both men acknowledged his arrival, but only Ollie raised a smile, and it was tepid at best.

"Do you have news for us, Detective Inspector?" Tony asked.

"Nothing new, but the inquiry is progressing."

Tony glanced at his friend. "That's policeman speak for I'm not going to tell you." Ollie smiled. "Isn't that right Mr McAdam?"

"Normally, yes. On this occasion, it's also true. We're still trying to establish a motive—"

"So... you're definitely treating this as a... what?" Ollie asked, shocked.

"As a murder, aye," Duncan said. By now, Alistair was by his side.

"You surprised by that, Ollie?" Alistair asked.

"Yeah... I am," Ollie said, shaking his head. "Who'd want to do something like that to Steve. I mean... he's a bit..."

"Do what?" Duncan asked. Ollie's mouth gaped and he glanced at Tony who was calm, icily calm. And it was Tony who replied.

"Do Steve harm, obviously," he said. Ollie nodded.

"You said Steve could be a bit... what was the end to that sentence?" Duncan asked.

"Well..." Ollie floundered. "It's not good form to speak ill of the dead... and he was a mate, so..."

"I think we'd rather you were honest," Duncan said. "I think your friend would want us to catch his killer, don't you?"

"Yes, of course," Ollie said.

"Or killers," Alistair added. Tony seemed to lock eyes with Alistair, both men bearing unreadable expressions. Ryan appeared through the French doors behind them, a cup of coffee in his hand.

"I thought I heard voices." He nodded to Duncan and Alistair. "How's it going with the investigation?"

"No news," Tony said, but he gestured behind them. "Although someone is paying us interest." They all turned to look, seeing Alex Brennan outside his cottage, looking over towards them. As soon as he realised they were all aware of his presence, he turned and disappeared back inside. "Are you visiting our gamekeeper for anything specific?"

"Just routine," Duncan said.

"A ha," Tony replied, flicking his eyebrows momentarily. "More police speak, only this time for *mind your own business*."

Duncan smiled. "I'm pleased to catch many of you all together. Two nights ago, you were all having a bit of a party, weren't you?"

"Every night's been a bit of a party," Ryan said, "aside from when we were out shooting. Why?"

"A few beers... a bit of food," Duncan said. They all agreed. "What about some recreational drugs?" Ollie averted his eyes from Duncan's but both Ryan and Tony were stone faced. Ryan sniffed, then sipped from his cup.

"Drugs aren't my thing," Ryan said flatly. "I have too much fun without them."

"Yes," Tony agreed. "We're not students anymore, Detective Inspector. We're a bit old for all of that."

"Really?" Alistair asked. "A few lines of the old Colombian marching powder to get you going for a night out? It doesn't interest you?"

"No, why would it?" Tony said, staring Alistair down but the DS was having none of it.

"Although, you'd probably keep it in the family if you did, wouldn't you?"

Tony held Alistair's gaze, then he smiled, but it was artificial. "I wondered how long it would be before you brought my father into this."

"Your father?" Ryan asked. Tony dismissed the question with a flick of his hand.

"What's that theory they have..." he said, thoughtfully. "Oh yes, *Godwin's Law*, that whatever subject you discuss, talk long enough and a comparison to the Nazis will eventually be made. With the Sinclairs... it always comes back to my father. Weird, isn't it?"

Duncan pursed his lips. "Your father has quite a name in criminal circles."

"Very little of what is attributed to him is provable," Tony said, seemingly enjoying the verbal sparring, with Alistair in particular. "And... it's quite a stretch to bring him into any of this, don't you think?"

Alistair smacked his lips. "It wouldn't be the first unexplained death that we happened upon revolving around his family though. I mean, you and Steven... along with Ryan, here, are all business partners and... being in business with a Sinclair can be... tough on your health."

"Are you insinuating something, Detective Sergeant?"

"Making an observation," Alistair countered.

"Good, because my father has been responsible for ending the careers of multiple keystone cops, people just like you, over the years and I doubt he'd be overly concerned about one more on that list."

Alistair smiled. He didn't frighten easily. Duncan, however, hadn't planned on pushing this particular line of inquiry just yet.

"So... are you confirming that no recreational drugs were sourced or have been taken since you came to the island?" he asked.

"None at all," Tony said. "Who's said otherwise?"

Duncan ignored the question. "I'd like it if all of you would be willing to provide us with a sample of DNA?"

Ollie looked nervous. "Why... why would you want that? We just said... we haven't taken any drugs—"

"Relax, Ollie," Tony said. "Mr McAdam doesn't care if we were stoned the other night... he wants DNA to compare with whatever they've found on Steve's body."

"Oh... right," Ollie said, frowning.

"Isn't that right, Detective Inspector?"

"That's correct, Mr Sinclair. Are you okay with that?"

"Of course," Tony said. "No problem for me at all." He looked at the other two. "How about you boys?"

Ryan shrugged. "I don't care at all."

"I suppose not," Ollie said, although he seemed less than happy about it.

"We'll need to speak to Neil and Nathan as well. Are they around?" Duncan asked, looking past them and into the building but he couldn't see anyone else.

"They've gone into town to get some food," Tony said. "They'll be back soon enough."

"Great," Duncan said. "I'll have one of my team come out and take the samples. It won't take long."

Tony smiled. "We'll be here. It's not like we can go anywhere, is it?"

Duncan cocked his head. "None of you are under arrest, and can leave at any time… however, I'd prefer it if you stayed put for the time being. Just in case we have any questions. It would be better if we can do it face to face—"

"How long do we have to stay?" Ollie asked. "I mean, I'm happy to help but… I do have work to get back to."

Duncan smiled. "We'll not keep you on the island any longer than absolutely necessary, I assure you."

Tony glanced over towards the Brennan's cottage. Alex was long gone, although his vehicle was still parked outside. "What did Brennan say to you?"

Duncan looked at him. "Who's to say he said anything?" Tony smirked, glancing at Ollie who shifted nervously in his seat. Ryan's expression remained unchanged. "Is there something you feel you need to say?"

Tony glanced at the other two, inclining his head. "I'd never want to be labelled a grass… my father wouldn't care for it, to put it mildly…"

"If you think it's pertinent to Steven's death, then I think you should tell us, Mr Sinclair," Duncan said.

Sinclair took a breath. "All right. Brennan took us out stalking… and the following day, things kind of kicked off."

"Between whom?" Duncan asked.

"Between Steve and Alex," Tony said.

"And when you say it *kicked off*, what do you mean exactly?"

Tony shrugged. "Two blokes... words exchanged, squaring up to each other. It looked like a bit of handbags for a moment..."

"Yeah, we all started laughing," Ollie said, glancing between Tony and Ryan. "Then..."

"A punch was thrown," Tony said. "Then it went off properly!"

"Steve threw a punch at Brennan?" Alistair asked.

"No! The opposite," Tony said. "It... escalated quickly, didn't it?" Tony said, looking at his friends. Ryan nodded and Ollie looked glum.

"I've never seen anything like it," Ollie said, shaking his head. "One minute they were doing a bit of pushing and then..."

"I had to separate them," Ryan said. "Steve's a powerful bloke, and I couldn't take him if I'm honest. Not if he saw me coming anyway."

"So, you restrained Alex Brennan?" Duncan asked. Ryan nodded. "And what was Steve doing at that point?"

"Laughing," Ollie said.

"*Laughing?*" Alistair asked. Ollie nodded.

"Yeah, he found it all pretty funny," Ryan said. "I didn't, but then I was manhandling the big man while this lot threw beer over Steve!"

Duncan exchanged a look with Alistair. "What happened next?"

Ryan shrugged. "Nothing. I walked Brennan away... and he went home. That's the end of it."

"And Steve?"

Tony smiled. "Took it in his stride."

"What was it over?" Duncan asked. "The fight, I mean."

"Steve said something about him being full of it," Tony said. "But he didn't elaborate."

Duncan turned to Ryan. "Did Brennan say anything to you?"

"Nah," Ryan said. "He'd had a couple himself. Not saying he was hammered, but I could smell it on his breath... and I sent him home, to sober up."

"When was this exactly?" Duncan asked.

They all looked at one another. "About three in the afternoon, wasn't it?" Tony suggested and the other two agreed.

"More or less," Ollie said. "And... Steve went out by himself later that night. We... er... didn't see him again until... well, until he was found."

"And he didn't tell you where he was going or what the fight was about?" Duncan asked. All three shook their heads. "And none of you thought it odd that he went out on his own that night, not telling any of you where he was going?"

"No," Ryan said. "Steve's a big boy, he had his grown-up pants on. He can go where he likes."

"And he wound up dead," Alistair said. Ryan met his eye but said nothing. "With friends like you lot, who needs enemies, eh?"

Ryan bristled at that, but Duncan took a step between them, breaking their eye contact. "Okay, we'll need that in your statements and, to be honest, that's information we could have had a lot earlier." He looked at Tony. "Is there anything else you might want to tell us that you've previously neglected to mention?" Tony shook his head.

They bid the men farewell and walked back to the pick-up, Duncan feeling eyes burning into his back with every step. Neither of them spoke until they were back in the cabin of the vehicle and Alistair had the engine running.

"Sorry about bringing up old man Sinclair," Alistair said. "I didn't mean to—"

"Don't worry about it," Duncan said, waving a hand casually in the air. "It would have come up sooner or later. Although, if you can avoid putting every person of interest's nose out of joint in this investigation, if only for a day, I'd appreciate it."

"Sorry about that," Alistair, said, but Duncan highly doubted he was sincere, seeing as he said it with a broad smile. "I don't mean to be antagonistic necessarily, it's just in my nature, so that's the way it comes out."

Duncan laughed. He looked towards the estate offices as they passed them. "Who does own this estate, anyway? Do we know?"

"Russell checked," Alistair said. "The named directors are UK based, but the estate's shares are held by a multinational company, based overseas if memory serves me." They reached the main road and Alistair turned right, beginning the drive back to Portree. "So... are you going to have their blood samples checked for drugs?"

"Aye," Duncan said. "It's what Charlie Lumsden said Brennan was buying them for and Alex doesn't look like the type to make use of illegal drugs himself."

"No, it's not something I'd expect from him. he's always been more of a drinker than anything else."

"So we've no reason to doubt that they were purchased for Tony and his cohort."

"Aye, right enough," Alistair said. "But I wouldn't have thought Brennan would be too keen on buying that lot drugs though either. Do you reckon the altercation had something to do with that?"

"No idea," Duncan said. "Maybe? If it was, then that would explain that lot's lack of detail on what caused the fight.

Maybe they didn't cover the cost as they were supposed to, and Brennan got the hump about it."

"Aye, or it's nothing to do with the drugs at all. Maybe Brennan tried to sell Steve his Walter Mitty nonsense and he got called out on it."

Duncan sucked air through his teeth. "Either way, I'd love to know."

"We could always turn back and ask Brennan," Alistair suggested.

"No, let's sit on it for a while. He saw us talking to them, so let's allow him to stew on it for a bit while we have a root around. There's this scrap they got involved in, in the town as well. I want to find out who else they offended locally."

Alistair concurred. "I have the impression that Tony Sinclair is used to getting what he wants, whenever he wants it as well though. I wouldn't put it past him to stitch Brennan up over a petty drug deal."

"Somehow," Duncan said, looking out of the window at the passing landscape, "I doubt the apple has fallen all that far from the tree. Even if Tony has distanced himself from his father's business empire, I should imagine he's still got something of his father about him. Don't you?"

"I wouldn't be surprised, aye."

"They weren't concerned about handing over their DNA though, were they?" Duncan said.

"Which means they had absolutely nothing to do with it, or…"

"Someone, maybe more than one of them, was very careful," Duncan said, finishing the comment.

"Do you think it could have something to do with Tony's father after all? All of this other stuff is just muddying the waters?" Alistair asked. "Tony doesn't seem overly concerned about his friend and business partner meeting a suspicious end or that it might mean he's in danger."

"No, he doesn't. Somehow, I reckon if he knew anything, he'd not tell us anyway. I'll bet he's been onto his father though."

Alistair laughed. "If not, he will have called him by the time we get back to Portree."

Duncan's mobile rang and he answered the call. It was Angus, back at the station in Portree. "What's up Angus?"

"Are you on your way back here, sir?"

"Aye."

"Well... the chief super is looking for you. Apparently, the media has got wind of Steven Phelps's murder... and they're pressing for information."

Duncan sighed. "I suppose that was to be expected sooner or later."

"The chief is issuing a statement, and he wants you to host a press conference later on."

"Right... a press conference, aye," Duncan said, glancing at Alistair beside him who grinned. He hung up, shaking his head.

"Have you got your best shirt on?" Alistair asked. "These HD tellies show all the stains, you know. Have you cleaned your teeth?"

"Another comment like that and I'll make sure you're sitting right beside me, Detective Sergeant!"

"I'd rather turn in my warrant card and move off the island."

"Both can be arranged, Alistair. Just say the word."

CHAPTER THIRTEEN

DC Angus Ross clicked his mouse and a new window appeared on his monitor. He scanned the details, seeking out the core pieces of information. "Alex Brennan joined the British Army aged twenty-two..." he said, glancing up at Duncan who was heading the afternoon briefing, "after having several documented run-ins with the Northern Constabulary," Angus said, referring to the regional police service prior to amalgamation into one force, Police Scotland.

"What trouble was he in?" Duncan asked. They'd returned to the station and Duncan was keen to learn as much as he could about the estate manager cum gamekeeper.

"Drink-related offences, mostly," Angus said, "and the associated situations he found himself in. Breach of the peace, fighting... an arrest for aggravated assault that never made it to trial, multiple cautions..."

"Anything drug related?"

Angus frowned, checking the file. He shook his head. "No, nothing. Why?"

"I'm wondering how he knows Charlie Lumsden, that's all."

Alistair scoffed. "Everyone knows Charlie, but he's not exactly considered a criminal mastermind. He's low-level, petty stuff. It saves him from having to get a proper job. Not that he could hold it down anyway."

Angus had searched for Charlie's file in the database and was now reading through it. "They went to the same high school... but several years apart."

"Everyone on the island went to Portree High school, Angus," Duncan said. "It's the only one on the island."

"Oh aye, right enough," Angus said, his face reddening. "But I can't see their paths crossing at any other point."

Alistair sniffed. "If you live on the island long enough, everyone knows everyone else... and if you don't, then you know someone who does. Brennan has been around long enough."

"What about his military career?" Duncan asked.

"As I say," Angus said, focusing on Brennan's file again, "he set out to join the Paras aged twenty-two, passing the aptitude course, he began the thirty-week combat infantry course at Catterick, wherever that is—"

"Yorkshire," Alistair said. "And it's brutal. The course, I mean, not Yorkshire. It's like Skye, just with more English folk."

"Right," Angus said, "but he never completed the training."

"Did he fail?" Duncan asked.

"It says here... in the file I got from the Ministry of Defence, that he had a medical issue," Angus said. "During something called *Pegasus*... he had a fall in the *Trainasium*... what's that, sarge?" he asked, looking at Alistair.

"The Trainasium is part of *Pegasus*, or what's known in the regiment as *P Company*. It's the eight-part pre-parachute selection course. It tests the candidates on their physical and mental endurance. You score points for aggression, determination, leadership... when I did it back in the day, you needed forty-five points to pass. I've no idea what they need now... five, probably."

"What if you failed?" Duncan asked.

"There's failing and there's *failing*. If you were close, they can put you back a bit and give you another shot... but if you just weren't ever going to make it, then you're done as a paratrooper."

"Then you leave the army?" Duncan asked.

Alistair chuckled. "No. When you take the King's shilling, your contract is with the army, not the Paras. They just shove you into another regiment. Where did Brennan wind up, because as much as he talks a great game about being an elite soldier, he never made the grade?"

"He went into the Royal Logistics Corps—"

"Aye, like I said, blanket stackers," Alistair said, smiling.

Angus continued, "He transferred to their training centre... but he was discharged before completing the course and never actually saw active service."

"So... he didn't win the war," Duncan said. Alistair smiled whereas Angus frowned, uncertain of the reference.

"Like I said, he's a *Walt*," Alistair stated.

"Has he been in trouble since he came back to the island?" Duncan asked.

"Only recently," Angus said. "In the last eighteen months he's been picked up in the town, oftentimes drunk but prior to that, there's no record of him."

"Ronnie knows him well," Alistair said to Duncan. "I think they used to go out shooting together every now and then. I don't know if they still do, mind."

"Might be worth asking Ronnie what he makes of Alex now," Duncan said. "I wonder what's been going on in his life recently to see him getting into trouble. Maybe it's the job, too much pressure with the responsibility or he's having some trouble in his personal life."

Alistair inclined his head. "Or he's just been better at getting away with stuff."

"You really dislike him, don't you, sarge?" Russell said. Alistair looked at him, stone faced. Russell shrugged. "I don't mean anything by it, but you've never really liked him, have you?"

"No. And, I'll have you know, I don't have to like everyone."

"Do you like anyone?" Russell asked, smiling.

"Aye," Alistair said, fixing his eye on the DC. "But you can go off some people." Russell laughed.

"What's the train... what was it called?" Angus asked.

"The *Trainasium*?" Alistair said. "It's an assault course. It's the only part of the *P Company* programme that doesn't earn you points towards passing the whole thing. It's specially designed to push you, to see if you have what it takes to be a paratrooper, a test of ability to overcome fear and prove you can follow orders when working at height. It's a straight pass or fail section."

"An assault course," Angus said, shrugging. "That doesn't sound so bad."

"No, piece of cake," Alistair said. "As long as you can handle completing the entire route sixty feet above the ground, that is."

"Ah... maybe not then," Angus replied, frowning.

"Right," Duncan said, drawing the briefing to a close, "I want blood samples from all of Steve's friends on the trip, and I want them processed by the lab as soon as possible. So far, we've got conflicting accounts and gaps in our timeline. We need to know whose accounts are on the level and who's leading us astray."

"What if they all are?" Alistair asked.

Duncan frowned. "We'll know soon enough."

"Are you ready for this evening?" Alistair asked.

"The public forum? Aye, as ready as I'll ever be."

DUNCAN'S EYES swept the room. There were perhaps fifty locals present, along with several journalists, and a television crew who were filming the event. Some of the members of the press had come across from the mainland, so he figured it must be a slow news week. He'd just finished reading the official press release, urging anyone with information they thought relevant to come forward and speak with officers. There were a couple of uniformed constables in attendance to both assist with crowd control and to make themselves available if necessary to take statements.

Taking a deep breath, Duncan settled in for the remaining moments of the forum, the time he wasn't looking forward to; questions from those assembled. There were a few raised hands, thankfully not too many. Perhaps this would be okay after all. He pointed to a man in the fourth row. He was well dressed, clean cut and Duncan figured it would be a sensible question.

"How many officers are working on this case?" he asked. "We'd like to know that we're safe to go about our business on the island."

"We have more than enough resources allocated to the inquiry," Duncan said. "And we have no reason to believe that there is an elevated risk to islanders. All I would say is for people to take care when they are out and about, much as you normally do." The man looked unhappy with the answer, but he sat back down. He pointed to a lady off to his right.

"There is talk that there might be a serial killer on the island. Are you considering that?"

This was what Duncan feared about events like this. He'd much rather have just released a simple statement and be done with it.

"No, there is no evidence that that's the case here. We have one man who has died under suspicious circumstances, and there is nothing to suggest an escalation. I would ask for everyone to, please, refrain from idle speculation that could cause alarm among the population. We have one deceased man which, although tragic, we have seen before on the island, and statistically, no doubt we will see again. This is not... unusual." He regretted his choice of phrase as soon as he'd uttered the words, but he maintained his composure.

"So, there's no truth to the rumour doing the rounds that this is gang related?" Duncan looked at the speaker, one of the local journalists and, inwardly, he thanked her for raising such a daft question. He had to suppress a smile.

"We have no *gang-related* issues on Skye," he said flatly. The member of the public who'd asked the question was still standing and she picked up where the journalist left off.

"How can you say that? We have people coming on and off the island all the time. No one knows who they are or where they're from. The numbers of visitors to the island are so much higher this year. How can you expect to keep us safe when you don't know who everyone is?"

"There's nothing to point to higher-than-normal visitors' numbers having any bearing on this case at all," Duncan said. "As I say, speculation is unhelpful in this matter, and only adds to anxiety levels. Please—"

"Are you actually going to do something about this or not?"

Duncan suppressed a sigh, catching sight of Alistair at the

back of the room. He could swear his DS had a trace of a smile on his slightly upturned lips.

Duncan was able to tie up the public forum soon afterwards and stood at the front of the room while his officers ushered people out. Alistair walked over to him, a spring in his step.

"You enjoyed that, didn't you?" Duncan said.

"I've always said this job would be great without the general public."

"Without the public, there would be no crime and therefore no need for us."

"Aye, it'd be dull. Best not to be promoted – like yourself – and then you don't have to deal with normal people... and only with the great unwashed.

CHAPTER FOURTEEN

DUNCAN ENTERED MCNABS, nodding to the man on the door. He only gave Duncan a cursory glance. It was midweek and the bar wasn't at its busiest with no event on tonight. The regulars were sitting at tables and a handful were propping up the bar making casual conversation. A football match was playing on one of the screens in the adjoining room, some friendly international fixture by the look of it, and a few excited comments could be heard.

Duncan approached the bar, looking for Grace. Two of the regulars looked at him, made eye contact and acknowledged his arrival. "Have you seen Grace?" Duncan asked.

"Aye, she's just downstairs in the cellar."

"Cheers," Duncan said, settling in to wait for her. His eyes drifted to the television mounted on the wall behind him. The sound was off, but subtitles were rolling across the screen, the presenter was reading the headline news. It wasn't long before the Steven Phelps murder investigation came up, his press conference and public forum following soon after.

"Are you close to catching the bastard?" one of the men

seated at the bar had asked, and Duncan turned around. Everyone present was watching him.

"Come on, Jimmy," Grace said, appearing from the back room, "give the man a break when he's off duty."

Jimmy nodded curtly, turning away and focusing on his pint once more. Others did likewise and Duncan smiled gratefully. Grace gestured with a tilt of her head and Duncan went to the far end of the bar and away from those present.

"So," she said, glancing over Duncan's shoulder and keeping her voice low, "are you any closer to catching him?"

Duncan thought about giving the generic answer, but this was Grace. "There's not an awful lot to work with at the moment... but we'll get there."

"Sounds ominous," she said.

"Aye, but it's my job. It'll be all right." He pursed his lips, and she was looking at him intently. "So... um... how have you been?"

Grace bobbed her head. "In the last couple of days since I saw you... I've been fine. You?"

"Fine," Duncan said, feeling awkward.

"So, we're both fine then."

"Apparently, yes," Duncan said, frowning. They eyed each other for a moment longer and then both cracked a smile, broadening when they saw it mirrored back at them.

"Look at the two of us, eh?" Grace said, shaking her head.

"Pathetic, isn't it?" Duncan replied. "Grace... I'm really sorry."

"So you should be. What are you sorry for?" she asked, leaning against the bar and crossing her arms. Duncan was puzzled.

"For... whatever it was that made you angry."

She laughed. "Honestly, Duncan... you're—"

"Look, I know I upset you, and I doubt very much it was because I referred to you as a..."

"Barmaid."

"Yeah," Duncan said, scrunching up his face. "It's more than that, but... I don't know what it is. Sue me!"

She laughed, looking around. "Okay, I know what I do isn't exactly... a career—"

"There's nothing wrong with it. Anyone who works for a living, doing whatever they do, has my respect."

Grace held up her hand. "And I don't plan on doing it forever, but you know how things are on the island. You earn money where you can, and then you figure it out in the longer term."

"Is that what this is about then, the longer term?"

She met his eye and nodded. "Yes."

Duncan rubbed his chin, considering what that meant. "Any chance of a drink while I try to figure out how much of my foot I can get into my mouth in this conversation?"

Grace tilted her head and took a glass from a shelf above the bar, pouring him a pint. She set it down in front of him and held out her hand. Duncan took out his wallet and Grace reached across, plucking out a ten-pound note. "Expensive pint," Duncan said.

"Well, you're buying me one too."

"Oh yeah, of course," he said, lifting his pint as she smiled at him. "So... the future," Duncan said, wiping his mouth with the back of his hand.

"Yes," Grace said, acknowledging a patron at the end of the bar who wanted a refill. "I've had a job offer," she said moving away.

"Oh aye, what's that about then?"

Grace poured a drink, carrying it to the end of the bar but

she seemed pensive now. She took payment and returned to where Duncan waited. "There's a wildlife observatory... a charitable trust who have secured some lottery funding, and they're looking for someone to document migration patterns, habitat... that sort of thing. Visually, you know, through photography. It's quite an opportunity." Grace had been acting as a freelance wildlife photographer for some time, having pictures published in magazines from time to time. She was talented.

"That's fantastic, well done," Duncan said. "When did this come about?"

She pursed her lips. "I had a letter about it last week... and a phone call yesterday."

"You never said anything." Duncan was surprised. It was great news. "I always said you were talented."

"Aye, not bad for a barmaid, huh?"

For a moment, he thought she was having a dig, but seeing her playful smile, he shook his head. "You nearly had me there."

She laughed. "The thing is... it's in Caerlaverock."

"Where's that?" Duncan asked, feeling his enthusiasm wane.

"On the northern side of the Solway Firth, south of Dumfries."

"The borders?"

"Aye," she said quietly. "The borders."

"That's... I mean..."

"It's a real opportunity for me to do what I love, Duncan... and... well, you and me we're..."

"We're good together," Duncan said. He saw her face drop, if only a little. "I mean, we're really good together."

"That's just it though, Duncan," Grace said glumly. "What

are we? Like you said, thirty is coming towards me at speed and I'm just working in a bar. I have this on, off relationship with a guy who struggles with commitment—"

"That's not fair!" Duncan said, cracking a bemused smile. "It's not like you've ever suggested we settle down."

"I'm not asking for a wedding ring, Duncan, but a girl needs to know she's not wasting her time." She wrinkled her nose. "You know what I mean?"

"Why do you think you're wasting your time?"

She fixed him with an earnest look. "Because you won't let me in."

He spread his arms wide. "Ask me anything, anything at all. I'll answer it."

"Duncan…" she looked away.

"Seriously! Anything," he repeated, leaning to one side and forcing himself into her eye line.

"All right," she said, leaning forward and resting her elbows on the bar, fixing her eyes on his. "What's the craic between you and Becky Mcinnes?"

"Oh… come on…" Duncan lifted his head and looked away.

"There… that's it. That's what I'm talking about."

"No… Grace, we were together years ago… and that's where it is, in the past—"

"And how many more ex-girlfriends can I expect to knock on your door in the middle of the night… that you'll run off to as soon as they call—"

"It's not what you think," Duncan said, remembering exactly the night Grace was referring to. It wasn't like he and Grace were even an item at that point, not really.

"I feel like I'm competing with your past, Duncan," she said sternly, "and I can't compete with a ghost. That's not fair on me… or you… but mostly, I'm thinking about me."

Duncan winced, his tongue firmly inside his cheek. "I... get it... I do, but you don't have to worry."

"One thing, Duncan. Whenever a man in my life tells me I don't need to worry, it usually signals that *I really need to be worried.*"

"Grace..."

"Hey, is that..." Grace said, talking over him and pointing at the television. Duncan looked over his shoulder, a picture of Steven Phelps was up on the screen. "Is he the guy you're investigating?"

"Aye, Steven Phelps. That's him."

"I know that guy," Grace said.

"What? Where from?"

"He was in here... at the weekend. Saturday, I think it was. Nasty piece of work too."

Duncan's curiosity was piqued. "Why, what happened?"

"He was in here with a group of lads. Usually, we don't let groups of single blokes come in together, especially when they've been pre-loading during the day. It often leads to trouble, but someone vouched for them to get them through the doors."

"Who?"

"I don't know. I'd have to ask the guys on shift that night."

"He was tanked up, you reckon?"

"They all were. There were about half a dozen of them, but one of them was getting married and they were up for a bit of a laugh, so they were allowed in." Grace frowned. "We should have known better."

"What happened?"

"I'm not sure how it started but your man there, what did you say his name was?"

"Phelps."

"Aye, the big man. He got a bit over friendly with a couple

of the local lasses, Jennifer McFaul was one of them. You know her?" Duncan shook his head. "She can talk for Scotland, that one. Anyway, Jennifer and her friends, not to mention the guys, took offence to the... er... how should I put it? The over-familiarity."

"Boyfriends?"

"Aye, I reckon. You know young Liam Maclennan... works at the garage just up the way, before you get to the industrial estate?"

"No, should I?"

"Probably not. He's a nice enough guy, but he's prone to using his mouth a little too much once he's had a couple. Anyway, he was pretty bullish and had a word. Then both groups got worked up and everything got a little heated."

"Did it kick off?"

"Oh aye, sure it did. Nothing too bad... a few punches were thrown, drinks spilled... and all of them were turfed out into the street in quick order."

"Anyone seriously hurt?"

"No, but I didn't follow them out, so I don't know what happened once they were all outside."

"And you're sure it was him? Phelps, I mean?"

"Yes, absolutely. It's all on camera if you want it." She gestured over her shoulder with her thumb. "The external cameras might have caught what went on once they left here, if you're lucky. I can get you a copy, if you want?"

"I'd appreciate that, cheers." Duncan took out his mobile and called Alistair. The detective sergeant picked up swiftly.

"Somebody had better be *deid*, because I'm about to eat my supper," Alistair said by way of a greeting.

"Eat fast, because we've got work to do." Duncan hung up, turning back to Grace but she was nowhere to be seen. His thoughts drifted back to their earlier conversation. The idea of Grace moving to the borders left him with a hollow feeling. Would she stay for him, if he asked her to? *Was it even fair of him to consider asking her to?*

CHAPTER FIFTEEN

THE FOLLOWING MORNING, Duncan pulled off the A87 and onto a petrol station forecourt. The garage set-up was around the back and he left his car at the perimeter fence and walked through the open gate between tall runs of chain-link fencing that surrounded the compound. The garage not only managed repairs and sold fuel but they also were the first port of call for recoveries across the island. Several flatbed trucks were parked up at the rear.

Duncan could hear the sound of activity coming from within the workshop, pneumatic tools were in use and raised voices carried to him. There were half a dozen people at work inside, with another couple of bodies visible through a window into the reception and the office beyond. One man, sporting navy overalls nodded towards Duncan.

"Can I help you, pal?"

Duncan smiled. "I'm looking for Liam. Is he around?"

"Depends who's asking."

Duncan brandished his warrant card. "Police." If the man was remotely bothered by that, he didn't show it. He inclined his head towards the reception desk and returned to fitting the new brake shoes on a Vauxhall Astra. "Thanks," Duncan said, setting off towards the entrance door.

"No bother, pal," the man said, without looking back.

The reception was small, the walls painted in an ochre colour which had seen better days and made the nearby waiting area, with its black imitation leather sofas, appear cramped. An American man was at the counter, the team handing over paperwork for some repair that'd been carried out on his hire car, and Duncan waited patiently.

He looked out into the compound where their cars were parked up either waiting to be worked on, collected or in such a state they'd be making their way to a scrapyard as soon as they could be loaded. Accidents on the island weren't common but in the summer season some of the roads away from the main routes could get overloaded and if you weren't used to them, then you could run into trouble. The odd wandering sheep could also lead to a coming together that favoured neither party.

"Good morning."

Duncan turned, the man at reception was looking at him. "Morning," Duncan replied, approaching the counter.

"Picking up or dropping off?"

"Neither," Duncan said, producing his warrant card again.

"Ah... right." He didn't sound surprised. Duncan cast an eye over him, presuming this was Liam. He had a black eye and a split lip which was healing but still showed signs of having been swollen. Duncan looked at his hands, resting on the counter and his attention was noticed, the hands withdrawn below the counter and out of sight.

"How are you doing, Liam?" Duncan asked.

"Do I know you?"

"DI McAdam," Duncan said. "And no, I don't think so. Are you feeling a bit sore?"

Liam cleared his throat, looking sheepish. He was in his early twenties and despite looking quite fit, Duncan wouldn't fancy the young man's chances going toe to toe with someone like Steven Phelps. "Aye, I'm all right."

"It looks like you took a bit of a hiding the other night."

Liam made to protest but Duncan's expression made him think better of it. "No big deal."

"Do you want to tell me about it?"

"No, not really."

Another man entered reception, lifting the flap at the far end of the counter and passing through, coming behind Liam and reaching for something on a shelf below. He looked at Duncan and must have clocked Liam's nervousness. "Everything okay, Liam?"

He was much older, perhaps in his fifties and Duncan guessed he was the general manager or a supervisor of some sort. "It's… er… it's the police, Ian. They just want a word."

"Oh, aye. Do they now?" He looked at Duncan and then gave his subordinate a suspicious look. "What have yous been up to?"

"Nothing… honest," Liam said without conviction.

"I just need a word with Liam, that's all," Duncan said.

"Right… well, don't be long. I need you onto that Mazda."

Liam nodded. "I'll be right there."

Ian left them alone, disappearing into the office behind them but Duncan figured he was making himself appear busy but still paying attention and probably listening in. "Do you want to take a quick walk with me?"

"Aye," Liam said and they both left the reception, walking out into the compound. They stood aside as one of Liam's colleagues came by them in a works van, Liam looking around to make sure they wouldn't be overheard.

"You seem nervous," Duncan said.

"No, it's not that... it's just... the boss is quite a taskmaster, and he wasn't too impressed when I turned up for work Monday morning with my face held together, you know?"

Duncan nodded. Any customer-facing role where the staff have clearly been getting into a spot of bother, would be frowned upon. "So, tell me about what happened?"

Liam looked glum. "What... er... have you heard?"

"Come on, Liam, don't mess me about. You don't think I'd be down here to talk to you about a drunken scrap on the weekend, do you? You must have seen the news—"

"Aye... but it was all a fuss over nothing. Just a few beers and a bit of aggro."

"Liam... don't mess me about."

"What happened to that guy had nothing to do with me! I swear."

"Then convince me or I can take you back to the station and we can go through it in an interview room—"

"There's no need for that..." Liam said, shaking his head. Duncan noticed he was walking with a slight limp. It didn't appear as if he was carrying an injury, but his upper body movement seemed robotic.

"Are you in pain?"

Liam smiled but the expression changed to a wince as they moved off, walking around the parked vehicles and away from the workshop and prying eyes. "Aye. Like you said... I bit off a bit more than I could chew."

"What was the fight over, a woman, I heard?"

Liam scoffed. "He was touching up the lasses, my missus included."

"Who was?"

"The big man, the one that's been all over the telly."

"Steven Phelps?"

"Aye, that's him." Liam frowned. "He said he mistook

Jennifer for a stripper. As if that makes any of it better. She's no' a stripper and that guy knew it. He was getting a bit handsy like..." Liam shrugged. "What was I supposed to do, me and the lads?"

"So you stepped in?"

"Aye, if you can call it that. I told him where to get off and... um... I might have said a few things that didn't really help matters."

"Who threw the first punch?" Liam shrugged, averting his eyes from Duncan's. "It's best to be honest with me now and save you a lot of trouble later."

Liam sighed. "All right... I did, but... I'd had a few and his attitude was pish, you know? He had it coming. Anyway, it all kicked off and we were slung out onto the street."

"What happened then?"

"Well, we were going to head off," Liam said. "I'd made my point and got ma head stoved into the floor as a result, so I'd had enough but..." he shook his head, "that guy, and his mates, they wouldn't leave it. It was like they were really up for a scrap."

"They kept it going?"

"We left and they followed. In the end we had a bit of a scuffle down Wentworth Street and then we legged it." He seemed embarrassed about making a run for it, but Duncan didn't think any less of him for doing so. The best way to end a fight is to not get involved, and so the young man made the right call in his book. "I mean, we were outnumbered as it was. And two of them were massive! And a bit mental."

"Did you do them any damage?" Duncan asked.

"Not enough to kill anyone!"

"That's not what I meant, Liam. Did you land any punches yourself?"

"Aye, one or two." He held out his hands, palms down,

showing Duncan the damage to the skin across the knuckles. "Those blokes were built like concrete."

"And who was with you, besides Jennifer?"

Liam looked around, his eyes settling beyond Duncan towards the workshop. Duncan glanced around but as soon as he did so, Liam started talking, rapidly. "It was a few of the guys, you know? I can't remember exactly who was there."

"Liam, don't mess me about."

"I…" he sighed. "It was three or four of my pals from…" he tilted his head, lips pursed.

"Work colleagues?" Duncan asked.

"Aye, they're my pals too."

"I want their names, Liam. All of them."

Liam relented, nodding but he remained staring at the ground. "No bother."

"Where were you three nights ago, the day after this altercation in the town?"

Liam's head snapped upright, looking terrified. "I was with Jennifer, at her mum's place. They'll both tell you… and then we went for a couple of drinks with friends, had some food at the Prince of India—"

"Okay, that sounds pretty comprehensive. It should be easy enough to confirm."

"I didn't have anything to do with what happened to that guy. I mean, I'm sorry he's dead like, but I don't even have a boat…"

"Who said anything about using a boat?"

"Ah… well, how else did he get over to Coruisk?" Liam laughed nervously. "Unless you reckon he could walk it." Duncan shrugged. "What, in the dark? He'd have to be mad."

"It takes all sorts," Duncan said. "I'm going to have one of my officers come out and take a formal statement from you.

It's just routine, and if I need to speak to you again, then I will, okay?"

"Aye, no problem."

"And we'll be speaking to Jennifer, her mum and anyone else who can vouch for your whereabouts three nights ago."

Liam nodded furiously, but he still seemed on edge. "Anything I can do, I'll do it," he said, looking nervously towards the workshop. Three of his colleagues, including his boss, Ian, were watching them. "Can I... can I go back to work?"

Duncan nodded. "Tell your pals I'll be speaking to them soon enough too." Liam glanced at him nervously, nodded and scurried across the compound, disappearing into the workshop. His boss was nowhere to be seen now, but the other two men were still eyeing Duncan warily. Liam seemed to be on the level, but he was nervous. The old adage of an innocent man has nothing to fear came to mind, but Duncan was experienced enough to know that wasn't always the case. History had proven that wrong on a number of occasions.

Liam's colleagues were taking a distinct interest in proceedings, however. His mobile rang and he answered it, walking back to his car around the front.

"Alistair, what's the craic with the lab tests?" Duncan asked. Alistair had stayed at the station to read the lab results following the processing of samples taken from Phelps's friends.

"Interesting," Alistair said. "And I don't mind telling you I'm a little bit surprised as well."

Duncan stopped, picking up on Alistair's tone. "What is it?"

"Well, I don't know whether Charlie Lumsden sold Brennan a pup, but whatever he supplied, it wasn't illicit, a narcotic or illegal."

"Say that again?"

"There are no traces of drugs in any of the blood samples provided."

"Nothing?"

"Nope."

A car horn sounded, and Duncan looked around, moving to the side of the road as a car made to leave the compound. It was a member of the workshop team, but Duncan hadn't spoken to him. The man acknowledged Duncan's move with a wave, drove across the forecourt and turned out onto the A87.

"So... either Charlie stitched Brennan up over their deal..."

"Or one or both of them are lying about pretty much everything," Alistair said. "Either way, shall we go and have a word."

"Aye, let's do that."

"Which one should we speak to first?"

"Brennan," Duncan said. "Let's see what he has to say for himself."

CHAPTER SIXTEEN

ALISTAIR DROVE Duncan out to the Maelruhba Estate. The Toyota Land Cruiser wasn't parked beside the house, but Duncan saw movement inside as they pulled up. Rain had been steadily falling during the drive down, but the clouds were now clearing and the sun was beaming down upon them.

Approaching the front door, Duncan looked to their right where a large barn was a short distance away. One of the double doors was open, caught on the wind having not been secured properly. Inside, he could see a quad bike, a small trailer and several kayaks mounted on a rack against the side wall.

They didn't need to ring the doorbell; it opened as they approached. Niamh Brennan stood in the gloomy interior, partially standing behind the open door. "I'm sorry, Alex isn't here," she said. Duncan exchanged a brief look with Alistair and he must have picked up on her reticence to open the door as well. Duncan took the initiative.

"That's okay, Mrs Brennan. We would like to speak to you anyway." She hesitated, peering out from behind the door and when it became obvious they weren't about to leave, she lowered her gaze and stepped back from the door. Duncan took that as an invitation and, as she headed back into the house, he eased the door open and both men followed.

The terrier they'd met on their last visit hopped off the sofa and came to inspect them, standing back and eyeing them warily for a moment before Duncan dropped to his haunches and, just as before, the dog came over to him.

"He's taken to you," Niamh said softly. Duncan glanced up, still stroking the dog's flank and only then did he see her properly in the light coming through the window. He stood up, the dog trotting back to the sofa, leaping up and settling down again but still kept an eye on Duncan.

"How did that happen?" he asked. Niamh lowered her eyes, pensive. Duncan could see the bruising beginning to show around her left eye.

"Oh... it's just one of those things." Her lips formed an artificial smile, but it faded rapidly. "It happens."

"Not in my house it doesn't," Alistair said sternly.

"Well..." she said trying to sound breezy, "we're not in your house, are we?" She thrust her hands into the pockets of her jeans, standing awkwardly. "As I said, Alex isn't home."

"Do you know when he'll be back?" Duncan asked. She shrugged.

"I'm not sure what he had on today... I think he might be up on the northern boundary. Some of the fencing failed and the livestock have spilled out."

"I'm sure we can catch up with him later," Duncan said. He pointed to her face. "Can you tell me what happened?"

She shrugged again, clearly reticent. "I was carrying some things..." she glanced at the dog, "and he got under my feet."

"Oh, did he aye?" Alistair said. Both men had seen enough signs of domestic violence in their time to see through that story. Duncan had been raised in the shadow of repeated instances of domestic abuse, seeing his mother and sister subjected to it and feeling the brunt himself of his own father's particular brand of violence.

"You shouldn't judge him too harshly, Alistair," Niamh admonished him. "Alex has been having a rough time of late."

"Tell us about it," Duncan said.

Niamh offered them a seat and Duncan sat down on the sofa while she took one of the armchairs next to the window. The terrier sidled up to Duncan, resting his head on Duncan's thigh and stretching out. Alistair chose to remain standing where he was. Niamh gathered herself, arms folded across her stomach. Duncan noted she winced as she sat down. It was very likely the black eye wasn't her only injury of note.

"Alex is a hardworking man, Detective Inspector," she said.

"Duncan, please," he said, smiling warmly. She inclined her head and her eyes flitted to Alistair.

"I know you don't rate him highly, Alistair," she said. He didn't respond, remaining impassive. "But he is a hardworking man who's only ever tried to better himself for... for his family." Her eyes moved to a photograph on the mantelpiece, the same one Duncan had seen on their previous visit; Alex, Niamh and a child. Duncan still couldn't see any sign of a child in the house, no toys, clothes or any of the things you see in a family home.

"Is that..." Duncan said, gesturing to the picture. Niamh stood up, crossed to the fireplace and picked up the frame, returning and handing it to Duncan.

"Freddie," she said. "Alex's son."

"Alex's?" Duncan asked. She nodded.

"Alex had a child with... a former partner."

"Oh, I thought..." Duncan hesitated and Niamh smiled.

"No, he's not mine but they shared custody... and I love

that little boy." Niamh's expression turned glum. "But Naomi moved away," she said, sighing, "after she married a guy from the central belt. Now... Alex doesn't get to see as much of Freddie as he'd like and Naomi seems less bothered about him being a fixture in his father's life, you know?"

"She's started afresh and wants to let go of the past?" Duncan asked.

"Aye, something like that, I suppose." She shrugged. "Whatever it is, she made things hard for Alex and... he's not good with adversity. Some people stand up and make themselves heard while others..."

"Fold," Alistair said.

Niamh looked up at him and nodded. "That's about the size of it." She fixed Alistair with a stern look. "He's really struggled of late, and the job doesn't help."

"What's going on?"

She shook her head. "It's just... he's expected to be everything to all parties. Sometimes I wonder if the owner has the first clue about what it means to run an estate such as this, tenant crofters, holiday accommodation and... bloody shooting parties."

"If he doesn't like his job, he should change it," Alistair said flatly. "There are plenty of other jobs around. A man of his talents should have nae bother."

Niamh shook her head. "It's not as simple as that."

"It is," Alistair replied. He was very candid, and Duncan figured they knew each other fairly well, otherwise his DS would never be so vocal with his opinions.

"It's not!" she said. "This house... the car... utilities... they all come with the job. I don't know if it's escaped your notice how tough things are these days unless you're fairly well off? If it was that easy then none of us would stick to jobs we didn't like, would we?"

Alistair took the chastisement with good grace, inclining his head which was about as much of an acceptance as she was ever going to get from him.

"Niamh," Duncan said, drawing her focus back to him, "can I ask you a question about Alex?" She nodded. "We know he likes a drink, and we've come across him in the past and again over the last eighteen months—"

"He... just needs a release is all," she said, sitting forward. "He's a good man, he doesn't mean any harm, it just... comes out of him when he's stressed."

"And is he stressed just now?" She averted her eyes from his gaze, but she did nod, even if it was almost imperceptible. "Does Alex take drugs?"

She lifted her eyes, meeting his. "I don't know why you're asking me that?"

"Because it's important," Duncan said. Niamh held his eye, and he didn't break contact. "Alex was seen the other night with a known dealer, in Portree, and we want to know what he was buying?"

She shook her head. "I don't know. Alex... likes a drink, and I've... never known him to take drugs. Are you sure it was Alex? I mean, maybe it was someone who looks like Alex?"

"His registration plate was seen and noted by a police officer, Niamh... and the dealer himself confirmed it."

She looked crestfallen, sitting back in her chair. "I–I don't know what to say."

"Did you notice anything different in him recently, particularly around the arrival of this group for their stalking event?" She was staring into space and Duncan sat forward, trying to get her attention. "Niamh?"

"Oh... sorry, I was miles away. Um... no, nothing out of the ordinary."

"Anything at all, a shift in his mannerisms... staying out later than usual? Anything?"

She looked at Duncan and her expression changed. it was like a veil lifting. "You... you actually think he might have... killed that man?"

"We have to examine—"

"My husband would never do such a thing!"

"Forgive me, but it would appear he has a volatile temperament."

"Raising a hand is one thing, but..." she glared at Duncan and then Alistair, "you can't think? He's not capable of something like that. He's a *good man*." Alistair arched his eyebrows, signalling he disagreed but he kept the thought to himself. "That night... Alex was at home, with me! All night!" she said fiercely. "And I'll say that to anyone who asks. Put me in court and I'll say it there too. We were here... watching the TV and then we went to bed."

"What did you watch?"

"What's that?" she asked, turning to Alistair.

"What did you watch on the telly?" he asked.

"I... I don't remember exactly. I'd need to... think about it."

Duncan glanced at Alistair, his expression unchanged. "Niamh, I think you should consider what you're saying. If it turns out to be untrue, then you could be getting yourself into a great deal of trouble—"

"He was with me," she said. "All night!" She looked at Alistair. "And I'm sorry if that's inconvenient for the two of you, but that's how it is."

Duncan accepted her defiance, tilting his head. "Thank you for your time," he said softly. Gently easing the dog's head from his leg, Duncan stood up. He took one of his contact cards from his wallet and extended his hand to Niamh. She looked at the card and then met Duncan's eye, but she didn't accept the card.

Duncan shot her a forlorn smile and set the card down on the coffee table in front of her. "If you ever need to talk, or need some help, I'll take your call at any time," he said softly. "Day or night, just pick up the phone."

Niamh Brennan remained in her chair, elbows resting on her knees, her expression one of thunder. "You can see your-selves out," she said. Duncan smiled and left the room, Alistair lingered for a moment longer, but he didn't say anything to her, and followed Duncan outside.

Light rain was falling again, and Duncan drew his coat about him. He glanced over his shoulder, and he swore he could see Niamh standing back from the window, watching them leave. He took a deep breath and glanced at Alistair.

"Well," Alistair said, "that went pretty well, under the circumstances."

Duncan smiled. "Hmm… she's digging her heels in."

"I'll never understand why women stay with men who hit them."

"It's never quite as simple as leaving, Alistair. You know that."

"Aye, yeah you're right. Maybe I just want to see an end to that kind of thing."

Duncan rubbed his chin. "Maybe she'll come around."

"You think Alex Brennan is our guy?"

"I think he's bottling something up," Duncan said, "but I don't know what it is."

Alistair nodded towards an imposing, steel-framed agri-cultural barn a short distance away. Estate staff were working inside. "Shall we go and have a word with some of the employees while we're here? You never know, one of them might be able to put Alex somewhere other than at home watching telly with his missus."

Duncan agreed and they started walking in that direction. "How do you know Niamh, by the way?"

"Huh?"

"Am I mistaken? You seem to know each other."

"Oh, she worked with my better half for a time, a few years back at the hospital. Niamh was an auxiliary nurse for a while, but she jacked it in pretty quickly. It wasn't for her. I don't know her very well, but well enough to know she'll be taken in by a bloke like Alex Brennan."

"Why's that do you think?"

"Well, he's full of it... talks a good game and she's..." he thought about it for a moment, "the anxious sort. I think she's been looking for somewhere to belong and men like that appeal to someone who's a bit inside themselves. If that makes any sense?"

"They say opposites attract though," Duncan said.

"Aye, and they also say *there's one born every minute* and Alex Brennan can pull the wool over people's eyes. He's the type. Scratch the surface and there's other stuff going on."

"Is he capable of murder, though?"

Alistair frowned. "To my mind, hit the right trigger points... and anyone is capable."

CHAPTER SEVENTEEN

THEY REACHED THE BARN, and their approach was noticed by one man who broke away from the other two. It looked like he'd been giving instructions, and he was a little older than them and therefore probably senior. He was sporting a large camouflage jacket and baseball cap. The skin of his face was tanned, by Skye standards at any rate, wrinkled and leathery. He clearly spent a lot of time outdoors.

"How are you?" Duncan asked, showing him his warrant card. "We're—"

He nodded curtly. "I know who you are." His welcome wasn't necessarily hostile, but nor was it welcoming. Duncan concluded it might just be his way. In the background, the other two staffers were leaving the barn via another door at the far end. One glanced back at them and catching Duncan's eye, he appeared to hasten his departure. Alistair saw it too.

"Do we smell or something?" Alistair asked with a wry smile.

"People dinnae like the police."

"Aye, the guilty ones," Alistair said, drawing a smile from the man.

"Can I ask who you are?" Duncan asked politely.

"Nicol," he said. "Nicol McLeod."

"And what do you do on the estate?"

He shrugged. "A bit o' everything." He looked past Duncan, over to the Brennans' cottage. "How is Niamh?"

"She's okay. Why do you ask?"

Again, he shrugged, turning away and walking over to the outboard motor he had mounted on a stand nearby. The casing was off, and he was carrying out some maintenance. "Just wondered. Not seen her about."

"You do usually?" Duncan asked, guessing why Niamh was keeping out of sight.

"Aye," Nicol said without looking at Duncan, focusing on selecting a spanner. "Nice lassie is Niamh."

"What about her husband?" Duncan asked.

Nicol made a show of loosening a nut, but he wasn't really paying attention to it. He glanced at Duncan, lips pursed, and didn't answer.

"You know what we are investigating, don't you?"

Nicol sighed, nodding. "I do, aye. Nasty business."

"Were you on that stalking party with Phelps?"

"The dead fella?" Nicol asked and Duncan nodded. "No, cannae say I was."

"How about those two?" Alistair asked, gesturing towards where the two younger men had been before leaving.

"Couldn't say."

Duncan found himself irritated. "Some might think you're being deliberately uncooperative."

Nicol met his eye, clicking his tongue as he arched his eyebrows. "Would they now, laddie? If you asked me a direct question, rather than dancing around the subject, then you might get what you're after."

"Alex Brennan."

"What about him?"

"Are you friends?"

Nicol smirked. "Alex does nae have any friends."

"Why not?"

Nicol shrugged. "I guess people are choosy about what company they keep."

"He's not popular then?"

Nicol set his spanner down, selecting a smaller one which he then toyed with in his palm. "Alex… likes to be in charge… and it goes to his head, in my opinion."

"He's a harsh taskmaster?" Duncan asked.

"That's the polite way of describing it," Nicol said.

"An arse?" Alistair said, and Nicol laughed.

"Aye, better." Nicol exhaled, looking over to Brennan's cottage again. "Alex can go over the top with his authority. The owner… is never about, and the rumour is that the whole estate is up for sale. He has a free rein at the moment… a free house, car… I'll bet he's never had it so good. The way he is around the place, it's almost as if…"

"As if what?" Duncan asked.

"He treats it like it's his estate. Somehow, he wound up running pretty much everything. I guess he'll milk it as long as it lasts."

"How does he treat you?"

Nicol laughed. "He treats me all right. I'm a bit long in the tooth to put up with any of his nonsense, and he knows it. He leaves me alone, which is better for his health, I should add."

"You don't like him either then?" Duncan asked.

"You got that from what I said?" Nicol replied, a trace of a knowing smile appearing at the corners of his mouth. "He rides the lads pretty hard. I mean, don't get me wrong, some of them need it or they'd take the mickey, you know? But…

even so, I think he gets off on the power side of it. He enjoys it a bit too much."

"Anyone ever stand up to him?" Duncan asked.

"Oh... Alex isn't daft. He never pushes it with anyone who'll bite... only those who won't answer back or feel they can't stand up for themselves."

"What about Steven Phelps?" Duncan asked.

Nicol eyed him warily, his expression clouding. "What about him?"

"Well... you have a guy who likes to be in charge and then a group show up... and they like calling the shots. It's conceivable that there would be a clash."

Nicol snorted. "Who's been talking?"

Duncan caught Alistair's glance his way in the corner of his eye, but he didn't acknowledge it. Nicol clearly thought they were aware of something, and that question was testing how much they did or didn't know. "Why don't you give us your side of it."

Nicol rolled his tongue along the inside of his cheek, evidently thinking, his eyes flitting between the two of them. He sighed. "I suppose it's out in the open, so my two-penn'orth won't make much of a difference."

"Go on."

"Like I said, Brennan likes to be in charge, to call the shots. Usually, when the tourists come out with us, they follow instructions, accept the briefing... listen to the way we do things." He shook his head. "Right from the off... this lot," he looked across towards the accommodation buildings, "were different."

"In what way?"

"Ah... the two guys in charge..."

"Phelps?"

"No, the groom an' his best pal... I don't remember the

names, but they were giving it some right from the off." He angled his head, looking stern and lowered his voice although no one was within earshot. The three of them were alone. "Entitled. That's how I'd describe them. They lorded it over everyone... throwing money around like they were celebrities – not handing it out, just showing off – making demands..."

"What sort of demands?" Duncan asked.

Nicol blew out his cheeks. "Think diva... and you'll be about there. Treated everyone like muck, they did, from the first moment they arrived. Mind you, I say that, but they've been different since your man was found out at Coruisk."

"Different how?" Duncan asked.

He shrugged. "Just different. They've been pretty quiet, kept to themselves a fair bit. I'm surprised they haven't left. Not that I think they're guilty of anything. It's just... I'm surprised, that's all."

"We've probably had something to do with that."

"Aye, probably."

"Including Brennan?"

"What's that?" Nicol asked.

"The guests treating people like muck. Does that include Alex Brennan?"

"Aye, especially Brennan. It's almost like... they singled him out because he was in charge." He shrugged. "At least, that's how it came across to me."

"And how did Alex take it?"

Nicol chuckled. "About as well as you might expect." He seemed to hesitate, as if he was about to say something and then changed his mind. "Anyway... I should probably be getting on." He made to carry on with his task and Duncan had to make it very clear they weren't about to leave before he reluctantly met his eye. "Is there something else I can help you with?"

"You can tell us what's on your mind," Duncan said.

"Ah... I still have to work here, you know?"

"I understand, but this is a murder investigation, so if there's anything... at all... that you think we might need to hear then now's the time to tell us."

Nicol, still reticent but thinking for a moment, finally nodded. "There was something that happened... nothing major and... it's probably nothing."

"Why don't you let us be the judge of that, Nicol," Duncan said.

"Alex took the group out for the day, stalking. They left a couple of hours before dawn, which is normal, and were gone much of the day." He shook his head. "Like I said, I wasn't with the group. I stayed here and when they got back..." he shook his head, "there was a real atmosphere among the group, but it was Alex who struck me as being different. Sometimes, with these groups, the going can get pretty tough and maybe some people don't enjoy it as much as they thought they would but with the guides, it's normal, you know. They're used to it."

"Something was up with Brennan?"

"Aye... he was off... like something had got to him."

"Like what?"

He shook his head. "I've no idea, but he wasn't himself and I saw some needle in the group."

"Between whom?"

"Phelps... and another guy, whose name I don't know. There were some words exchanged. I was over here, working, so I couldn't hear what was said but I could understand the tone. It wasn't hospitable, I can tell you that."

"Who instigated it?"

"No clue," Nicol said and as Duncan offered him a stern

look, he held his hands up. "I swear, I've no idea but Alex was nae happy about something."

"And Phelps?" Duncan asked.

"He was vocal but he was nae angry. It was more like he was... mocking in his tone, his body language."

"Mocking?" Duncan asked. "Who, Brennan?"

"Aye... I reckon so. A couple of his pals got in front of him, just as Alex tried to leave, and they stopped that Phelps guy from following Alex back to his house. He didn't look like he wanted it to stop. He was pushing his pals away and they had to get pretty forceful to encourage him to let Alex go."

"What could that have been about then?" Duncan asked.

"As I say, no clue," Nicol said. "Maybe he got a little loose with the firearms. We have firm safety rules when we're out on an organised shoot. Some people are a bit too casual, so maybe Alex called him out. Whatever it was, Phelps seemed to take exception to Alex, and he has my sympathy because Alex Brennan isn't exactly a people person, you know? He has that effect on a lot of people."

"Alex hasn't said anything about this to us."

Nicol raised his eyebrows, then focused on the outboard motor again. "Well... what does that tell you?" Alistair cast an eye over the motor.

"You go out on the water?"

"Aye, every now and again. It's a part of the package the estate offer; dolphin-spotting trips, seeing the island from the sea. We've got access to Loch Brittle, so it's an easy add-on. The estate needs all the money it can get, so I hear. Not that I'm a party to any of that stuff."

"Tell me," Duncan said, "did you ask him what happened between Phelps and Alex while they were out that day?"

"No, and I won't be asking him either." He shook his head,

then met Duncan's eye. "More than my job's worth to poke that particular bear."

"Did anyone else comment?"

Nicol shook his head. "It's better to be one of the three monkeys around here. I see no evil, speak no evil and I hear no evil. That way, I can lead a quiet life. Do you know what I mean?"

They then heard the sound of a car approaching them up the estate road. When they turned to look, it was Alex Brennan's Toyota. The driver watched them as he passed.

CHAPTER EIGHTEEN

ALEX BRENNAN DROVE around to the side of his cottage and pulled up in front of the small barn Duncan had seen open when they arrived. He glanced at Alistair's pick-up, but then went to the rear of his Toyota and dropped the tail gate, making a start at unloading the containers he was carrying.

Duncan and Alistair walked towards him. Duncan had planned to go straight back to Portree, but the conversation with Nicol had pushed Alex Brennan further forward into his sights. Brennan appeared to keep an eye on them as they approached but continued going about his business.

"Hello, Alex," Duncan said. He replied with a curt nod. Alistair didn't greet him at all and Brennan noticed, the two of them staring at one another momentarily before the latter broke eye contact. He was hauling a large water container from the front of the bed, it was empty, and he let go of it before he had to lift it from the truck.

"Detective Inspector," Brennan said. "What can I do for you today?"

"You can tell us about your altercation with Steven Phelps,

for starters," Duncan said. Brennan looked at him, puzzled. "At the weekend, when you returned from the stalking."

"I don't know what you're talking about."

"Really?" Duncan asked. Brennan looked beyond Duncan who glanced back but there was no sign of Nicol McLeod anywhere.

"Aye, I wonder where you got that idea."

"Answer the question," Alistair said flatly. "Or we'll go inside and ask your wife."

Brennan's eyes shifted, narrowing as he looked over at the cottage. Clearly, he didn't want them going in there. "I'll answer it, Alistair," he said. "Steven Phelps was a typical NCO in my experience. Good at dishing out orders but rubbish at taking them."

"That's your experience, is it?" Alistair asked, not bothering to keep the hint of mockery out of his tone.

"Aye... over-promoted and only with a rank due to his years in service. I'll bet there were dozens of soldiers better than him."

"And you got all of this from what, your two weeks sorting blankets and a day out with the man?"

Brennan shook his head, his expression darkening. "What would you know about it?"

"At least I served, unlike some others."

Brennan bristled, gearing up to counter but Duncan intervened. "I'd like to know what the problem was between the two of you," Duncan said. "You and he have a falling out and he winds up dead soon afterwards."

"Ah!" Brennan shook his head dismissively. "It was nothing, just him acting like he was in charge. It was my stalk, that's all. The guests... they're along for the ride."

"When did they arrive here?" Duncan asked.

"Some came up late on the Thursday night, others arrived during Friday."

"And Phelps?"

Brennan thought about it. "He was one of the first, Thursday night. They can come ahead of the allotted time as long as it's been agreed in advance."

"So, the trip was due to start Friday," Duncan said.

"The first excursion wasn't booked until the Saturday, but... aye, I suppose Friday was technically the first day. Those who arrive on the Thursday can make use of the facilities."

"And who did arrive early?"

Brennan seemed annoyed by these questions, his eyes flitting occasionally to Alistair who was still staring hard at him. "Steven Phelps... his army pal..."

"Ryan?"

"Aye, that's him. The... the builder as well, what's his name?"

"Nathan Aldred?"

"Aye."

"Did you interact with them?"

"Me personally?" he asked, and Duncan nodded. "Not really. The check-in is contactless these days, but they'd requested food. The estate will provide evening meals if prearranged."

"Who takes care of that?"

Brennan's irritation seemed to grow with each question. "What's so important about this stuff?"

"Is it a tricky question or something?" Alistair asked.

"Niamh is in charge of that side of things."

"I didn't realise your wife worked as part of the estate too," Duncan said.

"On occasion, aye."

"Bit hard for her to be customer facing, I should imagine," Alistair said. Brennan met his eye, and something passed unsaid between them. Brennan's gaze drifted over towards his cottage, almost as if he could see through the stone walls.

"Why would that be?"

"She's the anxious sort," Alistair said. "I doubt she likes to show her face very much, does she?"

"If you say so," Brennan said. Duncan took a step to his right, looking into the barn beyond them.

"Is this for your personal use?" Duncan asked, setting off for the barn. Brennan moved as well, and for a moment Duncan thought he was going to try intercepting him, but he fell into step beside him.

"I make use of it but it's estate property. Why?"

Duncan stopped at the entrance, glancing around at the interior. A boat trailer took up much of the floor space, but the walls were lined with racking, bearing an assortment of tools and equipment.

"Just curious," Duncan said absently, his eyes scanning the tools.

"Curious about what?"

Duncan glanced at Brennan. "It's in my nature." He smiled. "It comes with the warrant card." Brennan held Duncan's gaze for a moment longer and then looked to his right as another man approached. Duncan turned to see Tony Sinclair striding towards them. It struck Duncan that Tony had a rather odd gait.

"I want to speak to you, Detective Inspector," Sinclair said.

"Right... well if there's nothing else, I'll be getting on," Brennan said.

"Feel free," Duncan said and as Brennan made to return to his Toyota, Duncan had an afterthought. "I intend to request your mobile phone data, Mr Brennan."

Brennan halted, looking back. "My what?"

"I'm going to be in touch with your mobile phone service provider and have them give us everything they have on your phone; GPS locations, call duration... who you spoke with. Do you have a problem with that?"

Brennan stared at him, then he glanced at Alistair and shrugged. "Do what you like. I've nothing to hide." He returned to his Toyota, hauled the container out and set it down on the ground, slamming the tailgate shut. Duncan turned to Tony Sinclair who looked to be unsteady on his feet. The breeze shifted direction and Duncan understood, catching a strong smell of alcohol coming from the man.

"What can I do for you, Mr Sinclair?"

"I want to know when I'm allowed to leave?"

Duncan cast an eye over him. His hair was lank and hadn't been washed, and he had a day's growth of stubble. He was a far cry from the clean-cut professional he appeared to be when they first met. "I don't think you're in any state to go anywhere, do you?"

Sinclair's lip curled and he fixed Duncan with bloodshot eyes. "I'm getting married in less than four days—"

"And we appreciate your cooperation in this investigation," Duncan said. "If you could bear with us for a little while longer, I'd appreciate it."

"And what if I don't want to?"

Duncan shrugged. "It's a free country, Mr Sinclair. I have no authority to prevent you from leaving."

"Right, well... that's that then."

"Of course, I would have thought you'd wish to do all you could to help catch your friend's murderer though. Leaving so soon... could hinder that."

"And look bad for you," Alistair said. Sinclair looked at him.

"Of course I do." Sinclair looked across to where Alex Brennan was closing the double doors to his barn, keeping a watchful eye on all three of them whilst trying not to look like he was doing so. "It's just..." his brow furrowed, "I have things I need to do."

"I'm sure your partner has everything in hand," Duncan said, "and phones are incredibly useful devices. They work almost anywhere." Sinclair looked at him, studying Duncan's impassive expression as if trying to gauge his sincerity.

"Yeah... well," he said, looking glum. "I'll not be staying too much longer. That's all I'm saying." He jabbed a finger in the air at Duncan. "Do your job."

"We are, Mr Sinclair. I can assure you."

He made to leave and then hesitated. Turning back to face Duncan, Tony said, "You will catch who did this to Steve, won't you?"

"I give you my word we're doing everything we can."

Tony Sinclair took a deep breath, his eyes flicking between Duncan and Alistair one last time, and then he lurched to his left and stumbled away from them back towards the accommodation buildings.

"He's a curious one," Alistair said. "From what I've read about his old man, he wouldn't let the police tell him what to do."

"Agreed. I tell you what I'm finding curious."

"What's that?"

"We're looking into their friend's murder, and he had a falling out with Alex Brennan... and everyone who was present has failed to mention that to us."

Alistair inclined his head. "I hadn't considered that. It's odd."

"Maybe Brennan is telling the truth, and it was nothing at

all, but if his friends were hauling Phelps away... then I'd be wondering – if I was them – about it. Wouldn't you?"

"I would, aye." They both watched Tony, stumbling back to his accommodation, until he went inside. "What do you want to do next?"

"Obtain a warrant for Brennan's mobile phone records..." He looked towards the offices a short distance away, spotting security cameras mounted on the exterior. "And we'll have all the footage from the estate cameras as well, see what we can find out about people's movements over the weekend. It's surprising what some will do if they don't realise there's anyone watching."

"Why did you tell Brennan we were going to get his mobile phone records? We don't need his permission."

Duncan smiled. "I wanted to see how he'd react."

Alistair nodded. "He didn't seem bothered."

"No," Duncan replied, glancing towards Brennan's cottage. "He wasn't bothered at all."

CHAPTER NINETEEN

DUNCAN CLAPPED his hands together. taking position at the front of the room. All the background chatter wound down as all eyes turned towards him. Duncan scanned the room. His CID team were all present in the operations room and he'd managed to draft in some uniformed bodies to assist. Both Ronnie and Fraser Macdonald had been around long enough to be called veterans, they knew what to expect and, more importantly, what Duncan expected from them and he was confident they would be able to guide those less experienced colleagues.

Although the Isle of Skye saw its fair share of crime, major crime, murders specifically, were far from regular occurrences. What a police officer might experience in a month on the mainland, in Glasgow for instance, would arguably be what their counterparts on Skye might witness in their entire career.

Duncan nodded to Angus who dimmed the lights in the room. An image of the location was projected onto a screen behind Duncan and he pointed at it. "We're all now well aware of the Maelruhba Estate, and our suspect knows it much better than we do, so we will have a lot of ground to cover today.

Make no mistake, we need to pay attention and be thorough in the search." Duncan pointed to Caitlyn. "The first team will take the outbuildings and surrounding ground. The second team will be with DS MacEachran and prioritise the searching of the residence."

Duncan gestured to Angus and the young detective constable clicked a button on the remote in his hand and the image changed behind Duncan. "We obtained a warrant to search the estate after reviewing this CCTV footage," Duncan said, bringing up several stills lifted from the video. One image was of a white Defender, clearly visible was the estate logo emblazoned on the driver's side door.

The second image was a magnified section showing the driver. "This man, the driver, is Alex Brennan. He is the gamekeeper, the head groundsman of the estate. For those of you who don't know him, Brennan has a history of violence. He's come across our path before and we know he is an aggressive individual. There's no way of knowing how he might react to our presence, so be prepared. He has access to firearms and he also has military experience." Duncan glanced at Alistair, half expecting him to laugh but his DS seemed very focused.

"We are looking for anything that could link Alex Brennan to our victim, Steven Phelps. A weapon, clothing... any sign of Brennan having been out at Loch Coruisk that night. It could be as simple as a personal possession of Phelps's that Brennan brought home with him. If you come across anything at all that piques your interest, call a stop and have one of the core inquiry team come and take a look. No matter how small or obscure it is, let us decide. Now, does anyone have any questions?"

Fraser raised his hand briefly before folding his arms across his chest once again. "Not second guessing your investigation, sir, but what is it that has Brennan in the frame for this?"

"Brennan's alibi is his wife, Niamh. Both have stated he was at home with her on the night in question when we know Phelps was murdered." Duncan pointed to the stills taken from the estate security cameras. "This footage is time and date stamped and shows Alex Brennan leaving his house in an estate vehicle. I intend to ask him where he was going and why he lied to us."

"And… er…" Fraser said, frowning, "what do we think is his motive?"

"Apparently, words were exchanged between Phelps and Brennan the day before during their day's stalking and Phelps had to be hauled away by his friends once they returned to the estate. Now, what that falling out was over is unknown, Brennan certainly downplayed it to us and no one else has seen fit to mention it."

"Ah…" Fraser said, nodding. "So, we don't really have a motive."

Duncan inclined his head. "That's correct, Fraser. This is why we need to execute the search properly and obtain anything that can suggest his involvement."

"Right you are," Fraser said, smacking his lips and nodding. PC Fraser Macdonald wasn't one to question authority nor was he intentionally raising doubts about the search, Duncan was sure about that. On the outside, Fraser quietly went about his job, unfazed by any situation that came his way, but beneath the surface he was a very thoughtful officer. He was just prone to asking the questions that everyone else would think but dare not ask.

"Can we crack on with the search warrant now, Fraser?" Alistair asked drily.

"Oh, absolutely," Fraser said, nodding, the sarcasm dripping from the question completely passing him by. Several people sitting near him laughed.

THE TEAM DESCENDED upon the Maelrubha Estate, splitting up once inside the grounds with Alistair's team driving up to Alex Brennan's cottage and Caitlyn leading her group over to the estate outbuildings. DC Russell Mclean took two uniformed officers with him to the small office buildings. Duncan parked his car by the cottage and walked up to the front door.

He was met by Alex Brennan, standing in the doorway with his mouth agape. "What on earth is going on?" he asked, looking at the assembled officers. Angus was already leading several constables over to the barn where Brennan stored his belongings. Duncan approached and handed him a copy of the search warrant. Brennan gave the paper a cursory glance, shaking his head.

Niamh Brennan came to stand beside her husband, shock evident in her expression. Alex glanced at her, giving up on reading the detailed document in his hand. "They're here to turn our place upside down," he said despondently.

"Why?" she asked. Alistair was beside Duncan now, and he angled his head.

"Because the two of you have been telling porkies... that's why," he said.

"What?" Alex said, frowning. "I told you—"

"Enough to keep us looking elsewhere," Duncan said. "Please stand aside so my officers can search your property."

Brennan shook his head, Niamh looking defiant beside him. He steered her to one side, and she was about to protest but he shook his head, squeezing her hand. "We can't stop them," he said. "Let them get on with whatever they have to, and they'll be gone soon enough."

"Thank you, Mr Brennan," Duncan said. Alistair led Fraser and two other constables past them and into the house. Alex Brennan shook his head.

"Wipe your feet, gents," Alistair said. "We're not here to trash the place."

If Niamh, or Alex for that matter, appreciated the instruction then they didn't show it.

"I don't know what it is you're expecting to find," Brennan said.

"For your sake, I hope we find nothing at all," Duncan said quietly, looking past the couple and into the house. "Please keep out of the way and we'll be done as soon as possible."

Their arrival hadn't gone unnoticed and Duncan saw a small group gathering over at the accommodation buildings. He could already see Tony, Ollie and the unmistakable imposing frame of Ryan, and he assumed the others were also close by. They were watching proceedings closely.

Duncan held up his hand, gesturing for the couple to go back into the house and he would follow. Niamh looked positively furious, whereas Alex was far more pragmatic. He didn't seem too concerned by the search although he was clearly irritated.

"This is such a waste of time," Brennan said as they entered the kitchen. An officer was going through the kitchen cupboards already.

"Yours or ours?" Duncan asked.

"Everyone's," Brennan replied.

"Hey!" Niamh said as the constable dropped a cup which bounced on the counter but didn't break.

"Sorry," the constable said.

"You will be if you break any of my stuff!" Niamh said.

Sounds of drawers opening and movement in the next room sent Niamh to the doorway. She glared at Alistair and he winced apologetically. Niamh didn't say anything, but she did turn back to Duncan.

"We'll be through as soon as we can," he said. It didn't appease her at all. The constable continued going through the kitchen, moving to a small pantry where he began opening storage boxes and containers.

"Do you expect to find something in my bread flour?" she asked, sarcastically.

"Just let them do their work, love," Alex said. She scoffed at his response, meeting his expression with a look of disgust and he lowered his eyes to the floor. Noise came from upstairs, heavy footfalls on old wooden floorboards. Alex looked up at the ceiling, shaking his head. "I told you, I didn't do it," he said to Duncan.

"Only you haven't been entirely truthful with us, have you?" Duncan asked. Alex Brennan held Duncan's eye for a moment and then looked away. A moment later, they heard someone entering the cottage from the front door, making their way towards them. Ronnie Macdonald's head peered around the door smiling as he made eye contact with Duncan.

"Sir, you got a sec?" he asked. Duncan nodded and left the kitchen. As he passed, Ronnie smiled at Niamh and Alex, before falling into step behind Duncan.

"What have you found?" Duncan asked, aware of Alex Brennan's presence behind them. He seemed just as curious as Duncan or perhaps he was concerned they'd found something.

Once out of the house, Ronnie led them around the side and over to the barn. The double doors were open and two constables were inside, diligently working through the equipment stored on the racking. Duncan glanced at Alex, seeing his eyes lingering on the officers but he didn't say anything.

Ronnie passed the entrance, taking them down the side and around to the rear.

At the back of the barn, there was a little shack of a lean-to and beside that a log store. The cut wood was stacked taller than Duncan and was three metres wide and four logs deep. Some of the wood had been disturbed, piled up on the ground. Angus was standing to one side. He smiled at Duncan but the smile faded when Alex rounded the corner a step behind him.

"What have you found?" Duncan asked, joining Angus. The detective constable pointed to where they'd removed the cut wood from the stack. Duncan looked. There was a small space behind the wood, roughly a little over a foot in diameter and fashioned by way of stacking the logs a particular way. In the gap a sports holdall, black faux leather with twin white stripes running the length of it, had been wedged in between the rear wall of the barn and the wood.

Duncan peered in and saw the zip had been undone, the sides pulled apart to reveal the contents. Inside he saw some fabric material, clothing Duncan guessed, along with a pair of black gloves. Lying atop those was a ski mask. Duncan, donning a pair of forensic gloves, lifted the ski mask out, holding it aloft and showing it to Alex.

"T-that's not mine..." he said, for the first time his brash confidence appeared to be dented. He glanced between Duncan and Angus. Niamh came to stand beside her husband and he looked at her, shaking his head. "I swear it's not mine."

Angus carefully inspected the gloves, he gestured to Duncan who also looked closer. The gloves were leather and there was something smeared on the exterior of the glove heel and palm area. Whatever it was, it had dried, helping to glue detritus and dirt to the surface. Duncan and Angus exchanged a knowing look.

"Have it photographed and catalogued," Duncan said. Angus nodded.

"What is it?" Brennan asked. Duncan took a breath and faced him.

"I think you'll be coming with us, Mr Brennan."

Brennan's eyes narrowed, and he adopted a defensive posture. "Am I... under arrest?"

"Well, you can either come with us and we can have a conversation, or I'll arrest you and we'll have the conversation anyway. It's up to you."

Brennan glanced at his wife. Niamh was shocked and she took her husband's hand, holding onto it so tightly Duncan could see the whites of her knuckles. He smiled at her, doing his best to reassure her, then he looked back at Duncan. "I'll come with you."

CHAPTER TWENTY

DUNCAN BACKED into the interview room carrying two cups of coffee in his hands. Allowing the door to swing closed behind him, he set one cup down in front of Alex Brennan and gave the other one to Alistair. His DS was sitting opposite Brennan, arms folded across his chest, sitting back, his eyes firmly fixed on their suspect.

"Thanks," Brennan said, his fingers curling around the cup. It was from a vending machine and far too hot to drink, steam drifting off the surface and curling up into the air above it. He nodded to Alistair as Duncan pulled out a chair and sat down. "It's nice to have a human being to talk to."

"What's that?" Duncan asked.

"Your man here, he's said nothing since the moment you left the room."

"DS MacEachran tends only to speak when he has something constructive to say," Duncan replied, opening the folder that was already on the table in front of him.

"He must live in a monastery then," Brennan replied. Alistair didn't flinch, his eyes focused on Brennan, his gaze unwavering. Brennan seemed unsettled by this, which Duncan guessed was Alistair's strategy. Duncan made a show of looking through the file. Brennan shook his head, sitting back. "This is such a waste of my time."

Duncan's eyes lifted to him, and Brennan averted his own from Duncan's gaze. "I think it would be best for all parties, if I make that decision." Brennan sighed but said nothing. "I am obliged to remind you that you are entitled to legal representation—"

"What do I need a lawyer fer?" Brennan retorted. "I've no' done anything wrong."

"As you wish," Duncan said quietly. Someone knocked on the door and entered. It was Angus and he was clutching several evidence bags. He gave them to Alistair and then left.

Spacing the bags out before them, Duncan pointed to the largest which contained a hooded sweatshirt. It was black, plain with no motif. The second bag had the ski mask Duncan had picked up earlier in the day and the third contained the pair of leather gloves.

"Do you recognise these?" Duncan asked.

Brennan looked at the three bags. "Aye, but only because you found them outside my house this morning."

"You acknowledge they were on your property then?"

"They were on the estate, where my property is, and the first I saw of them was this morning. Same as you." He looked at Duncan then sat forward, staring at Alistair who'd adopted the same demeanour he'd had when Duncan returned to the interview room. "And they're no' mine."

"In which case," Duncan said, "how did they come to be in your wood store?"

"How the hell should I know!"

"I should tell you that we believe," Duncan said, placing a hand gently on the bag containing the gloves, "the substance we found on the gloves is blood. A sample has been sent to the laboratory for analysis."

"Good for you," Brennan said defiantly. "But it still has nothing to do with me."

"Are you used to burying ski masks and blood-stained gloves outside your house?" Alistair asked flatly. There was no hint of accusation in his tone and the question was delivered in a matter-of-fact manner.

"I told yer, none of this is mine," Brennan countered. Alistair arched his eyebrows.

"Aye, you said that once or twice."

"Because it's true!"

Alistair smiled, nodding slowly. "Oh, is it aye?"

"You've always had it in for me, Alistair. It doesn't matter what I say or do… you'll always see the worst in me."

"Why did you lie?" Duncan asked.

"Lie?" Brennan scoffed. "What did I lie about?"

"You said you were at home the night Steven Phelps was killed."

"All night," Alistair added. "At home with the wifey…"

Brennan stared at Alistair, then he looked away, his eyes dancing briefly before settling on Duncan.

"Aye, that's it," Duncan said. "The penny is dropping. We know you weren't at home."

"You said you were going to check my mobile data…" Brennan said. "That'll tell you where I was. I've seen it on those crime shows on the telly!"

"We have," Duncan said.

"There you are then!"

"And it tells us your mobile was at your house," Duncan said, reaching into the file and taking out the stills from the CCTV footage. He laid them out on the table and gently slid them towards Brennan, "but only your mobile. You… went elsewhere." Duncan placed his forefinger on the magnified image of Brennan at the wheel of the works vehicle. "Where were you going, Alex?"

Brennan stared at the images, his lips pursed. "I ducked out... not for long–"

"That's funny," Duncan said.

"I don't find anything about any of this funny, Detective Inspector," Brennan growled.

"How long were you out for?"

"What?"

"You said you went out, but not for long. How long were you out for?"

Brennan seemed pensive, and Duncan wondered if he was calculating timings in his head. "I... I'm not sure. Maybe... an hour or so."

"And where did you go?"

He shook his head. "I just needed to get some air."

"To get away from it all?" Duncan asked.

"Aye, that's it. Things... haven't been the best at home of late and sometimes it's just better... to take yourself out of a situation, walk away rather than stay put."

"Otherwise, accidents happen, aye?" Alistair asked. Brennan cocked his head.

"Accidents?"

"Slips, trips and falls," Alistair said. "Wives are notoriously clumsy people, aren't they?"

Brennan glared at him. "You know nothing about my life!"

Alistair smiled but without genuine humour. "I was speaking generally, but it's good to know you see your life in what I'm talking about."

"Where did you go?" Duncan asked again.

Brennan shook his head. "I told you, out and about. Nowhere specific... just out."

"You took an estate Defender rather than the Toyota, why?"

Brennan shrugged. "I have access to all manner of vehicles, and they're all owned by the estate. What difference does it make?"

"A Defender is an easy vehicle in which to hide a body, though," Duncan said.

"A *great* way to hide a body," Alistair agreed.

Brennan laughed. "And you think I could get Phelps... stick him in the back of that Defender and... then what, drive to the other side of the Cuillins and dump his body? That's stretching credibility a bit far, wouldn't you say?" He shook his head. "And here's me thinking you lot were bright."

Duncan silently agreed, but it didn't have to have gone down that way.

"If, and I do mean *if*, I could have overpowered Phelps," Brennan said, "how do you think I'd have managed to get him away from his pals? Answer me that, Sherlock!" He looked at Alistair. "And that would make you Dr Watson, but you're not smart enough, are you?"

Alistair remained impassive. He wouldn't rise to it, regardless of the provocation. Duncan allowed Brennan his brief moment of superiority before he took out another still image, taken from the same camera mounted close to the entrance gates to the estate. He laid it down in front of Brennan whose eyes drifted to it. Duncan saw his face drop as he read the time stamp in the bottom corner.

"Six-thirty in the morning," Duncan said, "of the following day." Brennan closed his eyes and Duncan could see he was breathing faster. "Did you duck out for another bit of fresh air or... were you in fact coming home?"

Brennan looked down into his lap but remained silent. Alistair sat forward, clearing his throat. "Because it's stretching credibility a bit far, wouldn't you say?"

Brennan, lips pursed, refused to look up. "Well?" Duncan asked.

"I've nothing to say," Brennan whispered.

"I have," Duncan replied. "You left the estate on that night, where you drove around with no fixed destination... and we have no footage of you arriving back at the estate until the following morning at six-thirty. So... unless you have a better explanation for where you were, we are seriously considering charging you with the murder of Steven Phelps."

Brennan's head snapped up and he pointed an accusatory finger at Duncan. "Oh hey... now you just hang on a minute. I didnae kill him or anyone else. This isn't on me!"

"Then where were you?"

He snorted. "Well, you're the police. You figure it out." He sat back in his chair and folded his arms defiantly across his chest. Duncan found his denial intriguing. By the look Alistair cast him a moment later, he could tell they were thinking similarly.

"Alex—"

"No!" Brennan said, sitting forward and cutting Duncan off. "I'm telling you I didn't do for that man. And, like I said, I've seen the shows on the telly. You cannae prove I did it, because I *know* I didnae. You understand?"

"It doesn't look good, Alex," Duncan said.

"Then charge me," he replied. Duncan glanced at Alistair who, lips pursed, inclined his head. Brennan saw the look and a trace of a smile marked the corners of his mouth. "You can't, can you? Because you don't have any evidence."

"Your alibi is shot," Alistair said.

"So what? I lied about where I was... I'm a naughty boy." He sat forward, picking up the coffee cup and sipping from it. "It's a big leap from there to brand me a killer for that though, isn't it?"

"We have seized the vehicle you were driving that night," Duncan said. Brennan shrugged. "And if we find any evidence that Steven Phelps was ever inside it, then—"

"Well, you will," Brennan said, grinning.

"We will?" Duncan asked.

"Aye, it was one of the vehicles we took out on the day we went stalking, so of course you're likely to find evidence he was in it. He was sitting in the rear on the way back to the estate."

Alistair's eyes darted to Duncan who tried very hard not to give away his disappointment. Brennan could be lying, or he could have chosen that particular vehicle in full knowledge that this scenario could happen. It would require a lot of planning, but it was possible. It also ruined a key element of the case they could build against him. It was as if Brennan expected them to find evidence of Phelps being transported in that vehicle.

"Where did you spend the night?" Duncan asked.

Brennan sniffed. "I slept in the back of the Defender."

"You expect us to believe that?" Duncan asked.

Brennan shook his head. "I don't really care what you believe, Mr McAdam."

There was a knock on the door, irritating Duncan but he turned to see Angus poke his head around the door. "I'm really sorry to interrupt, sir... but can I have a word."

Duncan glanced at Brennan who looked the happiest he'd been since they'd brought him in. He rose from his seat, suspended the interview and stepped out into the corridor with Angus, leaving Alistair in the room with Brennan.

"What is it, Angus? I'm in the middle of—"

"I know, sir, and I'm sorry," Angus said nervously. "But I've been reviewing all of the CCTV footage gathered from the estate."

"I know, we've been through it—"

"Aye, but there's a camera in a hide... near to the water's edge. It's part of a project financed by—"

"Angus," Duncan said, holding a hand up to stop him, "please get to the point, I'm in an interview..."

"The camera is motion activated, sir. It only functions when something passes by the hide. It's concealed, and no one can really see it unless you know it's there. We only found it this afternoon whilst carrying out the search of the estate. It's a small wooden box, about so big—" he made a box shape in the air with his hands and Duncan raised his eyebrows. Angus winced. "You have to see the footage. Alex Brennan wasn't the only one out and about that night."

CHAPTER TWENTY-ONE

DUNCAN ENTERED the ops room with Angus who hurried past him and brought his computer out of hibernation, clicking his mouse to open a file. Duncan could see multiple icons registering movie files. "These are the recordings," Angus said, pointing at the screen. "They are of varying duration depending on how much movement was picked up."

"Night vision?"

"Oh aye, absolutely," Angus said, clicking on one icon. The movie player started up, a deer stepping into view and getting up close with the camera. "Oh... sorry. Wrong one." Angus glanced at Duncan, his face reddening. He clicked on another file and this time the movement triggering the recording was further away, close to the water's edge.

Duncan squinted. "What am I supposed to be seeing in this?" he asked.

"Wait a second... there!" Angus said, and in the background they saw movement at the edge of the trees, and then two figures stepped out into view. Duncan stared at the footage.

"Who is that?"

Angus paused the footage, leaning forward and pointing to the second figure. "I reckon that's Ryan... as for the other one, they don't come into focus at all." He restarted the footage and Duncan watched as the two figures made their way along the tree line, their movements seemed abnormal but then Duncan remembered they were doing this at night. They couldn't necessarily see where they were going.

The two men disappeared back into the trees and, seconds later, the camera stopped recording. "When was that?" Duncan asked.

"It was recorded on the same night as we see Alex Brennan leaving the estate," Angus said. "The time stamp shows these two on the move twenty minutes after we know Brennan left."

"Have you checked the accuracy of the time?"

"I've put in a call to the organisation who manage the cameras to ask that very question, but I'm still waiting to hear back. From where we know the hide is located and the positioning of the camera, these guys came in from the direction of the accommodation building and are circumventing the Brennans' cottage and heading towards the old laird's house on the western edge of the estate."

"I wonder what they were up to," Duncan said, "no good I should imagine."

"Aye," Angus said, nodding. "Who goes prowling about in the dead of night if they're not up to no good?"

"But how does this affect us interviewing Alex Brennan?"

"Oh right, yeah," Angus said, clicking back to the file and selecting another recording. "I hadn't shown you this one."

The footage began and Duncan checked the time stamp. It was taken only a couple of minutes after the previous one. A lone figure creeps into view and Duncan leans closer to see. "That's Nathan Aldred... you can see his hair cut and the stud earrings..."

"You sure?" Angus asked.

"I reckon so, aye."

"Well... keep watching. It's about to get interesting." Duncan found his curiosity piqued and refrained from asking any more questions, watching the form of Nathan Aldred pass out of shot but before the camera switched off, another figure stepped into view. He hesitated, standing still and seemingly looking into the trees where Nathan had just disappeared. Instead of following, the man stood still, watching for almost a full minute. Duncan wondered if the footage had frozen seeing as he was motionless but then he moved off. However, he didn't follow the same course charted by Nathan or the previous two men into the trees but took a different route.

Duncan stood upright as the footage ceased playing. "Do they come back on any other recording?"

Angus shook his head. "No. None of them come back that way, or if they do, then they don't appear to have activated the camera."

"Film?"

"No, it's a digital set up so the camera doesn't run out of film at all. Maybe they kept to the trees or came back a different route, one not covered by the camera."

"Aye, maybe," Duncan said.

"What do you think they were playing at?" Angus asked. Duncan would like to know the answer to that question too. "Of course, if the time stamp is accurate on the recordings—"

"Yes, I get it, Angus," Duncan said, irritated. The DC frowned. He was well aware of the ramifications of the footage they'd just watched. Duncan took a deep breath. He'd have to go back down to the interview room. Alistair was not going to like this any more than he did, but if they could determine the time stamp was indeed accurate, then they'd have no choice.

"Funny you should mention Nathan Aldred, sir," Angus said, rooting around on his desk.

"Funny, how?" Duncan asked.

"I've been working on his background," Angus said, finally locating his notebook and triumphantly holding it aloft. "He's quite a character."

Duncan perched himself on the edge of the nearest desk. "Go on."

"Aldred is a builder by trade, right? When Caitlyn first looked him up, he is the director of five separate entities."

Duncan cupped his chin with his right hand. "And how is this significant? He can be a director of multiple businesses if he wants. That's not illegal."

"No, but he has an active case going through the civil courts at the moment related to one of his firms."

"Who is investigating?"

"Curiously, it's not investigating him directly. It's actually a challenge against His Majesty's Revenue and Customs for not prosecuting the firm in question," Angus said. "Seemingly, prior to Aldred's business voluntarily winding up, he set up another as a parent company, trading in the same field with a very similar name before folding the first."

"Sounds... interesting," Duncan said. "Why would he do that?"

"Because the business he shut down went under owing a small fortune to its creditors. Once you count up all the interested parties and the business's exposure to debt, we're talking millions."

"Yes, we know this," Duncan said. "Caitlyn told us."

"Right," Angus said. "It's what Caitlyn was talking about before; phoenixing. Had the business been forced into bankruptcy, then Nathan Aldred would have been automatically disqualified from holding a directorship of another company, managing or promoting another company. Basically, he'd be finished in business for anything from two to fifteen years. However, by going this route, of voluntary closure, he has every chance of keeping going and avoiding the penalty."

"What else have you found out about him?"

"He has financial problems," Angus said. "As far as I can tell, he's muddling along while this case plays out but his exposure to financial risk is damaging. His latest accounts for his various firms detail director's loans he's paid to himself over and above what the companies have in cash reserves and, from what I can tell, his business credit lines are stretched. I suspect he's living month to month, or worse. I couldn't find any social media presence, which in this day and age is unusual. When I went into the internet archive, I found out why."

"He's not popular?"

Angus smiled. "You could say that, aye. He was getting hammered on his personal as well as his business social media accounts prior to him closing them down. It looks like he's made a lot of enemies by folding that particular firm. There are a lot of really angry people who are out of pocket."

"Well," Duncan said, "being a terrible businessman isn't a crime and certainly doesn't point you in the direction of being a murder suspect—"

"Unless," Angus said, raising a finger in the air, "and this is where I have something new, there is a group of people who have banded together to try and bring you down." He passed Duncan a sheet of paper. On it was a list of names and Duncan concentrated, reading down, tracing the names with his fingertip. It was an extensive list.

"He really pissed a few people off, didn't he?" Duncan said, laughing. He stopped, his finger tapping the paper. He looked at Angus. "Is this…"

"Yes. Charles and Rebecca Phelps, aye," Angus said, arching his eyebrows. "I did a quick search and they're Steven Phelps's parents."

"I thought we couldn't find any next of kin?"

"That's right, we couldn't. They passed away in a car accident in Spain, late last year but," Angus nodded to the list in Duncan's hand, "the legal action was already underway."

"Phoenixing isn't a civil matter, though, is it?"

Angus shook his head. "Apparently, they were inspired to launch a civil claim for damages against Aldred. HMRC were not inclined to investigate, so they took it upon themselves." He shrugged. "Why HMRC didn't push it, I don't know. Either Aldred's misdemeanours were not considered large enough of a case to warrant the expenditure of an HMRC led prosecution or they accepted his version of events. What we do know is that this group came together to challenge that decision by the authorities in court, and at the same time brought a civil action against Aldred to try and recover their money. Or maybe they wanted to destroy him. Who knows? Whatever their motivation is, all we know for certain is that Nathan Aldred must have been, and probably still is, feeling the heat."

"Odd that Steven is pals with a man who's in debt to his parents. Do we know how much he's on the hook for with them specifically?"

"Very odd, I agree. Phelps's parents were very influential in this pressure group, even creating the social media accounts seemingly with the specific goal of highlighting what Aldred was up to. Look at this," Angus said, opening a different window and gesturing for Duncan to come closer and look. It was a social media page, under the title of *Cowboys Among Us*. Angus scrolled down the posts and there were photographs of part-finished building projects, and a lot of unhappy faces.

"That would strain a friendship, don't you think?" Angus

asked. "It could perhaps lead to arguments, and a motive for murder?"

Duncan sighed. "Can you think of anyone you'd be less likely to go away with for a week of relaxation and fun than someone who'd stiffed your parents?"

Angus cocked his head. "Assuming Steven Phelps actually liked his parents."

Duncan considered what he'd just seen on the camera footage. "Go back through the statements all of them made on the stag trip, and just make sure no one mentioned any nocturnal activities."

"Aye, will do. Then what?"

"Then we're going to ask them what they were up to, wandering around in the dead of night."

Duncan left Angus to it and made his way back down to the interview room, located close to the custody suite. Following a quick word with the custody sergeant, Duncan, accompanied by a uniformed constable, walked along the corridor to the interview room where Alistair waited with Alex Brennan. When he opened the door, Alistair shot him a quizzical look.

Duncan remained standing and Alex Brennan glanced up at him expectantly, both hands absently toying with the empty cup from the vending machine in front of him.

"All right, Alex," Duncan said, resignedly. "You're free to go."

"What?" Alistair asked, but Duncan merely offered him a glum look. Alex Brennan hesitated, perhaps considering this was a trick of some kind, but when Duncan encouraged him to stand, he slowly pushed back his chair and stood up.

"I can go home?"

"Aye, you can go home," Duncan said. "But, before you

do..." Brennan stopped, and met Duncan's gaze, "who were you buying the drugs for?"

"What?"

"The drugs you got from Charlie Lumsden. Who were you buying them for?"

Brennan smirked, seemingly buoyed by the confidence of his impending release. "I'm through answering your daft questions, Detective Inspector." He looked down at Alistair. "If you want to ask me anything else, you can do it with my solicitor present. You had your chance."

Duncan nodded to the constable and the uniformed officer beckoned Brennan over towards him before leading him out of the room and back to the custody suite to process his release.

Alistair stood up, having watched their chief suspect leave the room. "Any chance you could tell me what the hell just happened?"

Duncan smiled wryly. "We have some camera footage from the estate on the night we think Phelps was abducted or went missing."

"Aye, so what?"

Duncan recalled the footage in his mind. "Steven Phelps was present on the Maelrubha Estate, alive and well... half an hour after we saw Alex Brennan drive out of the gates."

Alistair sighed. "You're winding me up?"

Duncan pressed his fingers into his eyes feeling tired all of a sudden. "I'm not winding you up. If Brennan was responsible, then he had to come back and get Phelps later... and we've no evidence of him returning—"

"Until just before dawn the following day."

"Exactly right, Alistair." Duncan shook his head. "We're pretty much back to square one, unless the forensic work comes back and ties that little stash in the wood store to Phelps's murder."

"Anyone could have put that stuff there," Alistair said. "In the wood store, I mean."

Duncan scoffed. "Oh aye, you think he's innocent now, do you?"

"I'm just saying what any decent solicitor would say when it's put to them."

Duncan knew Alistair was right. They had nothing concrete on Brennan, and everything was circumstantial even if it still pointed in his direction. It wouldn't matter if they could prove Phelps was in Brennan's vehicle or if what they found in the search was related to the murder. Unless they could put Brennan and Phelps together at the time or location of his murder, then they had nothing that would convince the procurator fiscal to charge him, let alone a jury to convict.

They needed more. Much more.

"When we get the results back from the lab on the clothes we found stashed out the back of the cottage," Duncan said, "we might have further questions for him. Until then, he gets to go home."

"What are we going to do next?" Alistair asked.

"Ask the stag party what they were doing running around the estate after dark."

"They were... *doing what?*" Alistair asked. Duncan tilted his head and smiled ruefully. Alistair checked his watch, frowning. "How long did you leave me in this interview room for?"

CHAPTER TWENTY-TWO

ALISTAIR SLOWED his pick-up down as they entered the gates of the Maelrubha Estate, flagged down by PC Ronnie Macdonald whose turn it was to be the police presence. "How are you, Ronnie?" Alistair asked.

"Aye, I've had better days," he said glumly. He turned his face to the heavens and wrinkled his nose. "I'm hoping the rain holds off. I don't want to be sitting in the car all day."

"It's a tough life, Ronaldo," Alistair said with a smile. He nodded towards the office building nearby. "What's the craic?"

"Your man Brennan arrived back about ten minutes ago. He wasn't a happy camper."

"No, I get that."

Ronnie pointed towards the accommodation building where Alistair and Duncan were heading. "I think you should brace yourselves."

"What for?" Alistair asked.

Ronnie shook his head. "There's been a new arrival, and he stinks."

"What do you mean?" Duncan asked, looking over.

"He's driving a Bentley, wearing a sharp suit... he's got

bureaucratic nightmare written all over him. And... er... he's said if I'm going to be here, then I'm instructed to remain at the entrance here."

"Oh," Alistair said, "does he, aye?"

Duncan looked towards the house, seeing a Bentley parked apart from the other vehicles. "Who do you think he is?"

Ronnie shrugged. "I have the distinct impression he doesn't like the polis much. He barely gave me the time of day."

"Nah... maybe he's just met you before," Alistair said, smiling at him as he depressed the accelerator, slowly moving away.

"Aye, nothing but respect for you too, Alistair," Ronnie said, smiling, but they didn't see or hear him.

They drove up the drive, past the office buildings which seemed unoccupied today. Perhaps it was the detention of Alex Brennan or the police activity of the morning search which had driven people to either stay out of the way or maybe take an early finish.

They parked the pick-up and Alistair switched off the engine but Duncan stopped him as he cracked the door open. "Hang on a second," Duncan said, dialling a number on his phone. "Hey Angus, it's me. Do me a quick favour, would you?"

"Yes, sir. What do you need?"

"Run this registration plate for me," he said, reading out the Bentley's number plate. Duncan glanced sideways at Alistair and his DS nodded.

"I'll bet you a tenner it belongs to a lawyer," he said. Duncan smiled. "An expensive one at that." Angus relayed the details and Duncan thanked him before hanging up and clambering out of the vehicle, making their way to the communal entrance.

Once inside the building, they found themselves in a

double-height, vaulted lobby. At the far end was a reception desk, probably staffed when they had different parties occupying the accommodation, but Tony Sinclair's group had free run of all the rooms available, so the desk was empty. At the centre of the lobby was a seating area, leather sofas and chairs set out before a large wood burner, the flue rising up to the roof far above.

Duncan was surprised to find every member of Sinclair's group sitting there. Their arrival hadn't gone unnoticed, and as they approached Duncan realised they were all listening to one man. He was standing, addressing them all. In his late fifties, he had a shock of thinning white hair, swept up and away from his forehead, a tanned complexion indicative of spending time in the sun. Evidently, the way this summer was going, it wasn't a Scottish sun he was familiar with.

Duncan understood what Ronnie had meant when he took in his attire. The suit he was wearing probably cost more than Duncan took home in a month. He turned to face Duncan and smiled, revealing pearl white veneers, his tanned skin wrinkling around his eyes.

"Detective Inspector McAdam," he said warmly, offering his hand. "Delighted to meet you." Duncan took the hand, finding his skin was as smooth as his greeting.

"I don't believe we've met," Duncan said.

"Cameron Macintosh," he replied, looking past Duncan to Alistair. "DS MacEachran?"

"Aye," Alistair said, keeping his hands firmly by his sides.

Macintosh smiled, and although polished, Duncan knew it was as artificial as those teeth he was flashing. "I represent the business interests of Rhodry Sinclair."

"You owe me a tenner," Alistair said quietly.

"I beg your pardon, DS MacEachran, I didn't catch—"

"I was just saying you're a solicitor," Alistair said, smiling at him.

Macintosh nodded. "Correct. I have a longstanding history of working with the Sinclair family," he said, glancing at Tony who was looking down into his lap, his hands clasped before him. "As a result, I have been asked to come here and facilitate proceedings."

"That's a curious way of describing it," Alistair said.

"Of describing what?" Macintosh asked.

"Getting in the way."

Macintosh smiled. "Detective Sergeant, I can assure you I am here at the behest of the Sinclair family, and I will do all I can to close this matter down as quickly as possible."

"Aye, that's what I said."

Duncan shared Alistair's concerns but didn't voice them. "You said you represent the Sinclairs' business interests?"

"I do."

"And what interest is it of Mr Sinclair's as to what happens on the Maelrubha Estate?"

Macintosh smiled. "When an inquiry of this magnitude is underway and brings his son, Anthony, within its sphere it becomes of significant interest to my client."

"Right," Duncan said. "Fair enough." He looked around the group. All of them appeared very subdued. "We have some questions to ask you all regarding your activities on the night we believe Steven Phelps went missing." Duncan noted a couple of the men exchange quick glances whereas Tony Sinclair shifted in his seat.

"I'm sure everyone will be pleased to assist you, Detective Inspector. Are any of these men considered suspects in the untimely death of Mr Phelps?" Duncan looked at him. "Purely so we know whether or not you should be reminding them of their rights before answering questions."

"This is an informal process, Mr Macintosh. We are trying to fill in some gaps in our timeline of events leading up to Mr Phelps's death." He looked around the group and no one met his eye. "These are questions for witnesses, and indeed friends of the deceased."

"Hmm… even so," Macintosh said, also looking around the group, "perhaps it might be better for these gentlemen to consider their answers carefully."

"I'm sure they will," Duncan said. "May I continue?" Macintosh inclined his head, moving to stand on the periphery of the seating area but Duncan knew he had every intention of listening carefully and wouldn't hesitate to intercede if he felt it necessary. "When did you last see Steven?"

Tony Sinclair sat forward, and everyone seemed willing to defer to him. "We… er… had a meal planned for the evening, here," he said, lifting his hand and waving it in the air in a circular motion. "Then we had a few drinks… played a few hands of poker," he said, looking around at his friends. Two of whom agreed with slight nods. "A few more drinks… and then we all drifted off to bed. It was fairly quiet after hitting the bars in Portree on the Friday and being out on the hills all day Saturday."

"And you last saw Steven Phelps at what time?" Duncan asked.

Tony fixed Duncan with a stare, lips pursed. "I… um…"

"Didn't they already say that in their statements?" Macintosh said.

"Just clarifying," Duncan replied.

"Perhaps you could stick to a fresh line of questioning rather than wasting time rehashing old information," Macintosh said. "Otherwise, it might come across as if you're trying to catch someone out. Are you… trying to catch someone out, Mr McAdam?"

Duncan smiled. "So, you all called it a day around the same time that night then?" There was a murmur of general agreement. "You didn't do anything else? You stayed inside?"

"That's right," Tony said, looking around. "The last we saw of Steven was when he went off to bed."

"That is interesting," Duncan said, looking at Alistair who produced an envelope from inside his jacket. Tony Sinclair looked at his best man, Ollie, who shifted awkwardly in his seat. "This wasn't you then?" Duncan asked, opening the envelope and taking out some images lifted from the wildlife camera footage Angus showed him earlier. He passed the images to Tony and Duncan saw his mouth fall open as he flicked through them.

"I..."

"Don't know what to say?" Alistair finished for him.

"How about you, Ryan?" Duncan asked, passing him a photo of himself, his unmistakable physique and hair style clearly visible in the image.

Ryan gave the picture a cursory look and handed it back. "I needed to get some air. So what?" He looked at his friends. "This accommodation can get a bit stuffy."

Again, the group nodded along, although with less confidence as the images were passed around. Everyone was visible in the footage at some point, either moving alongside others or alone. Only Steven Phelps appeared to take a different route to the others. Duncan didn't know why, and he was keen to learn that along with what they were all doing.

"Getting some air, were you?" Alistair asked. "I thought maybe you were playing a bit of a nocturnal game of hide and seek?"

"What of it?" Tony asked, but he wasn't looking at Duncan, his eyes were trained on Macintosh who'd just studied the images.

"We're just curious as to what all of you were doing sneaking around the estate in the dead of night. It's a bit odd for grown men, wouldn't you say?"

Tony shrugged, and Duncan could see the family solicitor had lost some of his boldness, shooting Tony a dark look before turning to Duncan. "What is it you are seeking to learn with this... this theatre?" he asked, holding the images aloft before passing them to Alistair.

"Theatre? I'm just wondering what they were up to, as well as why they failed to mention this little night-time excursion out into the estate before now."

"Your question implies some calculation of wrongdoing on their part, am I correct?" Macintosh asked. "If so, I would ask you to be clearer with what you are suggesting."

"Not at all," Duncan countered. "However, I don't think it's me or my team that need to be clearer." He cast his eyes around. No one met his gaze. "Does anyone want to explain what you were doing running around in the woods?"

"I suspect some form of adult high jinks," Macintosh said, turning the corners of his mouth down. "Something that a group of young men away on a stag trip might get up to. Immature, perhaps, but no harm done."

"Then why not mention it?" Alistair asked.

Macintosh smiled. "Embarrassment... for grown men to be, how did you put it... *running around the woods at night*, could indeed be considered childish." His eyes swept the group briefly before settling on Tony. "And for a grown man to be considered acting in such a childish manner might see him lose face to those who love and care for them." Tony lowered his eyes.

Duncan realised he was going to get very little from these men. They'd been briefed, if not schooled, on what they were going to speak about. Cameron Macintosh had sorted that out before they arrived. Not that he could have known, unless there was more that Duncan was yet to learn about what transpired that night and over the course of the trip.

"It would appear from the footage we have seen that all of you were heading off towards the laird's house," Duncan said, and unsurprisingly, no one commented. "Steven, on the other hand, seemed to go off on a different route. Does anyone know where he might have been going or why he didn't follow the rest of you?"

"Oh, Detective Inspector," Macintosh said, smiling. "Surely, you cannot be asking any of these men to speculate on what their friend may or may not have been thinking on any night, let alone this particular one, where he met an untimely end?"

"They knew him better than we do," Duncan said, "and were with him for the days prior—"

"Honestly, Mr McAdam. You should know better than this with your experience."

Duncan found that interesting. Macintosh was clearly very thorough, and if he knew anything about Duncan then he must have researched him prior to arriving on the island. What was he doing here? Had he been dispatched to watch over his son, and if so was that because Rhodry Sinclair was simply looking out for his son or was Tony actually guilty of something? It was quite possible he was concerned that any suspicion of impropriety involving his son might give the police leverage over someone close to his business.

Macintosh was correct, Duncan's experience could cause the Sinclairs some trouble.

"We would like to have a look around the accommodation, if no one has any objections?"

Before anyone could answer, Cameron Macintosh nodded sagely. "I'm afraid, without a search warrant in place or in the absence of a crime being committed upon the premises, we will have to say no to that."

"We have a warrant," Duncan said.

"No, you have a search warrant for entering and searching the residence of Alex Brennan, and for a detailed search of the grounds. However, this doesn't encompass either the accommodation buildings or the laird's house itself."

Duncan took a deep breath. "We can arrange for a warrant, if you prefer?"

"Then I suggest you do so," Macintosh said, lifting his sleeve away from covering the face of his watch and checking the time. "Although, this late in the day, I suspect you would need a very good reason for one to be granted. Do you... have a good reason, Detective Inspector McAdam?"

"I can speak to the estate owner and have them grant us permission—"

"Not for the holiday accommodation, as I'm sure you know," Macintosh said. He glanced to his left and retrieved his briefcase that had been standing beside the chair Tony was seated upon. He set it down on the coffee table and opened it. "As for the laird's house," he said, searching for something inside the case, his eyebrows lifted momentarily as he found what he was looking for. "Here we are," he said jovially, standing up and passing the sheet of paper to Duncan.

"What's this?" Duncan asked, scanning the official-looking document and seeing Alistair in his peripheral vision, peering over his shoulder.

"That, Detective Inspector, is a pre-contract agreement between the registered owner of the Maelrubha Estate and my client, Mr Rhodry Sinclair, stating his intention to complete the purchase of this estate, along with all buildings, equipment and small holdings, tenanted or otherwise, as soon as the process can be concluded."

Duncan's eyes flickered to Macintosh and back at the document in his hand. "Now, why would he be so interested in a shotgun purchase of the estate?"

"My client has been carrying out his due diligence for quite some time, Mr McAdam." Macintosh glanced down at Tony. "In fact, he sent his son here to evaluate the status of the estate and to review his investment. His forthcoming marriage lent us the perfect opportunity to see how the estate is managed... warts and all, you might say."

Duncan sighed. "Okay, that's interesting."

"And tragic that an event as devastating as this one has happened at the same time..."

"Aye, tragic," Alistair said. "A real blow. But it hasn't changed your boss's mind then?"

"No, accidents happen."

"Murders happen too," Duncan said, "and your client has some experience of those as well."

Macintosh smiled. "Well, detectives... unless you have something more for us to discuss, I would say that this conversation is complete, wouldn't you?"

Duncan nodded. "I guess so." He looked around the faces and not everyone seemed pleased about this situation. "Oh, there is one more thing. Don't worry, Mr Macintosh, I don't think we need a warrant or for any of these men to require legal representation before we talk about it." He looked around at the group. "You're all still here."

Ryan, Ollie and Tony met his eye, but Nathan and Neil did not.

"I don't understand your meaning," Macintosh said. "It is my understanding that you requested these gentlemen remain here whilst you conducted your inquiries."

"I did," Duncan said, "but with one exception," he glanced

pointedly at Tony, "to a man, you've all complied without argument. I'm wondering why that is?"

Macintosh frowned. "You expect them to be less helpful in an investigation into their friend's death?"

"I would expect them to be more vocal... regarding everything. Whether they can leave, what's happening in the investigation... who might be responsible and perhaps seeking retribution against them. Only, they are all *very* quiet. And I find that odd."

"As they say, Mr McAdam, it takes all sorts," Macintosh said. "People react to traumatic incidents in different ways."

"Psychology is covered when you're studying law, is it?" Duncan asked.

"You would be surprised," Macintosh said.

"I'm sure," Duncan replied, holding the man's gaze.

"Well, if you'll excuse us, detectives. I think we are finished here." He took out a business card and passed it to Duncan. "Should you require anything from the estate; information, have access requests or look to serve a warrant... please do give me a call in the first instance. I have the authority of the current estate owners until it passes to my client."

Duncan smiled, holding the card aloft and slipping it into his pocket. "And I'm sure you'll be very accommodating."

"I am at your disposal, Detective Inspector."

Duncan turned and Alistair fell into step beside him. They didn't speak until they were outside and certain they wouldn't be overheard.

"What do you make of that?" Alistair asked. Duncan looked back towards the building when he reached the pickup. Movement to his right drew his attention and they both saw Niamh Brennan leaving the barn carrying a basket full of laundry, making her way back to the cottage. She glanced over at them, and Duncan was sure she'd seen them, but she didn't acknowledge their presence.

"Whatever they were up to that night," Duncan said, turning his attention back to Alistair, "it looks like they're not going to be talking."

"At least, not to us," Alistair said. "Which, from a personal point of view, I find their level of distrust of a highly decorated police officer a little upsetting."

"Highly decorated?"

"I'll have you know I've a commendation or two under my belt, from back in the day," Alistair said. "I've got them pinned to the fridge at home with wee magnets."

Duncan smiled, but it faded when he saw Cameron Macintosh leaving the building deep in conversation with Tony Sinclair. Tony's eyes darted to them and away again. "Do you ever have the impression you're not welcome somewhere?"

Alistair sniffed. "Everywhere I go," he said quietly. "Everywhere I go." He looked at Duncan. "Back to Portree?"

"Aye. Let's have a word with Ronnie first though, make sure he keeps his eyes open."

"You think they'll be up to something then?"

"Oh, aye," Duncan said, opening his door. "They're definitely up to something all right."

CHAPTER TWENTY-THREE

DUNCAN MADE his way down to the front lobby, greeting a couple of officers in the stairwell as he passed them. Opening the side door, he stepped into the station foyer and the clerk on the desk pointed to a woman sitting on a chair against the far wall. She had a baby in her arms, unsettled and grizzling. She made to stand as Duncan crossed the distance between them.

"Good morning," he said, "you asked to see me?"

"Mr McAdam," she said by way of greeting, adjusting her hold on the baby in her arms which did little to calm the child. Duncan recognised her.

"Lorna, isn't it?" he asked. "Lorna Lumsden?"

"Aye, well we're not married," she said with a curt nod, trying to soothe her child by putting a finger in its mouth. "But Charlie does live with me." The baby began sucking on the finger and quietened down. Lorna looked much as she had the first time he'd met her at the maisonette she shared with her partner, Charlie. She looked tired, as if she hadn't slept much but Duncan figured that was quite normal with a baby in the home. Not that he had experience of that, personally.

"What can I do for you?"

"Charlie's gone missing."

Duncan wasn't surprised. People like Charlie Lumsden were far from reliable members of society. From what Alistair told him, Charlie made a few quid here and there from selling recreational drugs, as well as anything else that came his way, legitimately or otherwise. Duncan doubted much came his way that wasn't either stolen or traded in lieu of debt. Such people were ten a penny in Duncan's experience, and for one of them to drop off the radar was hardly newsworthy.

Lorna must have seen this thought reflected in his expression because she scowled at him. "I know you don't like him—"

"It's not that, Lorna... it's..."

"What, Charlie's a wee bam, so he doesnae matter. Is that it?"

Duncan could see the anger in her tone wasn't matched by her expression. She was worried. "Okay," Duncan said, smiling to try and reassure her and gesturing for her to sit down again, "tell me what's going on?"

She retook her seat, and fortunately the baby didn't start crying when she withdrew her finger. She looked at Duncan earnestly as he sat down beside her.

"After you and Mr MacEachran came to see him, the other day, Charlie was all..." her brow furrowed as she sought the right word, "flustered. It was like you'd really got to him. I asked him what it was all about, yous coming to see him, but he said it was nothing. I knew full well it wasnae."

"Did you ask him what was wrong?"

"Aye, of course I did," she said, shaking her head. "But he told me it was just a bit o' business he was doing and you were asking questions. I have to say that got me a bit upset, because he's not supposed to be dealing anymore. He promised he'd cut it out when the baby came along."

"He said he'd stop dealing?"

"Aye, and he has... at least, I thought he had," she said, lowering her voice. "I told him, I cannae have people coming round the house all the time... you know?"

"Buying drugs?" Duncan asked.

"Aye... if the council were to find out, I'd likely be evicted... and I have my son and this one," she said, bouncing her child on her knee, "to think about as well now."

Duncan couldn't tell if it was a boy or a girl. He knew parents would often accessorise their child with a pink bow or a blue romper suit to help distinguish the sex of the baby if there was a doubt. This particular child could do with that, in his opinion.

"You reckoned he'd cleaned up his act?"

"I did, aye. He has, I'm sure of it." Duncan was sceptical, but Lorna seemed genuine enough in her belief. "Which is why it's all so odd."

"When did you last see him?"

"That morning, when you woke him up. He'd been on a bender the night before." Duncan arched his eyebrows. It didn't sound like someone stepping up and taking their responsibility seriously. "He'd only been in bed for an hour or two when you knocked on our door. As I said, after you left, Charlie was really upset about something."

"But he wouldn't say what it was?"

"Well, no... and I probably didn't help matters once I realised he must have been up to something. I mean, why else would you be calling round to ours?" She looked sheepish, her eyes darting from Duncan to her baby and back again. "I got a bit angry... and that set the wee man, here, off again. Charlie doesnae care for him crying."

So, it's a boy.

"You were angry that he might be up to no good?"

"Oh, I'm not daft, Mr McAdam. I know Charlie is always going to be up to something. He's the type, you know? But... he promised me he'd get off the drugs and definitely that he'd stop selling them."

"Maybe he just stopped selling from the house?"

She shook her head. "No, he's been clean since the wean came along." Duncan sighed, fixing her with a sceptical look. "I swear it, he has. I'd know if he wasnae, wouldn't I? I live with him." Duncan nodded, encouraging her to continue. "Anyway, the wean started kicking off... and Charlie was on at me to shut him up, getting really aggressive like, and he's not. Charlie is a sweet man most of the time."

Duncan found that hard to believe. "Go on, please."

"Well... as I said, it was all going off in the house. I mean, I was proper raging, you know? He wouldn't give me a straight answer... and he left."

"What? He walked out?"

"Sort of, aye. I was yelling at him and he sent a couple of texts... then he had a call. He pushed past me and went outside to speak to them... then he took off."

"He didn't say where he was going?"

She shook her head. "I saw him walk past the kitchen window and go down the stairs, but he never even looked back." She looked pained now. "And he hasn't been back home since."

Duncan thought about it. Charlie hadn't been gone very long at all but he sensed Lorna must be genuinely concerned to come into the station. She would know the police weren't likely to be particularly interested in someone like Charlie Lumsden.

"Who called him, any idea?" he asked.

She shook her head. "No, and he didna say anything at all, just pushed past me."

"Has he done this before, disappearing, I mean?"

"I'd be lying if I said you could always count on him... but he's been better since this one came along," she said, smiling at her child. "Honestly. It's... not like him."

"What about friends?"

"I've called them... or been round to their houses and asking if they've seen him. They haven't. I've been everywhere."

"And you trust their word?"

She laughed. "No! Like I said, I'm not daft... but... he's not answering his mobile, and my messages aren't being delivered. I even went round to his mam's place... and they haven't spoken in years, just in case because I cannae think of anywhere else he'd go. She's not seen him either."

"Is his phone off?" Duncan asked.

"Aye... I think so, but he wouldn't just disappear like this. He's got no reason to. I'm really worried, Mr McAdam."

He studied her face for a moment, seeing genuine fear in her eyes. Someone like Charlie, who moved among the circles he did, could easily get himself into trouble, but if Lorna was right, then something out of the ordinary may have occurred.

"Has anything strange happened recently? Has he said anything... or has anyone odd visited your home?"

"No, nothing like that," she said. "Things have been good. I'd worked some extra shifts before the baby came and we've been putting money aside."

"Do you still have it?" Duncan asked. Lorna looked puzzled. "The money, or has Charlie taken it?"

"I... I haven't looked." She went for her mobile, struggling with the baby in her lap. Without a word, she passed the child to Duncan. Instinctively, he took the child while she went to her pockets for the phone, holding him out from his body, the baby staring at him, wide eyed. "He's not going to explode."

"What?" Duncan asked, breaking eye contact with the child and looking at Lorna.

"He's not a hand grenade... he won't go off or anything."

"Aye, right," Duncan said, but he had never held a child before, even his niece was four years old before he spent any real time with her.

Lorna found her phone and tapped away at the screen. "Bloody hell," she whispered.

"What is it?" Duncan asked, feeling the strain in his biceps. This baby was heavy.

"It's gone."

"What has, the money?"

"Aye," she said, turning the screen so Duncan could see the balance. "He's... pretty much cleaned out the account."

In his mind, Duncan added, *or someone has*, but he kept the thought to himself.

Lorna seemed on the verge of tears. "Why... would he do that? It doesnae make any sense. We're happy!"

"All right," Duncan said. "It's not possible for me to launch a man-hunt or anything... but... I'll put the word around for people to keep an eye out for Charlie. We'll see if he turns up."

"Okay... thanks," Lorna said, dejected. She tucked her mobile back into her pocket and took the baby from him. "Why would he do this?" she asked again. Duncan didn't have an answer for her. Men like Charlie were notoriously unreliable, and the simplest answer is that he decided he didn't like family life and took off. Either for a break or permanently. Only time would tell. He wouldn't be the first to do so, but something about Lorna and her reaction to Charlie's vanishing act struck him as different, somehow.

The coincidence of Charlie's sudden departure following their visit nagged at Duncan, and he couldn't discount it.

CHAPTER TWENTY-FOUR

DUNCAN ROUNDED A CORNER, making his way back to the ops room, and almost collided with Angus. The detective constable took a step back. "Sorry, sir. I was just coming to find you."

"Well, here I am. What is it?"

"We've had a report back from the lab," Angus said. "The results are in from the testing done on those clothes we found in the wood store at the back of Brennan's."

"We could do with some good news," Duncan said, gesturing for Angus to accompany him back to ops. "Can we link it to the Phelps murder?"

"Yes," Angus said. "And no." Duncan stopped, fixing the young man with a quizzical look. "You'll understand," he said, setting off with a spring in his step.

"Can we or not?" Duncan asked as they entered the ops room. Alistair and Caitlyn were present, and Russell Mclean was seated behind his desk, arms folded, distracted by something he was reading on his monitor. Alistair looked at Duncan, a broad smile emanating from beneath his moustache.

"And we thought we had a puzzle on our hands as it is," he said. "This has just gone all *Twilight Zone* on us."

Duncan, his curiosity piqued, felt his mobile phone vibrate in his pocket and he quickly glanced at the screen, seeing it was an incoming call from Grace. He rejected the call, focusing on Alistair. He perched himself on the edge of a desk and nodded at his DS. "Go on then, confuse me more."

Alistair crossed to the information boards. Photographs of the clothing, a hooded sweatshirt, gloves and a ski mask, were stuck to the board, along with another showing where they were found at the back of the barn used by Alex Brennan. "The hoodie," Alistair said, tapping the picture, "has traces of DNA matching the samples we took from Alex Brennan. It's the right size for him, give or take." He pointed to the ski mask. "The lab found hair samples inside the ski mask, and those match the deceased, Steven Phelps."

Duncan felt a flash of excitement. "That links the clothing to our victim as well as our chief suspect, but it doesn't place them together at the time of death."

"It does not," Alistair agreed. "Although, we know they'd been together for an entire day beforehand. The technicians were unable to find either Phelps's DNA on the hoodie or Brennan's on the mask."

"Why should we expect that, it would make this far too simple," Duncan said, drawing a smile from several people in the room.

"Right," Alistair said. "We'll have to set aside the question of why Phelps was running around with a ski mask on. All we have left are the gloves."

Duncan looked at them. "The dried smear on the fingers, is it blood?"

"Yes, it's definitely blood, and positively confirmed as human. Although we can see the smear with the naked eye, the lab was able to see more under analysis. Both gloves show signs of blood on the leather, both the fingers and the palms, but here's the kicker; there are two blood types present. One person, who left the greater sample, suffered significant blood loss leaving a larger sample to draw a profile from." Alistair arched his eyebrows.

Duncan held his hands out, palms up. "And?"

Alistair smiled. "But that blood sample couldn't be matched to Steven Phelps. Nor is it Alex Brennan's, for the record."

"So... whose blood is it?" Duncan asked.

"That is the very question we are all puzzling over. The blood is old, and I mean really old, but they have managed to extract a strong DNA sample and are running it through the database, searching for a match. Nothing has come back so far."

"Do you have any good news?" Duncan asked.

"We have some fascinating news," Alistair said. "As I said, the majority of the blood on the gloves belongs to a person unknown, but we were able to pull a second DNA profile and that matches our victim, Steven Phelps."

"Which, together with the sample of DNA pulled from the sweatshirt that matches Brennan, places them together," Duncan said, "but as you say, we know they've been together. It proves nothing."

Alistair nodded. Duncan got up and walked over to where the crime scene photographs were displayed. He examined the images of Steven Phelps, looking at the man's hands. As he recalled, they were dirty, the skin rough and exposed with soil and dirt beneath the fingernails. "There's no sign of him wearing gloves the night he died or in the time leading up to his death."

"Aye, that's what I thought too," Alistair said. "The soil

beneath his fingernails was compared with that found in the treads of his boots. It matches... or as close as we can determine."

"So, he wasn't wearing gloves while he was scrambling across that hillside," Duncan said.

"Those gloves..." Russell said, and all eyes turned to him, "are bothering me." Duncan encouraged him to continue. He was talking to them but focusing on his monitor. "I've got a classic car—"

"You have an *old car*," Alistair said. "And being old doesn't make something a classic. It just makes it old."

"Aye, that's what I hear your missus says about you, sarge," Russell retorted.

"What have you got?" Duncan asked him, curious.

"My car, sir – my classic car – has leather seats but they're a bit weathered and the previous owners didn't take care of the covering as they should have. The leather is cracked and... that doesn't matter," he said, glancing up and seeing Duncan's expression. He chose to get to the point sooner. "The gloves look old to me, well worn."

"So?"

"Well... seeing the label there," he said, pointing absently to the photo of the gloves, "I've never heard of the manufacturer, so I've just done a search on the internet. The company who manufactured them disappeared a decade ago... they were bought out by a rival and the brand evolved."

"Maybe they are old, were broken in and comfortable," Alistair said.

"Aye, your missus says that about you too," Russell quipped, but dropped his smile when he saw the change in Alistair's expression. "Anyway... moving on..."

"Phelps or Brennan, whoever owned them, may have kept

them," Duncan said, agreeing with Alistair. "Is there anything else there that might be useful."

"Maybe," Russell said. "I've probably never heard of the brand because they made military equipment."

"For military issue?" Duncan asked.

"Aye... but that doesn't mean much," Alistair said. "Military issue kit like this can be supplied direct to base stores or to army surplus shops. You'd have been able to buy them in every town and city around the country where there was an army base nearby, as well as those where there wasn't. Catering for the weekend warrior who likes a bit of paintball." Alistair frowned. "An interesting find, Russell, but I don't think it helps us at all. Both men spent time in the army, so either of them could have owned the gloves."

"You said Phelps's DNA was inside?" Duncan asked him, and Alistair nodded. "So, the assumption is they were his gloves, right."

"Gloves he wasn't wearing the night he died," Alistair said, "or had removed them prior to his night-time walk through the Cuillins."

Duncan couldn't shake the feeling that they were missing something in all of this. Everyone involved in the case seemed to be working against them. Alex Brennan had been uncooperative right from the outset, but from what he could gather, that was the nature of the man. He was unpopular for a reason, and Duncan could see he wasn't what you might describe as a *people person*. Whoever was responsible could have killed Phelps and then put the gloves on, thereby transferring his DNA into the gloves. The gloves simply added complexity and ambiguity rather than clarity.

Niamh's attitude could also be understood; spouses often backing their partner regardless of what they are accused of. A couple were joined at the hip, their future lives, both economic and reputational, were dependent on one another. That's why spousal testimony in relation to alibis was always considered to be of lower value by defence advocates. It couldn't be relied upon.

As for Steven Phelps's friends, they were all hiding something, but whether that tied into his death, Duncan had no idea. With the arrival of Cameron Macintosh, the Sinclair family solicitor, he didn't expect a lot of help from there. The only person that Duncan could have confidence was levelling with them was Lorna, Charlie's partner. Unfortunately, she was just as much in the dark as they were.

Duncan's mobile vibrated again, and he saw it was Grace. "I'll be back in a minute," he said, stepping out of the room into the empty corridor and answering the call. "Hey."

"Duncan…"

He sensed something was wrong. She was at work, he could hear music and raised voices in the background. "Grace, everything all right?"

"Can you… er… come down to the bar?"

"Now?" he asked. "I'm a little—"

"It's important," she said. He checked his watch. McNabs, the bar where Grace worked, was only around the corner.

"Sure. I can be there in ten minutes."

"Make it five," she said, abruptly hanging up.

Duncan walked back into the ops room, beckoning Alistair over to him and lowering his voice. "I need to duck out for half an hour."

"Is everything okay?"

"Aye, sure," Duncan said. "I'll not be long. Find out who the blood stain belongs to," he said, referring to the gloves. Alistair nodded and Duncan left.

McNabs was on the street parallel to the police station and Duncan simply had to walk around the building to reach the main entrance. There was no one on the door tonight, but on a midweek evening it wasn't necessary. The nightlife of Portree was a far cry from Sauchiehall Street in Glasgow, and there was rarely trouble. Which is why Duncan was surprised to see a patrol car parked across the pavement, hazard indicator lights flashing.

He went inside, quickening his pace. The main bar had a half dozen patrons inside whereas the next room had almost twice that as far as Duncan could see. Grace was behind the bar and, as he approached, her eyes flitted to the far corner where Duncan could see Fraser Macdonald standing over a table, looking menacing. As menacing as Fraser could get anyway. It wasn't his style to be intimidating despite his ample size.

Beyond Fraser, he saw two people at the table. Becky Mcinnes... and her son – Duncan's son – Callum. He hadn't seen either of them for months. Having made a conscious decision not to interfere in his son's life. To get involved would likely tear the teenager's life to pieces, but also do harm to both Becky and the daughter she shared with her husband, Davey. So, he'd kept his distance and made no attempt at contacting either of them.

The last time he'd had any contact was when he rejected a call from Becky. She'd made three and he'd declined all of them. The final one had been in February, months ago, and he still felt guilty about doing it. But it was a necessary step. He was certain of that.

Callum had a face like thunder and appeared to be clutching a paper towel to his face. Becky had an arm around her son's shoulder, and she hadn't seen Duncan's arrival.

"What's going on?" Duncan asked Grace as she approached.

"Young Callum has—"

"Needs locking up!" a voice shrieked from behind them. Duncan turned to see one of the regulars, Travis, a local man who was a known alcoholic but harmless enough, leaning against the bar with a bar towel, seemingly packed with ice, pressed against his bearded cheek. "That boy's mental."

"All right, calm down, Trav," Grace said, turning away from the seething regular, and steering Duncan out of earshot.

"What's the craic?"

Grace shook her head. "Callum's been in pretty much since the doors opened. He's... drinking heavily."

"He's drunk?"

"Aye."

"Then why did you keep serving him?"

Grace smiled. "It's not my fault he can't hold his booze, is it? He's not had that many. But he has got out of line. Travis there..." she glanced back at him, moaning to anyone near him who was prepared to listen, "thought he'd have a bit of fun at Callum's expense. He... um... didn't care for it."

Duncan's brow furrowed. "Callum started this?" He could tell there had been an altercation between the two men and neither appeared to have come away from it unscathed.

"Aye, he landed the first punch," Grace said. "It seems like he has his father's temperament." Duncan's gaze narrowed and Grace reacted with a puzzled look. "Davey Mcinnes, he's got a hair trigger temper on him... and a lack of a sense of humour." She frowned at Duncan. "I thought you knew him from way back?"

"Aye, yes of course," he said, turning his focus back to the table where Callum sat with his mum, under the watchful eye of Fraser. Becky caught his eye, and she leaned in, said something to Callum who glanced across towards Duncan before Becky got up and weaved her way through the tables towards him. "Why did you call me?" he asked quickly, keen to hear the answer before Becky reached him.

"He refused to leave – Callum – and so I had no choice but to call your colleagues. He's flatly refused to go... and so far, Fraser has been incredibly patient, but sooner or later, he's going to have to go." Duncan could see Grace had her eye trained on Becky, approaching with a determined look on her face. "And... I know you two have... something going on."

"We don't—" But Grace had already turned away and was making her way back to the bar. Becky came to stand before Duncan, hesitant, and smiling awkwardly.

"Hi, Duncan," she said. He smiled and she glanced back at Callum. "How... have you been?" she asked, nervously trying to find a home for her hands.

"I'm okay," he said. "You?"

"Okay," she replied. "Callum... he's... erm..."

"Not staying out of trouble," Duncan said. "You know if he gets into bother, his suspended sentence—"

"I know!" Becky snapped, and then smiled, trying to soften her demeanour. "I know," she repeated. "He's a good boy, it's just he's struggling a bit just now, that's all."

Duncan stroked his chin with the palm of his hand, theorising that Fraser was doing his level best not to arrest the teenager. The best thing they could do was to get him out of the bar and home. With the fractious nature of Becky's marriage, home might not be the best place for him to be but he couldn't be out in the bars drinking and getting into trouble.

"How are things at home?" Duncan asked.

Becky smiled awkwardly. "Davey's Davey," she said. "He tries... and we're—"

"I mean with regard to Callum," Duncan said quietly. He cared about Becky, he really did, but she'd made her choice to stay with her husband despite his abusive past. Duncan couldn't get involved because if he did, he'd likely make matters worse, not better, and the more he knew, the more he was likely to get involved.

"He's okay with Callum," Becky said and Duncan could hear something in her tone. Was it regret? Disappointment perhaps.

Duncan saw Fraser lean over and say something to Callum whose eyes drifted over to meet Duncan's. The teenager threw back his chair, Fraser instinctively taking a step back, but Callum wasn't aggressive. He picked up his coat from the back of the chair, put it on and then gathered the paper towel he was using to stem the flow of blood from his nose, then moved away from the table. Fraser met Duncan's eye, winked, and fell into step alongside Callum who stalked purposefully towards the exit.

Duncan had the sense Fraser had just used the threat of Duncan's arrival as a lever to get him to leave the bar. He felt a pang in his chest, fearing that Fraser had intimidated his son with his presence. Duncan didn't know quite how he felt about that. Becky reached out her hand, touching Duncan's forearm. "I'll make sure he gets home... and stays out of trouble."

"Aye, okay."

Becky took a step away and then turned back to him. "It's good to see you, Duncan." He nodded and she hurried after her son. Duncan watched her go and when he turned his head around, he saw Grace watching him intently from her place behind the bar. He moved towards her, but she put the glass she had in her hands into the mini dishwasher behind the bar, loudly announcing she had to change a barrel, and hurried into the back room.

Those sitting at the bar didn't pay her any attention, and

Duncan figured she was speaking to him more than anyone else. Travis sidled up to him.

"That boy's got something wrong with him, the same as his father! What are you going to do about it?"

Duncan shot him a dark look, and Travis backtracked to the bar, taking his seat without another word. Duncan sighed, standing alone in the bar now and unsure of how he should handle the situation with Grace. She was going to leave the island soon, unless he did something about it. Even then, she might still leave.

It wasn't fair to her, to broach the subject while she was at work, so he took out his mobile and typed out a text message. *Call me when you're off shift. I love you. D x.*

He hesitated briefly before tapping send. Duncan had a few laps of the track under his belt, and he knew this probably wasn't the best timing, but he'd chosen the words carefully. He wasn't going to allow Grace to leave without at least giving her something else to think about.

He just hoped he wasn't overplaying his hand.

CHAPTER TWENTY-FIVE

ALISTAIR WAS SURPRISED NOT to see a patrol car parked at the entrance to the Maelrubha Estate as he and Duncan passed through the gates.

"Where's Ronnie?"

"Word from upstairs," Duncan said. "An official request has been made that the police presence is no longer required on the estate and has been withdrawn."

"When was this decided?"

"Last night apparently," Duncan said. "I should imagine Cameron Macintosh thought we had someone there purely to keep an eye on what was going on."

"Aye... well, he'd be right, wouldn't he?" Alistair said, smiling. It was true. Duncan didn't expect anyone on the estate to be under threat, certainly not once the investigation spooled up. Someone had gone to great lengths to dispose of Steven Phelps in a remote location. The notion that the perpetrator would return here was unlikely. Duncan had wanted to keep tabs on comings and goings.

Macintosh was experienced enough to know how to

scupper criminal investigations, working closely as he does, with the Sinclairs.

"What's all this then?" Duncan said, pointing towards the accommodation building. Two members of the estate staff were loading items into the back of an estate pick-up truck. Whatever it was they were carrying, was wrapped in protective packaging and being handled with care. "Take us a bit closer, would you, Alistair?"

"Aye," he said, changing course and slowly driving up to them. Duncan recognised one of the men, Nicol McLeod, and he nodded to Duncan as they drew up alongside him.

"Morning," Duncan said.

"Mr McAdam," Nicol said.

"What are you up to?" Duncan glanced over trying to see what they'd put in the bed of the truck.

"Just... er... moving some stuff around... back to the main house."

"Antiques and things?" Duncan asked, seeing how carefully the items were being loaded. They didn't seem to be large pieces, and he couldn't think what else they might be. Nicol's eyebrows lifted momentarily but before he could answer, Cameron Macintosh appeared in the doorway and Nicol left Duncan and walked past Macintosh, back inside the building without another word.

"Good morning, Detective Inspector McAdam," Macintosh said, striding purposefully towards the pick-up. "What a surprise to see you here on the estate, unannounced."

Duncan smiled. "We're not here to see you," Duncan said. He glanced at the next item being carried out of the accommodation building. "Having a clear out?"

"Nothing like that, just rearranging things is all," Macintosh said. "I presume you are here to see Alex Brennan?"

Duncan didn't want to tell the man anything at all. "Just checking in on them."

Macintosh's expression was such that he doubted Duncan's reason was genuine, but he didn't question it. "Well, be quick, Detective Inspector. We have a business to run and all of this... nasty business is distracting for the staff." He smiled at Duncan. "Please excuse me." He turned and went back inside.

"What are they up to do you think?" Alistair said as Duncan wound his window up and they pulled away, resuming their course to the Brennans' cottage.

"No idea."

Alistair pulled up in front of the cottage and they both got out. The blue Toyota Alex Brennan drove wasn't present. Their dog ran from the back of the house, coming to investigate the sound of someone arriving and Duncan dropped to his haunches, ruffling the dog's fur as it leaned into him.

"That dog seems to like you," Alistair said.

"He's a good judge of character," Niamh Brennan said and both men looked up to see her coming down the side of the house. She had her hair tied back and was wearing gardening gloves and holding a small trowel.

Duncan smiled. "Thanks."

"Well... his judgement is far from perfect," Niamh said flatly, bringing a smile from Alistair. "Alex isn't here."

"That's okay," Duncan said, rising. The dog retreated from him, trotting to stand beside Niamh. "It's you we're here to see anyway."

"Right," Niamh said, turning and heading to the rear of the house. "Well, you can talk to me while I work."

Duncan exchanged a look with Alistair and both of them followed her. The estate pick-up passed them, with Nicol at the wheel, heading towards the laird's house. The sun was shining today, and it felt warm on Duncan's skin. Niamh was at the foot of the garden, walled on three sides to offer shelter from the prevailing wind. Back in the day, this area would have been used to grow vegetables for whoever lived here as part of the croft. Now though, it was a well-tended garden, hardy plants and shrubs making up most of the boundary in front of the wall, several of which were flowering.

Niamh was weeding the beds, and she knelt on a pad to protect her knees and Duncan was sure she'd winced as she tentatively knelt.

"How are you feeling?" he asked. The bruising to the side of her face and around the eye had really come out in the last day or so, deep shades of purple and black replacing the swelling.

"Oh, you know… improving." She didn't look at them and went on with her efforts. Duncan had thought, perhaps naively, that Alex had only struck his wife once in the face, regardless of the explanation she'd given him before. Now, it seemed like there had been more to it by the way her movement was clearly restricted.

"Where's Alex?" Duncan asked.

She still didn't look up and she didn't speak for a moment. When she did, she was very matter of fact. "He didn't want to be here," she said, finally meeting Duncan's eye. "After you let him go, he came back for a bit but… he had a meeting, at the estate."

"So, he's at work?"

She chuckled briefly but without genuine humour. "No… and he won't be here much longer."

Duncan picked up on something unsaid. "What do you mean?"

Niamh sat up on her haunches, resting on her heels and toying with the trowel in her hands. "It would appear the new owners want to take the estate management in a new direction," she said. Duncan glanced at Alistair.

"They are letting him go?"

She scoffed. "That's a polite way of putting it, yes."

"Did they give a reason?"

"No," she said, looking at Duncan glumly. She thrust the trowel into the soil. "You know, I don't know why I'm bothering with this." She looked around the garden. It was obvious she spent quite a lot of time caring for the borders and controlling the growth. "But... it is something I love to do."

"You'll be leaving as well then?"

She nodded. "I do a bit of work here and there, cooking for guests... if they request it. It's only for a bit extra, you know how it is on the island, you find bits to do here and there, and it all adds up."

"Where will you go?"

"I don't know." She shrugged. "Something will turn up."

"How did Alex take the news?"

She laughed, shaking her head and then took a deep breath. "About as well as he takes any trial or adversity that comes his way... badly. Alex is a simple creature, like most men. If you take care of his most basic needs, tickle his ego from time to time, then he'll bump along just fine." She inclined her head. "On the other hand, take away his toys, tell him he's pretty much useless... he'll crumble before your eyes or run away and hide."

"Cynical," Alistair said.

"Pragmatic," she replied. Removing her gloves and putting them in her lap, she brushed her hands together briefly. "But I'm sure you didn't drive all the way out here to discuss the facile nature of mankind," she glanced around her garden, "nor for gardening tips, I should imagine." She offered Duncan a forlorn smile. "What is it you want?"

"I want to know why you covered for your husband, when you knew he wasn't with you the night of Steven Phelps's murder."

"Did I cover for him?" she asked. "Did I lie?"

"He wasn't home all night as you said, Niamh."

She seemed pensive, resigned to the reality of being caught out in her deception. "Are you married, Mr McAdam?"

"No."

"Do you have someone special in your life… someone you want to keep safe from all the horrors this brutal little world has waiting in store for us?"

"I do, yes."

"Then… it shouldn't be too hard for you to understand why I said what I said."

"I think I would draw the line when it comes to a murder investigation, though," Duncan countered.

She nodded. "And if you couldn't countenance any possible way that they could be a party to something so awful… wouldn't you do anything within your power to protect them? You mean to tell me you've never crossed a line or bent the rules… if only a little?"

"I'm not here for a philosophical debate, Niamh," Duncan said. "Your husband may have been involved in a murder, and that trumps your gut instincts."

"Maybe yours, Mr McAdam, but not mine. I *know* my husband… and despite what you might think of him," she said, her eyes flitting between the two detectives, "I know him like no one else." She shook her head. "He's not a killer. I know it."

"Forgive me," Duncan said, "but he has a violent streak. You know it as well as we do, even if you won't say it aloud. I suspect you also know full well what time Alex left your house that night."

"I do, yes. And so do you, seeing as you have him driving away on camera." She gave them a knowing look. "Yes, Alex told me when he came home, after you released him."

"So, there's no need to lie anymore," Duncan said. "What time did he come home?" He already knew but he wanted to put her to the test, see if the accuracy of her memory had improved.

Niamh held Duncan's gaze, then looked away before answering. "In the morning... a little before sunrise as I remember."

Duncan saw no need to chastise her further for her earlier indiscretion. She knew he'd been gone all night and had given her husband an alibi anyway. He could arrest her for having done so, and still might when all was said and done, depending on how things panned out.

"Did you ask him where he'd been?" She pursed her lips, clearly reticent. "Niamh, it's important. Be truthful."

"No, I didn't ask," she said. Duncan found that hard to believe but before he could press her, she held up a hand. "There was no need to ask."

"You already knew, didn't you," Duncan said, and Niamh nodded. "Where was he?"

Niamh closed her eyes, taking a deep breath. "It's not... it's not as easy as that."

"I will find out," Duncan said firmly, "and in my experience, it would be better for all concerned if you shared it with us because if I have to start knocking on doors and causing a fuss, I will. I hope there's a good reason for all of this otherwise you—"

"Okay!" Niamh said, flustered. She couldn't keep it quiet any longer but clearly she was pained by whatever she was being forced to reveal. "The honest answer is... I don't know for sure where he was... but he will have gone where he always goes when... when we fall out or..." she sighed, "when he... feels the need." Duncan waited expectantly. Niamh shook her head. "Ullinish. That's where he will have gone. I'm sure."

"And what's there for him, in Ullinish?" Duncan asked.

"She's there," Niamh said, meeting Duncan's eye. "Kara." She almost spat the name and as she said it, she seemed overcome with both frustration and sadness, as if speaking of it somehow made it more real for her. "Kara McGarrell, that's who he would have gone to." Her eyes glassed over and she tensed. "That's where he always goes... and I'll wager that's where he is just now."

CHAPTER TWENTY-SIX

ULLINISH WAS a small crofting township on the banks of *Loch Bracadale*, on the west coast of the island, west of Struan and situated on a small peninsula overlooked by the low basalt cliffs of the Cuillin Hills. The single access road bypassed *Cnoc Ullinish*, a small hill to the east of the township, and wound its way down to *Ullinish Point*, where at low tide there was a causeway out to the island of *Oronsay*.

"There's been some building out this way in recent years," Alistair said. Duncan looked around. The buildings he could see were a mixture of old stone croft houses, similar to his own, and newer constructions built in the style of timber long-houses. The weather front had cleared, as was common, during their drive up from Glenbrittle and blue skies belied the Atlantic wind rattling across the island.

Looking to his right, to the northwest, Duncan could see the peaks of *Healabhal Beag* and *Healabhal Mhòr*, collectively better known as MacLeod's Tables towering over the land-scape beyond *Harlosh Island* and Loch Bracadale. If he had to live anywhere else on the island, other than in his family croft in Balmaqueen, then he couldn't have chosen a better spot.

Ullinish was hemmed in by lochs on three sides with stunning views of Skye's landscapes in almost every direction.

A vehicle rounded the bend in front of them and Alistair pulled to one side in plenty of time to let it pass, but the driver had his head down, seemingly fiddling with something and he paid them no attention. It was none other than Alex Brennan, but neither Duncan nor Alistair made eye contact with him, and Brennan accelerated up the road without noticing who he'd passed.

"Seems preoccupied," Alistair said.

"Doesn't he," Duncan agreed. Alistair pulled out onto the road and continued on. They were approaching the headland now and here the road forked offering access to the last handful of residences in the township. It wasn't overly large, with a small population made up mostly with traditional crofts, but there were one or two businesses now catering to the tourists who wanted to make the short walk across to *Oronsay*.

Coming to a fork in the road, Alistair looked to the right, "I think we go that way and then… aye, that's it," he said, turning the wheel and setting off. They came to a white-painted stone house and there was a five-bar gate to the left giving access to another track that wound its way around a small brae. Just visible was another building, sheltering in the lee of the hill. The gate was open and Alistair made his way down the track.

The property they arrived at was constructed in the style of a traditional longhouse, but the skylights in the roof indicated it was two-storey, likely a four- or perhaps five-bedroomed property. The front of the house faced east and on the northern edge of the plot was a large double garage, built in the same style, clad in larch, and Duncan spied a small powerboat, under cover, beside a Mercedes parked in the garage.

The driveway was lined with black basalt chippings, common on the island and quarried locally, and the sound of the large wheels of Alistair's pick-up crunching could be heard within the property because a figure appeared at a large window to witness their arrival. They got out and approached the front door, to be met by a woman in her early forties, Duncan guessed.

Kara McGarrell struck an elegant figure, dressed in a pale blue trouser suit, her clothing and make-up fastidiously presented. She was a brunette, her hair hanging to just below her shoulders, stylish, and she greeted them with the whitest, most perfect smile Duncan had ever seen. She didn't seem fazed at all by two unknown men arriving unannounced on her doorstep. She appraised the two of them, her eyes settling on Duncan.

"Good morning," she said, her smile broadening.

"Good morning," Duncan replied, "Kara McGarrell?"

"Yes," she replied, and Duncan produced his warrant card.

"DI McAdam and DS MacEachran," he said, showing her his identification. "We would like to speak to you about a friend of yours, if you can spare us some of your time?"

"Oh? Sounds intriguing," she said, curious. "Who?"

"Alex Brennan."

She nodded. "You had better come in then," she said, glancing at her watch, a two-tone yellow gold and steel Rolex. The front door was already wide open, and she beckoned them into the entrance hall which was as large as Duncan's living room at home.

Duncan cast an eye around the interior. The floors were solid oak. Having recently finished renovating his old house, he could tell the difference between a cheaper veneer, engineered floor covering and the real deal. The walls were all painted white and the windows were triple glazed, and aluminium clad, perfect for what weather would be thrown at them living in the Inner Hebrides.

Kara led them through the house into an open-plan living area, encompassing the kitchen, dining room and an expansive living room with a huge glazed wall overlooking Loch Caroy all the way to *Harlosh Island*. A telescope was mounted on a tripod at the far end and once the sun set, if the skies were clear, then the views from here would be just as spectacular at night as they were in the daytime.

"Tell me," Kara said, rounding a granite-surfaced island and turning on an expensive-looking coffee machine mounted at chest height, beside two matching ovens, in a bank of cabinets lining one wall, "what has Alex got himself involved in this time?"

"This time?" Alistair asked.

She smiled knowingly. "I'm sure we all know he's been in trouble from time to time. It seems to follow Alex wherever he goes. He has... a bit of a dark side to him."

"A dark side?" Duncan asked, surprised by her candour seeing as she was yet to learn why they were here.

"Darker... is probably a better description, Detective Inspector...?"

"McAdam," he reminded her.

"Yes, a *dark side* makes it sound like he's some kind of a demon," she said, smiling. "I don't mean that. Alex... is Alex," she said with a shrug, "and I doubt he's all that dissimilar to any other man who lives on this island." She cast an eye over both of them. "You two included."

"May I ask the nature of your relationship with Alex Brennan?" Duncan asked.

"How very forward of you, DI McAdam," Kara said, pressing a button and the machine began grinding unseen coffee beans. "Would you like a cup of coffee?"

"I'm okay, thanks," Duncan said. Alistair seemed ready to ask her for one but thought better of it when Duncan caught his eye. Duncan was keen to observe her as they talked, and he didn't want the opportunity of distraction to present itself.

"Please yourself," she said, placing a cup beneath the head. The machine began filtering coffee and the pleasant aroma soon permeated the space.

"Alex Brennan?" Duncan asked again when she took her espresso from the machine, cradling the cup with one hand.

"He's a friend of mine... ours, I should say. My husband and I."

"How do you know him?" Duncan asked. She didn't have a local accent, and if he had to guess, he figured she was from somewhere down in the borders, south of Edinburgh he guessed.

"Known him for years," Kara said, blowing steam from the top of her liquid and sipping at the coffee.

"You can't have lived here for very long," Duncan said. He figured the house must have been constructed in the last few years and no more than four, based on the condition of the property and the decking outside.

"We built this place three years ago," Kara said, looking around. "It was always a bit of a side project James had lusted after."

"James?"

"My husband," she said. "He's been involved in property all of his working life, construction projects in several countries, not least in Scotland... but this place... is something of a bolt hole. Somewhere to get away from the rat race, recuperate... *be at one with nature*."

"Is that what you think, or your husband?"

She laughed. "I love it here. It's quiet, peaceful... and you can be as involved with the community as you wish to be.

Personally, I like my own space and James... well, he comes here to get away from people, not to see them."

"You don't live here all the time then, I'm guessing?" Duncan asked.

"No, but I'm here more often than James. He'd come across more, but his business keeps him very occupied."

"Property, you say?"

"Yes, commercial property in the main," she said, "offices, retail units..."

"Where is he based?"

"The central belt," Kara said. "His office is in Glasgow, but as I say, he has investments all over."

"He's not here just now then?"

Kara met Duncan's eye, her smile still in place but her eyes had a steel to them, peering over the rim of her coffee cup. "No. I'm here alone."

"And how often do you see Alex?"

She set her cup down, slipping her hands into her trouser pockets, inclining her head. "What is it about my relationship with Alex that so interests you, DI McAdam? So far, you've paid me far more attention than you have him, and you're yet to tell me why it is you're here."

"Forgive me," Duncan said. "We have been led to believe that you and Alex have... an intimate relationship."

Kara smiled, unfazed. "Ah... I wonder who might have told you that." She didn't wait for an answer. "But what business is it of yours whether that's the case or not?"

"Last weekend, a man was killed—"

"The poor man you found over at Coruisk?"

"Yes."

"That was awfully tragic to hear he'd died."

"Murdered," Alistair said.

"I beg your pardon?" Kara asked.

"You said died, he was actually murdered."

"Yes, of course. I heard it on the news. Awful."

"Well, the deceased," Duncan explained, "was part of a group staying on the Maelrubha Estate, and Alex had taken them hunting the day before this man went missing."

Kara moved her gaze from Alistair back to Duncan. "And?"

"Alex had an issue with the man—"

"Surely, you can't think Alex killed him?" she asked, incredulous, smiling in disbelief. "I know I said he had a darker side, but all I meant…"

"All you meant?" Duncan pressed.

She shook her head. "That he can be a bit of a rogue… not that he… I mean, that's ridiculous."

"The day the victim went missing, he told us he was at home with his wife, all night." Duncan absently scratched his temple with his index finger. "We now know that isn't true. He left home late that night, and he didn't return until just before dawn the next day."

Kara maintained her gaze on Duncan, her expression impassive. "I see." She shrugged. "How does this information bring you to my house?"

Duncan exchanged a look with Alistair. "Our understanding is that he may have spent the night here, with you."

She grinned. "With me? I see, that's why you're here."

"Did Alex Brennan spend a night here last weekend?"

Her smile faded, fixing Duncan with the steely gaze that had only been present in her eyes previously. "Has Alex cited *me* as his… what do you say, his alibi?"

"No, he hasn't, but Niamh has confirmed he wasn't at home as she'd stated."

"And she told you he was here with me?" Kara said pointedly.

Duncan nodded. "That's a possibility she floated with us, yes."

Kara scoffed. "I'll bet she did, the poisonous little cow." The venom in her tone caught Duncan by surprise. Up until this point, Kara McGarrell had been as elegant in her tone as she was in her presentation. She must have seen Duncan's reaction because she softened a little. "You have to understand, Mr McAdam... Alex and Niamh's relationship – their marriage – isn't quite what it seems from outward appearances."

CHAPTER TWENTY-SEVEN

"COULD YOU EXPAND ON THAT?" Duncan asked, his curiosity piqued.

She cocked her head, picking up her coffee cup again and leaning back against the counter, her eyes drifting out of the picture window above the sink, overlooking the *Harlosh Island*. "Their marriage has its problems," she said quietly. "Don't they all?"

Alistair made a face. "Mine is perfect."

Kara looked over at him. "That might be what you think, but I wonder if your wife thinks differently."

"Oh, she'd be sure to let me know if she did," Alistair said with a trace of a smile.

"Well, not everyone is as good at communicating as you are, DS MacEachran," Kara said.

"Aye, that's probably true," Alistair replied, with a wink.

"The Brennans?" Duncan asked.

"Alex took up with Niamh shortly after his divorce was finalised," Kara said. "He was a bit of a mess back then, unsurprisingly. The breakup was rough on him, what with his ex taking his child over to the mainland."

"Aye, we heard that," Duncan said. "He hit the bottle a bit too hard, started getting himself into scrapes around town."

"Yes, that sort of thing," Kara said. "Anyway, he got the job on the estate, although it wasn't the estate then. It was much smaller... more of a groundsman job, you know, but it gave him purpose and a bit of his dignity back. He met Niamh around then too."

"She was working there?"

Kara frowned. "I'm not sure what she was doing there, but they met... and hit it off, I guess. They were both... looking for something, and it suited them."

"Isn't everyone looking for something in life?" Duncan asked, sensing there was more behind her choice of phrasing it.

"Yes, of course... but... I don't think you understand..."

"Then explain it to me," he said.

Kara's brow creased in thought. Duncan figured she must have Botox injections or something because her facial features were too smooth, too rigid and unnatural.

"Don't get me wrong," Kara said, "I suppose Niamh is... a nice enough woman, if you like that sort of thing. I knew she was wrong for Alex right from the outset. She was looking for... someone who would look out for her. She needed strength... reliability—"

"And she saw that in Alex?" Alistair said, failing to keep his scepticism out of his tone. "Give me strength!"

"I didn't say Alex was without his faults, did I? Far from it... but that was her motivation." She tilted her head. "In my opinion."

"And what was he looking for?" Duncan asked.

"Classic... rebound, looking for purpose, someone to care for who would love him," Kara said. "I spoke to him, so did

James... and I think Niamh just suited what Alex was seeking. She was lost... vulnerable, maybe?"

"So where do the marriage problems come into this?" Duncan asked.

Kara smiled ruefully. "Well, I'm not a therapist... but what works at the outset, for both parties, doesn't necessarily work when you're years down the line. There's no growth for the two of them. Niamh got her security – as secure as you can get with Alex – and he got a wife, but she couldn't give him what he really wants."

"Which is?"

Kara shrugged. "A family. That's what Alex wanted, a family to replace the one he lost."

"That's hardly healthy ground to build a successful marriage on," Alistair said.

"I'll not disagree with you, Detective Sergeant," Kara said. "But I'm only telling you what I think."

Duncan contemplated what she'd said. Kara finished her coffee, putting the cup into the dishwasher. "So... Niamh doesn't want children or... can't have them?"

Kara thought about it. "I don't know. She *says* she can't... but I'm not convinced of that."

"You doubt her honesty?"

Kara seemed pensive, and Duncan was inclined to wait. The longer a silence continued, the more the majority of people feel compelled to end it. It was a proven sales technique which also happened to work quite well in this scenario.

"I don't know, but you would think her husband would, but Alex... doesn't know... because she's never in the marital bed."

Duncan shot her a quizzical look. "I'm not sure I understand."

"Imagine being married to someone who denies all physical contact, Mr McAdam." She arched her eyebrows. "In my opinion, and it is only my opinion... Niamh loves her husband, but their marriage is pretty much a platonic friendship more than a loving partnership."

"And what about Alex?" Duncan asked. Kara looked at him, unsure of what question he was asking. "Does Alex love his wife?"

She looked away from Duncan, glumly. "I think... Alex needs someone in his life. He's not good by himself. Does he love her?" she asked herself, sucking air through her teeth. "I believe he wants to, but... I don't know, not anymore."

"Sounds complicated," Duncan said.

"Adult relationships... marriages, are complex things, Mr McAdam," Kara said. "And it takes all sorts to make the world go around."

"Okay... so, can you confirm whether Alex was here last weekend, or not?" Duncan asked. The sound of a car pulling up outside drew their attention and Kara glanced at a small tablet screen on the counter to her left. The house had security cameras and the feed from the one overlooking the drive was displayed. Kara looked momentarily shocked but, catching sight of Duncan observing her, she forced a smile and brightened.

"That's James," she said, smiling somewhat nervously.

"Oh... your husband's home," Alistair said dryly, with a big smile. "It'll be lovely to meet him."

Kara ignored the comment and moments later the front door opened, and a man backed through the door, a small suitcase in one hand and a bunch of flowers in the other. "Darling, whose big truck is that parked outside?"

Kara hurried to the doorway, where James McGarrell

dropped his suitcase, offering his wife the flowers and she greeted him with a warm smile and a kiss on the cheek. "Hello, darling, this is a nice surprise," she said as he looked past her at Duncan and Alistair.

"Well, my meeting this afternoon was put back to next week, so I thought I'd come up and spend a bit of time with you."

"Ah..." Alistair said, wrinkling his nose. "Isn't that *lovely*!"

James McGarrell looked at him and then Duncan, easing his wife aside. He stepped forward, offering his hand. "James," he said, and Duncan accepted the offer.

"Duncan McAdam," he said, nodding a greeting. James looked at him, smiled and then glanced at his wife.

"They're with the police," Kara said.

"The police? Is everything all right?"

"Oh, I'm sure it's absolutely fine," Alistair replied, turning the corners of his mouth down, exaggerating the expression. "Nothing to see here at all."

Kara glared at him, but James seemed puzzled and missed the passing look on his wife's face. Duncan was far more discreet. "We were just here to speak to your wife about Alex Brennan."

"Alex?" James said, surprised. He raised a thumb over his shoulder. "I've just passed him on the way here."

"Oh, did yer, aye?" Alistair said.

"Yes, he didn't see me though," James said. "In a world of his own, I think. Is everything all right with him?" Alistair looked ready to make another quip, but Duncan glanced his way, silently advising him not to. Alistair simply smiled.

"Alex... has got himself involved in that case I told you about, the dead man they found over—"

"Oh, that can't be right! Alex wouldn't be involved in anything like that, surely?" James asked, looking at Duncan.

"He was leading a hunting party the victim was involved in, that's all, Mr McGarrell," Duncan said.

"Ah… that makes more sense. You had me worried for a moment there," James replied. "So, what brings you out here to talk to Kara?"

Duncan's eyes flitted to Kara's and he frowned. "We're just seeking some background information at this time, sir," he said. "From people who are friends with him, that's all."

"With Alex?" James asked, putting his arm around his wife's shoulder. "Well, that's certainly us, isn't it, darling?" Kara nodded. "We've been his friend for years."

"You know him well then?"

"Oh yes! Alex and I go way back… in fact," he said, jabbing a finger in the air, "I got him that job down Glenbrittle way. Well, I vouched for his character anyway."

"Ah, that's nice," Alistair said. "It's good to have pals, isn't it?"

James looked at Alistair, slightly confused. "Yes… yes, it is. So, what can we do for you?"

"Oh…" Duncan said, "we—"

"It's okay, James," Kara said. "The detectives have got what they needed and were just leaving. Isn't that correct, DI McAdam?"

"Well, in that case," James said, offering Duncan his hand again, "I've had a bugger of a drive up from Glasgow, so I'm going to take a shower and freshen up a little." Duncan shook hands and Kara slipped away from her husband's arm, putting the flowers down on the kitchen island.

"I'll see you out," she said.

Duncan nodded, and Alistair smiled warmly at James, before they both followed Kara to the front door. James passed them in the entrance hall, collecting his suitcase before making his way upstairs. Kara opened the door and accompanied them outside, pulling the door closed behind her.

She walked with them to Alistair's pick-up, arms folded across her chest. She looked concerned now, awkwardly glancing back towards the house.

"Thank you," she said to Duncan.

"What for?"

She inclined her head, smiling sheepishly. "You could have handled that very differently." Her eyes flicked to Alistair, the smile disappearing. He had that effect on some people, Duncan noticed. It was the sledgehammer subtlety that not everyone appreciated but you always knew where you stood with him.

"We're not here to cause trouble," Duncan said. "Either for you, Alex or anyone else."

"Thank you," she repeated.

"You know, Alex may well have to revise his statement," Duncan said, "and when he does, you could find this situation rapidly spins out of your control."

She nodded, despondently. "Look," she said, keeping her voice low and moving hair, blown across by the breeze, aside from her face, "I'll say the same thing to you that I said to Alex when he came by earlier... don't expect to have me confirm he was here. If you put me in an interview room or, God forbid, inside a courtroom, I'll say the same thing no matter what; *he wasn't here with me*."

"You would perjure yourself?" Duncan asked. He glanced at the camera mounted above the front door. She followed his gaze.

"The cameras can be switched off with the tap of a button, DI McAdam, and you'll see we are not overlooked. My husband values his privacy, and we chose this building plot well."

"Your *friend* could be facing a murder charge," Alistair said. She looked at him earnestly.

"I know, but that's not for me to decide." Turning back to Duncan, she said, "But it is up to you to prosecute a man you believe to have an alibi, even if he can't prove it." Again, she looked at Alistair. "You make a moral judgement on my behaviour... but if you try to prosecute an innocent man, what would that say about you?"

Duncan shook his head. "That's a hell of a risky game you're playing."

"Not really. From where I stand, I have nothing to gain and..." she glanced over her shoulder, back at the house, "... everything to lose." She read their expressions and turned introspective for a moment. "I won't ask you not to judge me... because we all do it, don't we, make judgements of people we barely know? But things are rarely as they seem on the surface, and you never truly know what's going on behind closed doors. You must see that in your job?"

"Aye," Duncan said. "That's true."

"Perhaps where James and I are concerned..." she said, her voice cracking, "maybe we didn't get all that we were looking for in our marriage either."

Without another word, Kara McGarrell turned and walked back into the house. She didn't look back and Duncan watched her go. Alistair caught his eye and Duncan glanced at him. Alistair's forefinger subtly pointed to the house and Duncan glanced at the upstairs windows where he could see James was watching them through one of the large skylights.

As soon as Duncan met his eye, James turned and disappeared from view. The front door was closed, and Kara was also nowhere to be seen. Alistair heaved a deep sigh, unlocking the pick-up and hauling open the door. "I'm so glad I married my wife, I tell you," he said as he climbed in.

Duncan's thoughts drifted to Grace, and not for the first time, he found the notion of her leaving the island gnawing at him. He got into the passenger seat.

"Working in property certainly pays, doesn't it?" Alistair said, pointing at the nearly new BMW parked alongside theirs, then glancing at the Mercedes in the garage. "Do you ever think we're in the wrong line of work?"

"Property developers... looks like fun on all the TV shows but when the cycle ends and the economy tanks, you're exposed," Duncan said. "There's one thing in our job that is always guaranteed."

"What's that then?"

"A never-ending supply of people who'll take the easy route. We'll never be short of work, whatever happens in the wider world."

Alistair nodded and then his brow furrowed as something occurred to him. "Change of subject, I wonder what he's been up to?"

"Who, James?"

"Aye, why's he bought her flowers?"

"There has to be an underlying reason?"

"Aye... it speaks to a guilty conscience," Alistair said.

Duncan laughed. "A husband can't surprise his wife with flowers?"

"He's up to something," Alistair said.

"You've never come home with flowers for your wife?"

"Nope." Alistair shook his head. "I've never had the need to."

"The need?"

"Because I haven't done anything wrong."

"Cynical," Duncan said.

"Aye, I tell you now, if I walked in at home with a bunch of

flowers in my hands, she'd be asking me *what's been going on?*"
Alistair looked thoughtful. "He suspects something. I'll bet
you good money."

"No," Duncan said. "I already owe you a tenner for recognising Macintosh as a lawyer, as it is."

CHAPTER TWENTY-EIGHT

BACK IN THE OPERATIONS ROOM, Duncan was met by an excited Angus Ross, bounding up to them before they'd taken off their jackets. "Sir! We've found a match."

"A match? For the blood—"

"On the gloves, aye," Angus said. "We've been running it through the system, and something came back half an hour ago."

"Whose is it?" Duncan asked.

"Sharon Caulfield," Angus said, returning to his desk.

"That's not a name I recognise."

"You won't, sir," Angus said.

"She died a decade ago," Russell said from behind his desk. Duncan looked over at him and saw Angus crestfallen that DC Mclean appeared to have stolen his thunder. "Suicide."

Duncan didn't know what surprised him more, the fact the woman had died ten years previously or that it was by her own hand. "Tell me about her?"

Angus nodded. "When she died, she'd been in the army for four years. She was stationed in Yorkshire to attend a training course. She took her own life while she was on that rotation. At the time, there was a bit of controversy around it."

"What was the controversy?" Duncan asked.

"Because there were allegations of – and an investigation into – bullying that'd supposedly taken place involving members of her company in the months prior to her death. The family weren't happy with the conclusion of the investigation which was a joint military and police inquiry—"

"A joint investigation?" Alistair asked. "No such thing when it comes to the army, I can assure you of that."

"Aye," Angus said. "What I meant is that there were two investigations that delivered conclusions: one by the local police and the other by the RMP—"

"Aye, but let's not get too carried away with the capabilities of a bunch of guys and girls who spend their time handing out speeding fines and breaking up drunken brawls," Alistair said.

"You're not a fan of the Royal Military Police then, Alistair?" Duncan asked. Alistair shook his head. Duncan sat down, trying to understand how these threads could possibly come together on the Isle of Skye. "What regiment was she in?"

"The Royal Logistics Corps, sir," Angus said.

"Where was she based?"

Angus looked down. "She was at Leconfield, sir. It's in East Yorkshire, in England."

Duncan frowned, glancing at Alistair. "Logistics... Alex Brennan was in the—"

"Blanket stackers," Alistair said. "Aye, for a while he was."

"At the same time?" Duncan asked Angus who clicked through several open windows on his computer. "I'm looking... but... oh aye, here it is." He lifted his eyes, disappointed. "No, I don't think they were. Caulfield dies in... the May of that year and Brennan was out of the army in the December of the previous year. Damn. I got all excited there for a second. I'm not sure Brennan was ever based in Leconfield either."

Duncan exhaled. "Well, I suppose that would have been way too easy. Steven Phelps, he was—"

"Parachute Regiment," Alistair said. "No help there either."

Duncan sat back, putting his hands behind his head and interlocking his fingers. There had to be a connection. "Sharon Caulfield didn't wipe her blood on those gloves from beyond the grave, a decade on. What's the connection?"

Angus looked at him apologetically. "I can't find one, sir."

"Well, let's start with the basics. How did she die?"

"A single gunshot wound to the head, sir," Angus said. "She discharged her rifle beside the perimeter fence. Her body was discovered soon afterwards by the camp security, and she was pronounced dead at the scene."

"Her own rifle?" Duncan asked.

Angus nodded. "Aye, that's what the report said. As I say, the family weren't happy. The official report stated she went on a solo patrol around the base perimeter which was against regulations. However, the family spoke to colleagues, past and present – at the time – and found friends of hers who said she'd been bullied. They were of the opinion that their daughter was preparing to raise a formal complaint and that was why she was silenced."

Duncan considered it. "So, they suggested she... what? She was killed to keep her from doing so?"

"From what I can gather, aye," Angus said. "I've not read the official report but it's all in the public domain."

"Hearsay though," Duncan said.

"An alternative theory is that she was so badly bullied she took her own life rather than go through the process of reporting it," Angus said. "The family didn't agree. They pushed for an independent inquiry, especially seeing as there had been other cases in the previous... three years."

"What cases?" Duncan asked.

Angus looked to Russell who picked up the narrative. "As Angus said, there was another death at the camp a few months prior to Caulfield's. That was also ruled as a suicide, a young female recruit who was alleged to have suffered bullying from non-commissioned officers. Two years earlier there had been another unexplained death which was left with an open verdict by the coroner, although suicide had been considered in that case, too. The deceased in that case had taken a drug overdose, but it wasn't determined whether that was accidental or intentional."

"Did the family of Caulfield get their wish for an independent inquiry?" Duncan asked.

"No," Russell said, "but there was a review carried out three years after her death by an independent coroner and the police did, under pressure, submit to another team from a neighbouring force reviewing their investigation."

"The results?"

"Both the coroner and the case review team drew the same conclusions. I have requested a copy of the full files, but they've not come through yet. I did a bit of internet research because the cases generated a lot of interest in the press... the tabloids love this kind of thing, don't they?"

"And?"

"The lieutenant colonel who was in charge of the base came under intense criticism for apparent failings in the duty of care to the lower rank and file. There was a lot of coverage of a poor culture in terms of how fresh recruits were trained as well as a culture of *toxic masculinity*, whatever that means," Russell said.

Alistair nodded. "That's what they call *being arseholes* these days."

"Were any prosecutions brought?" Duncan asked.

"No, sir," Russell said. "As I say, plenty of coverage in the media, but no names were put up in lights, so to speak."

"All right," Duncan said. "There's a connection between Brennan, Phelps and this young soldier, Sharon Caulfield. We need to find it. Angus, get onto the Ministry of Defence and get a list of people stationed at the camp when Caulfield was there. Go through it and find the link."

"Sir... that will be hundreds, if not thousands of names..."

"Aye, have you got anything better to be doing?"

"No..." Angus said, sitting down and lowering his voice, "I was just saying."

"There's a link. Find it," Duncan said. He turned to Russell. "Once you have copies of the files, I want you going through all of them looking for anything that might have been missed, the police files, the coroner's inquest and the independent case review." He pointed at the image of Steven Phelps on the information board. "Somewhere along the line, Phelps inter-cepts with Caulfield and Brennan. If we find that, then we find out who killed him and probably why."

Russell nodded. "I'm on it."

Duncan looked at Alistair. "We're getting closer, Alistair. I can feel it."

His mobile rang, it was Grace and he stepped into his office, closing the door behind him. "I'm sorry I didn't call after my shift yesterday, but it was late and—"

"No, no, don't worry," Duncan said. "Is everything all right?"

"Yes, of course. I mean... I have a lot on my mind, you know?"

"Aye... listen, we need to talk..."

"Do you have time for a cup of coffee? I'm working the back shift again tonight, so..."

Duncan checked his watch. He didn't have time, not really but if he wanted Grace to feel like she mattered to him then he'd have to make time. "Of course. Where?"

"The Granary? In about a quarter of an hour?"

"Aye, I'll see you there."

The coffee shop was only across Somerled Square, barely a stone's throw from the station.

The sun was shining as he left the station, although the ground was still damp from an earlier passing shower, steam gently rising from areas in direct sunlight. The sun felt warm upon Duncan's skin. Patrons were sitting at the tables outside the coffee shop now, still sporting their big coats because of the stiff breeze.

He met Grace at the door. She looked nervous and they hugged awkwardly before going inside and joining the queue. The tourist season was well underway, although visitors came to the island all year round, it was particularly popular at this time of year. The hope of catching a settled spell of weather while the children were off school was a big draw.

Little did most people know that May or October were arguably the sweet spots to come to Skye, being less crowded with a good chance to explore the island in settled conditions, but the biggest positive was that the island's midges – the bane of outdoor pursuits – were yet to hatch. As soon as the sun dips below the horizon, and the wind drops, if you're caught outside their presence would make themselves known.

Duncan bought two coffees and Grace led them outside to a small table at the back of the seating area. They made small talk but that lasted only a couple of minutes before the elephant in the room made its presence known.

"I'm thinking of taking the job," Grace said. He'd been

expecting her to say that to be fair. Thus far he had failed to offer a counter argument, so why wouldn't she take up the opportunity on offer to explore her passion. Although, her hesitation left him with a glimmer of hope that she hadn't made her final decision.

"That's...um..." he said quietly, "a decision." She laughed. Duncan looked at her, irritated that she was mocking him but he saw genuine mirth in her expression and he smiled. "I guess that's stating the obvious."

"Yes, it is," she said, the laughter subsiding. "So... what do you think?"

Duncan frowned, unsure of how to respond. He didn't want her to go, of that he was certain, but at the same time was it his decision – his right – to stop her if that was what she wanted? "Erm... I... would rather you didn't." The words sounded hollow because he was wrestling with that dilemma in his head.

"Wow," Grace said. "Straight from the heart."

He met her eye, and she wasn't angry or mocking, and she seemed curious. "You would miss me?"

He smiled. "Aye... without question."

"But not enough to ask me to stay?"

He grimaced. "I don't want to be in the position of telling you what you should or shouldn't do. If it all goes pear-shaped, then I'll be the one to blame."

"I wouldn't blame you," she said, sipping her coffee.

"Aye, you say that now."

Grace nodded. "It is a woman's prerogative to change her mind—"

"At any given moment, on any given situation," Duncan said with a smile. Grace arched her eyebrows and Duncan cleared his throat awkwardly. "So... when do you leave?"

"If I leave," Grace said and Duncan's spirit lifted. "I have to work my notice at the bar. I wouldn't like to leave them in the lurch."

"I'm hoping it's a lengthy notice period... say three months?"

"Try four weeks," she said.

Duncan winced. "That'll... fly past."

"It will," Grace said, sitting forward. "Which gives you approximately a fortnight to make up your mind."

"About what?"

"Convincing me that I have a reason to stay here on Skye."

He knew what that meant. She wasn't expecting a marriage proposal, at least he hoped not, but she wanted to know if they had a future. He took a mouthful of coffee, wiping the foam from his lips with the back of his hand. "Hang on, you said four weeks. How come I only get two?"

"Because," she said, peering at him over the rim of her cup, "if it takes you longer than that to decide, then the decision has already been made... by both of us."

Duncan detected something in her tone. He was under the distinct impression that he had much less than two weeks. Someone caught his eye and Duncan looked over Grace's shoulder, seeing two men together, chatting outside the hostel across the street. The building was painted in a vivid yellow with blue detailing. However, the two men weren't the average backpackers.

"Duncan?"

"Sorry, what?"

"What do you think?"

He forced himself to look away from the two men having, what to Duncan, looked like an animated, if not a heated, conversation whilst fumbling in his jacket for his mobile as he met Grace's eye. "Think about what?"

She shot him a dark look. "What do you think *about what I just said?*"

"I... one second," he said, holding up a finger and dialling Alistair's number. His DS picked up immediately.

"Can't you have a cup of coffee with a beautiful woman without phoning me for a—"

"He's here," Duncan said, standing up and looking across towards the hostel. "Charlie Lumsden... he's here."

"Where?"

"Outside the hostel... fifty yards from me and he's talking to—"

As soon as he uttered the name, it was as if Charlie's sixth sense tingled and he glanced to his right, meeting Duncan's eye. Immediately he shoved aside the man he was talking to and bolted.

"He's on the move!" Duncan barked, bumping into his table, spilling his and Grace's drinks before almost knocking an elderly couple over as they made to sit down at the table adjacent to theirs.

"Duncan!" Grace said. He took his mobile away from his ear, hurriedly walking backwards and looking apologetic.

"I'll call you... I promise!" How she took that, he didn't know because he'd already turned and was sprinting down the road, seeing Charlie disappearing from view down the passageway alongside the hostel. "He's headed down into *Lisigarry Court!*" Duncan shouted into his mobile, hearing tyres screeching as wheels spun on a no doubt slippery surface, but he paid it no heed, so intent was he on pursuing Charlie.

CHAPTER TWENTY-NINE

DUNCAN CAME to an abrupt halt at the main road, seeking a break in the traffic to cross, frustrated by the number of vehicles. He edged to his right, staring down the passageway hoping to see which direction Charlie would take at the end, but there were several sets of steps down and Charlie was hidden from him.

Duncan took a chance, running between two sets of vehicles and a truck driver blasted his horn as Duncan ran out in front of him and took off down the passage. "Hey!" a man, making his way up from the car park below, shouted at him as Duncan hustled between him and his children, but Duncan was unrepentant.

The passage opened up into a long-stay visitors' car park, utilised by cars and coachloads of tourists, which wrapped around a shallow inlet of Loch Portree. The tide was out, revealing the mud and seaweed of the inlet, the smell carrying on the breeze. The sun glinted from the shallows and Duncan looked to his left and right. There was another set of steeper steps back up to the main road a hundred feet away but even the most athletic people would struggle to have run up those in the time Charlie had. And Charlie Lumsden was far from a picture of health.

The access road down to the car park was to his right and a fleeing figure would be easily visible in the open expanse of ground. Directly in front of him was the waterfront, wrapping around to the headland. There were blocks of flats, three storeys high overlooking the area, but there was no sign of Charlie. He couldn't have got too far. Duncan gambled and set off at a run to his left, heading for Bayfield Road on the far side of the car park.

This was barely more than a track, accessed from the newer car-parking facilities, which ran down between a mixture of old garages and ramshackle shacks, lined with corrugated steel sheeting, leading to a line of stone terraced houses once inhabited by local fishermen. Crossing the distance, Duncan pocketed his mobile and as he rounded the corner of the first building, he caught sight of Charlie, doubled over, hands resting on his knees and panting hard.

"Charlie!" Duncan yelled and that only spurred the man into action. Seemingly gaining a second wind, Charlie took off in the opposite direction. "Me and my big mouth!" Duncan muttered, giving chase.

The road surface was pitted and uneven, Charlie stumbling as he fled. Their route brought them close to the water's edge where a number of old fishing boats had been pulled up onto dry land, several looking like they hadn't touched water in years. Charlie rounded the next bend, slipping on the wet earth and tumbling to the ground.

Duncan wasn't close enough to take advantage and Charlie got back to his feet and set off again like a gazelle. Duncan couldn't believe how much pace he had in his legs, feeling his own becoming more leaden with each step. He was breathing hard but he also knew Charlie was running deeper onto the headland. The houses lining the banks of the bay were built in front of the hillside and unless Charlie was good at climbing, he was going to run out of road soon enough.

Unfazed, Charlie stumbled on but as Duncan tired, so did he. The length of his strides began to shorten and he slowed, Duncan gaining ground as the minutes passed. Before long, Charlie pulled up beside the foundations of a partially constructed home at the end of the road. The tide was out, and if he was so inclined, Charlie could continue on where the road terminated but he'd have to clamber over rocks and make his way around the headland to the harbour or ascend a steep, tree-lined embankment to his left.

Evidently, Charlie wasn't up for that. He turned, facing Duncan, doubled over and breathing heavily.

"Fancy... meeting you here," Duncan said, between deep intakes of breath, hands on his knees, grimacing.

"Just out... for a bit of a jog," Charlie said, perspiring heavily. "I think that was a personal best I just did there." He was clutching his side with his left hand, probably suffering from a stitch.

Duncan ambled up to him, shaking his head. "Why did you run?"

Charlie sniffed, wiping his runny nose with the heel of his hand. "Why did you chase me?" he retorted through gritted teeth.

"Lorna is worried about you."

Charlie waved his comment aside. "She's a worrier, that's for sure, but I can take care of myself."

Duncan righted himself, still breathing heavily and standing on shaky legs. He was comfortable with his stamina levels but, clearly, he needed to do a bit more work on his cardio fitness. "Why did you take yourself off, Charlie?"

He shrugged. "A man in my line of work... needs to stay out of the public eye."

"The public eye? What do you think you are, an influencer or something?"

"I've got a million subscribers on YouTube," Charlie said, smiling weakly. Duncan arched his eyebrows. Charlie relented. "All right... I'm not on YouTube. It's just... being on the police's radar isn't good for me, you know? It keeps people away."

"Customers, you mean?"

"Everyone," Charlie said. "It's bad form. People can have all manner of funny ideas about what I'm up to... or what I'm saying."

"No one thinks you're a grass, Charlie. What on earth do you know about..." Duncan reflected momentarily, "anything at all?"

"Aye, you'd be surprised, Detective Inspector. Really, you would."

"Tell me about it," Duncan said.

Charlie made to speak and then hesitated, his eyes narrowing. Then his face split into a broad grin and he wagged a telling finger in Duncan's direction, trying to catch his breath. "Ah... you nearly had me there. You... you're a wily one, you are Mr McAdam."

"So... what did Alex want?"

"What's that yer say?" Charlie asked, still grimacing as he inhaled ragged gasps.

"Alex Brennan," Duncan said, thumbing over his shoulder. "You were chatting to him back there."

Charlie met Duncan's gaze with an innocent expression. "Nah... I don't know any Alex..."

"Have you had a bang to the head or something? Alex Brennan."

"I think you're mistaken—"

Duncan stepped forward, confident no one was around to see them and took hold of Charlie's coat, forcefully hauling him upright. "Stop wasting my time!" he barked, his face only inches from Charlie's. Charlie held up both hands, angling his head back from Duncan's face, fearful. Duncan released him and Charlie took a step back.

"All right, Mr McAdam... *I* was mistaken... that's what I meant to say."

"What were you talking to Brennan about?"

"He wants to get his missus something nice for her birthday—" Duncan took a step towards him and Charlie recoiled, but the sound of an approaching vehicle made Duncan hesitate. He turned to see Alistair's pick-up bouncing along the narrow road towards them. He drew up, and wound down his window, blinking in the sunshine.

"Nice day for a wee stroll, lads," he said, smiling. He switched off the engine and got out, coming to stand beside Duncan, his long coat flapping in the breeze. He cast an eye over the two men. "I don't know which of you is more out of shape."

Charlie pointed at Duncan. "Him."

"Alistair," Duncan said flatly, gesturing to Charlie, "nick him."

"What fer?" Charlie protested.

"Well, we can make a start with conspiracy to commit murder, intention to supply... maybe a section 90 offence while we're at it—"

Charlie frowned. "What the hell is a section..."

"Ninety," Duncan said. "Impeding a police officer in carrying out his duty."

"You've got to be having me on?" Charlie protested. "I've no' done any of this."

Duncan, clutching the stitch in his side, stepped forward and put a restraining hand on Charlie's upper arm, pushing him towards Alistair. "You're right, Charlie. I'm a wily one... and you can sit in a cell and have a think about what you've got yourself into and, more importantly, how you're going to get yourself out of it."

Alistair took a firm hold of him, but Charlie didn't appear to be a flight risk, seemingly resigned to his fate. Duncan made to walk away, heading back down the road. "Do you not want a lift back to the station?" Alistair said as he set off.

"No thanks. I'll walk," Duncan replied, glancing at Charlie. "I need air."

"Do you see that," Alistair said to Charlie, roughly propelling him towards his pick-up. "You've only gone and upset the man now."

"Me? He's the one chasing after me for no good reason."

"Oh, is that so," Alistair said. "Then how come you find yourself on the naughty step?" He marched Charlie towards his pick-up, one hand on his collar at the scruff of his neck. "And if you make my truck smell, I swear I'll handcuff you to the bumper and drag you back to the station."

CHAPTER THIRTY

DUNCAN WAS BREATHING HEAVILY ONCE AGAIN as he climbed the steps up towards the town centre. Halfway up to the top, he could hear a number of idling engines and the siren of an approaching ambulance. A gaggle of people were blocking the pavement at the top, watching something and Duncan wasn't surprised to see the traffic in one direction stationary and nothing was coming from his right.

Easing his way through the crowd of people, blue lights flickering in his peripheral vision, Duncan stared down the road. He could see two police cars and the ambulance pulled up a moment later having managed to get through the press of vehicles. Fraser Macdonald stood in the middle of the road, signalling to waiting drivers that they had to stay where they were, and Duncan found his curiosity piqued.

"Anyone see what happened?" Duncan asked no one in particular.

"Some guy was hit crossing the road."

Duncan made his way along the pavement, easing people aside and soon came upon the scene. The paramedics were now tending to the victim, lying in the street, his left leg bent at an angle that immediately told Duncan it had been dislocated at the hip, probably also at the knee if not broken. A pool of blood was also spreading out from beneath the body.

"Oh, hey there, sir," Fraser said, holding a hand in the air to the onlooking driver of the nearest car who may have been considering whether or not he could squeeze by the scene. "Bit of a nasty one," he said in his usual, matter-of-fact tone.

"What happened?"

"I'm not sure just yet," Fraser said. "A few conflicting accounts." He nodded towards a shocked bystander, an older man with a woman beside him who Duncan assumed was his partner, who was watching on from the nearby pavement. "Your man there says the car mounted the pavement..." he grimaced, "the poor sod didn't even see it coming, upended him and dumped him in the road."

Duncan heaved a deep sigh. "Painful."

"Aye, and that lassie over there," Fraser said, pointing to a young woman in her early twenties, "says after the car struck him, the driver behaved erratically, reversing back over him."

"Really?"

"Aye, that's what she says. The driver was probably in shock and hit the wrong pedals. You know how it is. Did you see that video clip about the Porsche driver who pressed the accelerator rather than the brake and stuffed it into a wall?" Fraser winced. "Total write off that was... must be over a hundred thousand pounds on that car—"

"Who was the driver?" Duncan asked, looking around for a vehicle with damage to the front but he couldn't see one.

"Hit and run, sir," Fraser said, shaking his head. "They'll turn themselves in tomorrow... once they've come to their senses," he said glumly, "or sobered up, which is more like it."

Duncan left Fraser to manage the growing irritation in the waiting drivers. This was the main circuitous route through Portree and up the east coast of the island. To get around this blockage would push traffic onto roads that just weren't designed for the sheer volume of vehicles that were now backed up in both directions. The town was always busy, the streets of an old fishing town were never designed for the hundreds of thousands of tourists who came to the island annually, and all of them in vehicles of one sort or another.

Ronnie was the other uniformed officer in attendance, and he'd administered first aid to the victim prior to the paramedics arriving. Duncan came to stand on his shoulder, looking down at the stricken man who was shrouded by the working medics. He was conscious though, moaning, and clearly in a significant amount of pain. His right arm was twisted awkwardly, and Duncan figured he wouldn't be leaving hospital any time soon.

"Now there's a man who's having his fair share of bad luck this week!" Ronnie said. Duncan offered him a quizzical look. Ronnie nodded at the victim. "Brennan there... and it always comes in threes, doesn't it?" he said, shaking his head. Duncan took a step to his right, Alex Brennan's face visible to him for the first time. He moved to kneel beside him, catching Alex's eye. This was too much of a coincidence.

"Alex? Can you hear me?" Duncan asked. There was a flicker of recognition, his eyes widening but he was forced to blink away blood running from a deep laceration above his right eye. "Did you see who hit you?"

Brennan groaned, tried to move his lips but whatever he was trying to say was virtually inaudible but definitely incoherent.

"Excuse me, mate, could you move back and give us space to work," one of the paramedics said.

"I'm a police officer," Duncan replied.

"Aye, and I'm a paramedic," he replied, "and you still need to move back. What's his name?"

"Alex," Duncan said. The paramedic leaned close to him.

"Alex! I'm a paramedic. Can you speak to me?" Brennan said nothing, his pupils dilating. Duncan was pretty sure he'd lost control of his vision which wasn't a good sign at all. Glancing down at the pool of blood Brennan was lying in, it was a lighter shade of crimson which was a good sign. He wasn't bleeding from any major bodily organs. If he was, the colour would be a deeper shade, closer to burgundy.

"Can you hear me, Alex? If you can, please blink for me."

Brennan's eyes didn't move at all, staring straight ahead. Duncan thought he was still conscious, just about. "Alex?" he said, raising his voice.

"Can you move back please, sir," the paramedic said, without looking at Duncan.

"I need to know who did this to him."

"Well, if you don't clear off," the medic said, offering Duncan a withering look, "you're never going to get the chance to ask him."

Duncan leaned closer. "Alex, can you tell me who did this?"

Alex Brennan's eyelids flickered this time, but he seemed on the verge of drifting into unconsciousness. Reluctantly, Duncan rose and backed away. The paramedics ignored him. They were incredibly focused with only one thing in mind, and that must have been to keep him alive. Duncan wasn't sure whether he'd make it.

Duncan beckoned Ronnie over to him. "Have a few more officers come down here to join you." His eyes swept the people nearby, all watching goings on with a morbid fascination. "I need witnesses to tell us what they saw, driver, vehicle... whether they thought it was intentional—"

"Intentional?" Ronnie asked, surprised.

"Aye, did they mean it," Duncan said. "I'll send Angus and Caitlyn down to give you a hand but keep as many of these people here as you can."

"Who'd want to run him over?"

Duncan exhaled deeply. "Like Fraser just said to me, he's having a bad week. Either he's the unluckiest man on the island or someone's out to get him."

Duncan walked back towards the intersection where cars pulled out of Somerled Square, hearing two blasts of a horn coming from further down the street. He looked and saw Alistair, who had been stuck in the traffic, pull out onto the wrong side of the road and drive down towards him. Alistair pulled up alongside Duncan, winding his window down.

"What's the craic?"

"Alex Brennan... he's had an accident," Duncan said and immediately looked at Charlie in the passenger seat who averted his eyes from Duncan's.

"Is it serious?"

Duncan cocked his head. "Aye, it's not good." He pointed a casual finger at Charlie Lumsden. "Keep him in a cell. I'm going to speak to him later." Alistair must have picked up something from Duncan's tone because he nodded solemnly.

"Don't worry, we'll get him tucked up in his own private room, a wee stainless-steel toilet in the corner, and a plastic sheet for his mattress. He'll love it."

Charlie glared at Alistair who shot him a warm smile in return.

"Good. You'll be back in ops before I am," Duncan said. "Have Angus and Caitlyn come down here and give Fraser and Robbie a hand."

"Doing what?"

"I want to know exactly what happened to Alex Brennan."

Duncan looked up and down the street, spotting CCTV cameras mounted on a couple of buildings. "Have them obtain the camera footage too."

"You don't think it was an accident, do you?"

"No, Alistair. I don't."

Duncan stepped out of the road, indicating for two vehicles to back up a little to make room for Alistair, who took the left turn into Somerled Square. The paramedics were still working on Alex in the street, moving with some urgency now which indicated to Duncan that his condition was worsening. With so many broken bones they would normally take a lot of time to stabilise someone before risking moving them, just in case they made his injuries worse.

However, on this occasion, getting him to a hospital as soon as possible was probably the lesser of two evils. Fraser acknowledged him with a nod and Duncan rounded the corner and made his way back to the police station.

Duncan's mobile rang and he answered it just as a bus started its engines, preparing to leave the bus station in front of the station. He had to press one hand against his free ear to hear the caller.

"DI McAdam?"

"Yes, who is this?" he asked, hurrying to get into the sanctuary of the station foyer and away from the rumble of the diesel engine.

"It's Kara," she said. "Kara McGarrell."

Duncan stopped in the foyer, his mind whirring as he detected nerves in her tone. "What can I do for you, Kara?"

"I... I'm worried about my husband, James."

"What's happened?"

"After you left our house earlier... James and I... we had..." she drew a deep breath and he thought her voice might crack, "an open and frank conversation," she said, almost with a shudder. He could picture her anxiously pacing her kitchen as she talked.

"Your husband knows?" Duncan asked. "About your relationship with Alex?"

"Yes, he does. I told him." He could hear her breath being drawn in in short intakes. She was emotional.

"Where is James now?" Duncan asked.

"I don't know. He left... and I'm worried he's going to see them."

"Them?"

"Alex and Niamh. You see..." she paused, and Duncan thought she might break down, "Niamh knew as well. In a way... she sort of condoned it."

"I thought you were all friends," Duncan said.

"Don't get me wrong, I don't think she was necessarily happy about it, but... she couldn't meet Alex's needs... and I could. It made Alex happy and, weird as it might sound, that made her happy. If you follow?"

Duncan found it odd, but then adult relationships could be odd, and he'd met plenty of people who lived lives outside of the norm over the years. "I see. James... he's as unhappy with Niamh as he is with Alex?"

"Yes, I think so. James and Niamh... they were an item once, a long time ago when they were teenagers, back before she left the island."

Duncan thought about the accident Brennan just suffered and couldn't help but wonder where James McGarrell was at that time. "When did James leave yours, do you remember?"

"Um... three quarters of an hour ago... maybe a bit more..."

Duncan sensed she was holding back. "Kara, what is it?"

"I-I... I called Niamh. I thought it best to warn her but...

she's not picking up, at home or on her mobile. I think James might have done something stupid."

"Okay, try not to worry," Duncan said.

"Should I go over to the Maelrubha... see if I can find Niamh and maybe intercept James if he goes there?"

"No, stay where you are," Duncan said, making his way through the station and out towards the rear compound where his car was parked. "If James comes home, I want you to call me straight away." Kara didn't speak and Duncan stopped where he was in the corridor, acknowledging the greeting of a passing uniformed colleague. "Kara... you being there might inflame matters. I need you to stay put. Can you do that for me?"

"Yes... I can do that."

Duncan hung up, then resumed his course to where his car was parked, picking up the pace.

CHAPTER THIRTY-ONE

DUNCAN SAT IN HIS CAR, mobile pressed against his ear but the call went unanswered, eventually diverting to voicemail. He put the phone down and started the car, drawing his seat belt across his chest as he reversed out of the space and drove to the side gate. The gates were already opening and he allowed a liveried van to enter, waving to the driver as it passed him, and then he left the station.

His mobile was connected to the car now and he called Alistair. "Charlie Lumsden is tucked up in bed," he said jovially. "Now, are you going to tell me why?"

"He was talking to Alex Brennan in the street. When he clocked me looking at him, Charlie took off in one direction and Alex in the other."

"I presume he was unwilling to confide in you what they were talking about?"

"Aye, that's right. They bolted rather than let me catch them together."

"If Brennan took off running, maybe that's why he wasn't paying attention when he crossed the road," Alistair said.

"I'm not sure that's the case," Duncan replied. "I didn't

really pick up on it at the time, because I was focused on grabbing Charlie before he pulled another disappearing act, but I heard a set of tyres squealing as I chased him. That would have been around the same time as Brennan did his road-runner act."

"You mean..." Alistair said, thoughtfully, "that someone ran him over on purpose?"

"Exactly that."

"Hang on... where are you?"

"I'm on my way out to the Brennans' house. Niamh isn't answering her phone."

"Don't bother. We can have uniform take care of that—"

"No, I've just spoken to Kara McGarrell and James has gone off on one. Kara thinks he might be going after the Brennans."

"Both of them?"

"Aye, and thinking about it," Duncan said, "he might have already got to Alex."

"You reckon it was him?"

"It's possible... but then there's Tony Sinclair and his pals."

"What about them?"

"They've stuck around all week, as I asked them to, but I never thought they would keep to it, not all of them. What might motivate them to stay here?"

"To find out what happened to their pal?"

"Aye," Duncan said, negotiating a tight junction, "but they can keep abreast of things by phone or even by reading the news. Why would they have to be here?"

"To be close, just in case..." Alistair said, "we find out who was responsible."

"And what do you think they might do if they figured out who was responsible?"

Alistair sat down, exhaling deeply as he got himself

comfortable in his chair. "By that logic, if they were to think it was Alex Brennan... then they might go after him as well."

"I know," Duncan said. "If it's one or two of them who ran Brennan over, then I wouldn't be surprised if the rest of the group put up an alibi and help them clean up the car before we get to it."

Alistair seemingly sipped from a cup of tea, smacking his lips after doing so. "Then time is pressing," he said. "We'd have to get to the vehicle before they bleach it, burn it or... do whatever."

"That's one reason I'm heading over there but mainly I'm concerned about James McGarrell and what he might do."

"Not to Niamh, surely?"

"According to Kara, he and Niamh used to have a thing, so he might feel extra betrayal."

"Even so—"

"Who knows what daft things some people will do when their partner cheats on them," Duncan said, recalling finding his clothes lying in the gutter outside the West End apartment he shared with his former girlfriend when he worked down in Glasgow.

"Should I come out... or maybe I could send Russell? He's no sodding use here anyway," Alistair said, raising his voice presumably so Russell would hear him.

"No, keep everyone at it with you. Get the footage of the incident, if you can. Make sure we get as many witness statements as possible... and..."

"And?"

"Have someone go to the hospital and stand as close to Alex Brennan as they can, just in case he has something useful to say before..."

"Before he pops his clogs?"

"Aye." Duncan hoped he would be fine, but whoever had

struck him did so at some speed and with force. If the one witness was correct and the driver had then reversed the car back over him, then his internal injuries were likely to be severe.

He hung up, then dialled Niamh's phone number once more. This time, the mobile cut to voicemail within two rings. Shaking his head, Duncan ended the call without leaving a message.

The drive across the island to *Glenbrittle* took much longer than he'd expected, having to navigate the narrow roads packed with cars, camper vans, and mobile homes. Despite expanding the parking facilities at the Fairy Pools, one of the island's favourite attractions, especially during the summer, the traffic often backed up. Once away from the main road passing through from *Sligachan* to *Merkadale*, the going tended to slow significantly.

It was late in the afternoon when Duncan finally made it onto the Maelrubha Estate, driving through the gates and heading for the Brennans' cottage. Alex's blue Toyota was present, parked outside the cottage and Duncan wondered what he'd used for the drive into Portree.

He walked up to the front door and rang the bell, stepping back and peering through the nearest window for signs of movement. He didn't see any. Half expecting to hear the dog bark, he was surprised to hear no response from inside at all.

Making his way down the side of the house, Duncan looked into the Toyota, noticing a mobile phone lying on the central console. He tried the driver's door and found it unlocked. Glancing around, he saw no one about and opened the door, leaned in and cast an eye around the interior.

Picking up the mobile, he found it was locked, but when he brought up the lock screen the background image was a picture of Niamh and Alex, arm in arm, standing behind a cairn on the summit of a mountain Duncan didn't recognise. There were multiple missed-call notifications, so Duncan figured this was Niamh's and not Alex's mobile.

A set of keys were loose in the driver's side door pocket and Duncan found that odd. He picked them up, noting several keys that looked like standard house keys plus a few more that probably fitted padlocks to gates or locked rooms elsewhere on the estate. He had no authority to remove the keys and seeing as they were on the estate, with only estate staff or visitors who were likely to come by, Duncan put them back where he'd found them.

Resuming his walk to the rear of the property, Duncan entered the walled garden, half expecting to find Niamh weeding or pruning seeing as it was a hobby she seemed to care about. But she wasn't there. The rear door to the cottage was wide open and he stopped at the threshold, peering inside. He rapped his knuckles on the glass pane of the door.

"Hello! Mrs Brennan?" He waited patiently for a reply. When he received no response, Duncan tentatively entered the kitchen. Plates with partially eaten food were on a small table at one end and he saw a glass had been knocked over, spilling its contents across the tablecloth. "Hello! Niamh?" he called again, raising his voice.

When he reached the doorway into the living room, he hesitated. He had no just cause to enter the property, seeing as a crime hadn't been committed as far as he knew. Something caught his eye in his peripheral vision, at the far end of the kitchen beyond the table. Duncan slowly walked towards it, his heart sinking as he came across the still form of the Brennans' dog, lying on its side.

Duncan dropped to his haunches. At first glance he thought the creature might be asleep, his legs stretched out to the side, but the eyes were open, lifeless. He made to reach out but hesitated, seeing a shimmering liquid on the surface of the dog's fur around the neck. It was blood. Duncan withdrew his hand, heaving a sigh and reaching for his mobile.

He stood up and when Alistair answered the call, Duncan was already back outside. "How did you get on with Niamh?" Alistair asked.

"She's not here," Duncan said, "as far as I can tell." he cast an eye over the house, looking at the upstairs windows. "I'll have a look upstairs in a minute, but..."

"But what? I know that tone..."

"It's like the Marie Celeste here," Duncan said. "It's odd... and the dog is dead."

"Dead?"

"Aye, it looks like someone... strangled it with a wire or something, I don't know. They left it on the floor in the kitchen."

"That's... demented. Is there any other sign of violence?"

"No... only that... which some might argue, me included, is weird enough."

"What do you want to do?"

Duncan exhaled. "I can't do anything without more to work with. Have you had any joy with finding a witness to Brennan's accident?"

"Accident is stretching it," Alistair said. "We have two separate people who claim the car mounted the pavement and ran him over. One guy even says they must have been aiming for him because the car changed direction... twice, you know, to make sure they got him."

Duncan thought about it. "What about reversing back over him?"

"No one else has claimed that so far, but you know what people are like. They were probably on their mobiles until they heard his head hit the windscreen."

"Hmm… what about the car, did we get an index, make or model?"

"Oh aye," Alistair said. "So far we have a black minivan, with two occupants, one male, one female… a pale coloured SUV, possibly Japanese or German, depending on who you speak to… or a grey executive saloon with one or three occupants. Honestly, I despair with the general public. Someone will say JFK did it next."

Duncan sighed. "All right, listen… put the word out on James McGarrell. Maybe he's taken himself off the island and back down to Glasgow, but if his wife thinks he's after revenge then we should take it as a credible threat."

"What about Niamh?"

"I'll have a nose about the rest of the house, and then ask around the estate while I'm here. Hey, she could be having a cup of tea at a neighbour's house… but…"

"The dog?"

"Aye… and from what people have said, Niamh doesn't seem like the sociable, neighbourly sort." Duncan was about to hang up but thought of something else. "What about Alex Brennan, how's he getting on?"

"No word yet but we've sent Fraser down there. He's good at sitting about looking uninterested, but he'll keep his ears open, don't worry about that."

Duncan hung up and went back into the house. The cottage was small, little more than two rooms downstairs with a narrow hall leading to the front door. From here, there were stairs up to two bedrooms and a small bathroom. There was no sign of Niamh in any of the rooms and Duncan lingered in the largest bedroom.

Curiously, as he looked around, he could see the room had a woman's touch. It was neat and tidy with everything allotted its own place. There were two pillows on the bed, but they were stacked upon each other and positioned in the centre of the bed. The mattress also appeared to bow in the middle as if one person slept there. Duncan didn't wish to pry, although doing so did come with the warrant card, and he opened the wardrobes, casually inspecting the contents. He only found women's clothing.

Duncan was far from a clothes horse himself, but he did have enough items to fill a wardrobe. He tried the next wardrobe and, again, he found nothing that he could attribute to Alex. Moving back into the smaller bedroom, a single bed was pushed up against one wall, the headboard butting up against a radiator beneath the window.

There was one cupboard and when Duncan opened it, he found what he was looking for, a rack and shelving bearing Alex Brennan's belongings. Beneath the bed, he found a couple of slimline storage boxes containing shoes, gloves and any other items that seemingly wouldn't have a place in the cupboard including a small selection of adult magazines.

Duncan slid the storage boxes back into place and backed out of the room, making his way back downstairs, an uneasy sensation permeating his thoughts. What happened here today and just where is Niamh Brennan?

CHAPTER THIRTY-TWO

RETURNING to the front of the cottage, Duncan saw activity over at the accommodation buildings. By the look of it, the group had decided to depart. Duncan was surprised it had taken this long. He could see Neil and Ollie carrying their bags to their respective vehicles, loading them into the boot.

"Hello, Mr McAdam."

Duncan turned to see Nicol McLeod approaching. "Afternoon," he said, then nodded towards the people making ready to leave. "I see they're heading off."

"Aye, not before too long either."

Duncan glanced at him, curious. "You'll be pleased to see the back of them, then?"

Nicol snorted. "Their sort can stay away as far as I'm concerned, troublemakers, one and all."

"Aye? What kind of trouble?"

Nicol inclined his head. "Piss heads... coming up here, behaving like children," he said, shaking his head, "or criminals, depending on your standpoint."

"Criminals?"

Nicol nodded. "Getting tanked up and running about the estate in the dead of night, up to no good."

Duncan hadn't found Nicol this forthcoming when he'd spoken to him previously. In fact, it was quite the opposite, he'd been guarded. Nicol caught Duncan studying him and smiled. "I know. I should have said something before... but..." he shrugged. "You have to be careful, don't you? It's not like jobs are ten a penny in these parts."

"So why say something now? What's changed?"

"The ownership's changed," Nicol said. "From what I can gather things are going to be different on the estate going forward."

"What are they planning?"

He shrugged. "They're not going to tell the likes of me, but your man Alex Brennan has been given his marching orders. I'll wager he'll no' be the last one out either."

"So..." Duncan said casually, "what were they doing *running around the estate in the dead of night?*"

"Like I said, behaving like children, playing silly games, daring each other to do daft things."

"For example?"

Nicol wrinkled his nose. "Ah, I suppose it doesn't matter now. They dared each other to steal the most expensive item they could lay their hands on."

"What?" Duncan asked, thinking that sounded preposterous and indeed, daft.

"Aye," Nicol said, nodding towards the laird's house across from them, just about visible through a thick copse situated between the accommodation buildings and the historic property, "breaking in and thieving antiques... jewellery, and whatever else caught their fancy. Daft as a brush, all of them."

"*That's* what they were doing?"

"Aye, and all caught on the security cameras too. I mean,"

he said, smiling and shaking his head, "how thick do you have to be? I've done some silly things in the past, back when I was a teen and that, but if you're going to get up to stuff you can get into real trouble for, make it something worthwhile so when you're caught, it doesn't make you look stupid."

"When did you know about all of this?"

"Monday morning! As soon as the first staff member opened the doors... windows smashed, muddy footprints all over the place." Nicol laughed. "It was like the chimps had gone mad at the tea party."

"No one called the police," Duncan said.

Nicol laughed. "That's above my pay grade, sadly. And, like I said... jobs are hard to come by in this neck of the woods." He turned and started walking away, back to where he was working in a nearby outbuilding.

"Nicol, have you seen anything of Niamh today?"

Nicol turned; his brow creased in thought. "This morning, walking that wee dog of hers," he said, looking down towards the water's edge. "She takes the same route every morning, at the same time... creature of habit. Not seen her since, though."

"Was she okay?"

"Aye. She waved... same as usual. Why?"

"Did you see anyone hanging around the cottage?"

Nicol shook his head. "No... but I've been out on the boundary for much of the day. Why, what's going on?"

Duncan smiled. "Nothing, don't worry. If you do see her, could you let me know?"

"Aye, will do," Nicol said with a slight nod and went back to work. Duncan stood where he was, watching the stag party who'd noticed his presence. Duncan decided to have a word and walked in their direction.

The men were idly chatting as he approached them, and once Duncan was within earshot, all chatter ceased, wary eyes turned towards him. "Afternoon, gentlemen," Duncan said, his eyes drifting across all of them. Only Neil, the shy one who worked in IT, failed to meet Duncan's eye. The best man, Ollie, offered him a smile by way of greeting. Nathan also said hello, but Tony Sinclair simply nodded and, at best, it was a curt gesture. Only Ryan wasn't present. "Heading away?" Duncan asked.

"Is that why they made you a detective?" Tony asked. "Because you're good at stating the bloody obvious?"

Duncan smiled at the barb, and he was sure there was more behind it than simple banter. None of his friends laughed and all of them seemed awkward the moment Tony said it. "Yes, very good," he said simply.

"You can't keep us here," Tony said.

Duncan shrugged. "I'm not planning to. I know where to find you, if the need arises."

"Good... well," Ollie said, smiling, "I have a long drive ahead of me so..." He glanced at Tony, and they shook hands.

"I'm going to hit the road as well," Neil said, stepping across and hugging Tony. He leaned away from him but remained in the embrace. "I'm sorry about... how it's turned out. If you need to talk..."

"I'll know where to find you," Tony said. That exchange piqued Duncan's curiosity.

"May I have a quick word, Tony?" he asked. Tony Sinclair nodded, said a quick goodbye to his friend, Nathan, who was keen to get into his pick-up and be away quickly, before falling into step alongside Duncan. They walked to the edge of the turning area, Tony's friends getting into their vehicles while they looked on.

"So... what do you want?" Tony asked flatly. "I'm looking to be away soon as well."

"I know what you lot were doing in the woods that night."

Tony sighed. "Is that so?"

"High jinks... and immature," Duncan said, "but hardly something you needed to conceal from us."

Tony looked at Duncan with a wry smile. "Really? Rhodry Sinclair's son arrested for burglary... you don't think that'll shift a needle somewhere?"

"I don't know what you mean."

"Someone would use that as leverage... either your lot or one of my father's competitors."

Duncan laughed. "Don't you have a high opinion of yourself? I guess it doesn't matter now, does it?"

"No," Tony said, "you can't be arrested for stealing what's already yours..." He shrugged. "Well, your father's anyway."

"You had your father buy the estate to get you out of trouble?"

Tony scoffed. "As if! You think I had a choice in this?"

"Go on."

"DI McAdam, I've hated my father since I was thirteen, when I found out what he did for a living. I've spent most of my adult life putting as much distance as humanly possible between us..."

"And yet, here we are," Duncan said.

"Yeah, here we are."

Duncan frowned. "You might hate the man, but you can't deny he's helped you dodge a potential banana skin, however insignificant it might be. I've checked your record, you're clean. You'd have got a rap on the knuckles, at worst."

Tony laughed. "You're still thinking any of this is about me. This is about him."

Duncan tilted his head. "Children never appreciate the efforts of their parents, do they? You should be happy! You can go and get married, safe in the knowledge that I'm not going to feel your collar anytime soon."

"He didn't do me any favours," Tony said, his tone laced with bitterness. Duncan turned to face him, curious. "I've been with my fiancée a very long time... and she is well aware of the world I've come from, my father... as well as how hard I've worked to keep myself away from all of that... nonsense. So, we could have a future, a family away from that world. I've *never* asked my father for anything."

"It sounds like he wasn't listening."

Tony shook his head. "He needs people around him he can trust, and if you can't trust your family, then who can you?"

"You could stay clear," Duncan countered. "There's no need for you to go back into the fold, unless you're telling me he's blackmailing you?"

Tony laughed. "No, don't be silly. But... there was one condition attached when Sarah, my partner, agreed to marry me, to be a part of my life at all."

"Which is?"

"I can't be involved with my father in any way. The moment I am, she walks away... she's always said that."

"Well," Duncan said, looking around the grounds of the estate as the last of Tony's friends passed through the gate at the end of the drive, "I guess you're kind of involved now." He looked at Tony. "Aren't you?"

Tony took a deep breath. "Which is why the wedding's off, Detective Inspector."

Duncan arched his eyebrows. "She'll come around."

Tony laughed bitterly. "You don't know Sarah."

"I don't, that's true," he said, "but if the apple truly fell some distance from the tree... then give her a chance. She just might surprise you."

Tony looked sideways at him and nodded. "Maybe. The thing is... I know who I am and where I come from. And I can stay away... but it's always going to be there, in the background." He sighed. "Maybe the best thing for her is to be well clear of me." He exhaled glumly.

"Tell me this," Duncan said. "If you knew this was how she was likely to react, why did you even tell her?"

"About my father?"

"Aye."

Tony smiled. "If you're going to commit to another person, then you have to give yourself to them *in your entirety*, warts and all. You can't go through life keeping secrets from one another. It's not healthy... for either of you. "Goodbye, Mr McAdam," he said, offering Duncan his hand. Duncan accepted it. "You will keep me advised of what happens in Steven's case, won't you? I know you think I haven't helped, but my attitude hasn't been because I don't care," he nodded towards where his friends were last seen, "and they care, too."

Duncan nodded and Tony walked towards his car. Duncan saw an SUV parked on its own now that the others all had left. "One thing," Duncan called after him. Tony stopped and turned. "Where's Ryan?" He looked around. "I've not seen him."

Tony shrugged. "He was Steve's invite, not mine." He shrugged. "I've no idea where he is, barely seen him the last couple of days."

Duncan nodded and Tony resumed his walk to his car, getting in and not looking back. He drove away, raising his fingers from the steering in the smallest of farewell waves.

CHAPTER THIRTY-THREE

DUNCAN RETURNED TO PORTREE, parking in the rear yard of the police station and heading into the building via the custody suite. It was a busier than usual evening with several members of two shinty teams being processed inside the station. Tempers were flared, and Duncan had to move through the press as the custody sergeant sought to maintain order.

"What's this all about?" Duncan asked the nearest officer who wasn't occupied, standing on the periphery watching proceedings.

"A reserve team match... supposed to be a friendly, but not a lot friendly about it."

Duncan smiled. It was a great game, one of the few sports he'd really enjoyed as a teenager, a cross between hockey and open clan warfare. However, Duncan hadn't heard of arrests being made at a match before. If there were issues, then they tended to be settled during the game on the field of play, if not in the car park after the match.

"Sir!"

Duncan turned to see one of the civilian desk clerks trying to get his attention. "What is it?"

"There's someone to see you at the front desk."

Duncan changed course and made the short walk across the station to the foyer where a dishevelled figure waited for him, hand braced against the counter, standing on unsteady feet. Duncan could smell alcohol on him as soon as he entered the foyer.

James McGarrell met Duncan's eye and then lowered his gaze to the floor.

"Mr McGarrell," Duncan said. "We've had an eye out for you."

James nodded, lifting his eyes which were bloodshot, the skin around them red and puffy. He'd been crying, a lot. "I know," he said quietly, slowly swaying. Duncan wondered if he was about to fall over.

"Do you think you should sit down?" Duncan asked him.

James cackled at the suggestion. "If I let go of this..." he looked at the counter, "then I'll be on the floor."

He was in a right state. Duncan guessed he'd been on the sauce for much of the day. He wouldn't be fit to interview for hours, perhaps not until the following day. "Come on, we'd better get you somewhere to put your head down." Duncan took him by the upper arm and made to guide him through the station to the custody suite. He might not sleep very well with a cell block packed with irate shinty players, but at least he'd have somewhere safe to sleep it off.

"I didn't set out to hurt him," James said as he shuffled forward, Duncan's grip all that stopped him from pitching forward.

"What's that?"

"Alex..." he said, sheepishly. "I only wanted to have it out with him..."

"You're in no fit state to tell me what happened," Duncan

told him, knowing anything he said wouldn't be admissible in court due to his intoxication. "Save it until later."

"No," James said, trying to pull his arm away from Duncan's grasp. "You don't understand."

"What?" Duncan asked, refusing to let him go because he was all that was keeping James from winding up face down on the floor.

"He *betrayed* me," James said. "Me! His best pal... and he's been carrying on with my wife!"

Duncan nodded. "Not a reason to run him over though, is it?"

"He deserved it... but I lost my mind when I saw him... and... and I just put my foot down."

Duncan nodded. That was one question answered at least. James had made a snap decision, so he claims, and now he'd be facing charges. It could even be a murder charge if Alex Brennan didn't make it through.

"Save it, and we'll speak later," Duncan said, hauling him through the door. They could hear shouting coming from the custody suite and James seemed startled.

"W-where are we going?" he asked, fearfully.

"To put you somewhere safe," Duncan said.

"Can you... call my wife and—"

"I'll let Kara know you're here," Duncan said. They reached the booking desk, and it was still three deep with a couple of players looking to reignite whatever it was that had seen them detained in the first place. Duncan caught the sergeant's eye and gestured to James McGarrell beside him. The sergeant rolled his eyes, elbowed a constable beside him and yelled to Duncan.

"Cell two! And I'll get to him when I can."

Duncan steered James around the gaggle of people, meeting the constable who held the keys to the cells. He walked James to the door of cell number two and handed him off to the constable who would remove James's belt, shoelaces and anything else he might be able to use to fashion a noose to hang himself with.

"Where do you have Charlie?" Duncan asked the constable who was helping James sit down on the bench, lined with a thin plastic-covered mattress that doubled as a sleeping pallet.

"Lumsden? He's in four."

"Can I have a word with him?"

The constable nodded and handed Duncan his keys. Duncan crossed the narrow corridor, opening the viewing slot of Charlie's cell. He was sitting at the far end of the twelve foot by six foot cell, knees hugged to his chest. His eyes lifted to the door as Duncan peered through the slot at him, but he didn't flinch, even when Duncan unlocked it and opened the door wide.

"It's about damn time you came to see me," Charlie said. "It's turned into a circus down here... and now they've sent me a clown!"

Duncan smiled. He'd been called far worse. "I let Lorna know where you are," he said.

Charlie's mood lifted slightly. "Thanks. Is she okay?"

"A wee bit annoyed with you, I reckon, but aye."

Charlie nodded glumly. "I'll be for it when I get home, that's for sure."

"Do you want to go home?"

"Aye, of course."

"Good," Duncan said. "I think my custody sergeant needs the space."

Charlie's eyes narrowed. "I can go?"

"Aye," Duncan said, leaning against the wall, arms folded across his chest.

"What's the catch?"

"You have to tell me what Brennan wanted from you. More drugs?" Charlie rolled his eyes. "Come on, Charlie. You want to go home and, quite frankly, I'm sick of dealing with you. Tell me what's going on, and we can both crack on with our lives."

Charlie pursed his lips, glancing around the cell. He was no stranger to a police cell, but he couldn't be comfortable with having been cooped up for much of the day. Charlie Lumsden wasn't the sort to find incarceration easy. Clearly, having weighed up his options, he relented, nodding. "What do you want to know?"

"What was Alex Brennan doing with you today... and how did he find you when your own missus couldn't?"

Charlie laughed. "I called Niamh... and Alex picked up."

"Why?"

Charlie frowned. "Because he picked up her mobile, I suppose—"

"No, why did you call Niamh?" Duncan asked.

"Ah... we go way back. I was at school with her back in the day, you know?"

"Why were you calling her in the first place?"

"Because..."

"Come on, Charlie, out with it."

He sighed, lifting his eyes to the ceiling in resignation. "Because I wanted to know what she'd done with... with the drugs I sold... no," he held up a hand, "gave... her. That's right, the drugs *I gave her*."

Duncan was taken aback. "The drugs?"

"Aye... after you and Mr MacEachran kicked my door down—"

"Lorna let us in, but whatever story you tell yourself is fine."

"Ah, right... aye, that was it." He shrugged. "Anyway... I

knew it was likely to kick off at some point, so I figured I'd make myself scarce for a bit."

"We spoke to you... and so you took off, with no idea why you should?" Duncan asked. Charlie nodded. Duncan guessed it was a logical course of action... if you were a bit of a smack head. "And you're telling me, now, that you sold—"

"Gave!"

"I don't care if you're dealing," Duncan said. "You gave drugs to... Niamh, and not Alex?"

Charlie nodded firmly. "Aye."

"Then why did you say you were with Alex when we asked you?"

Charlie snorted. "I didnae! *You* said it was Alex, I just... didn't correct you."

Duncan relived the moment in his mind, and had to admit, Charlie's recollection was accurate. "So why didn't you tell us?"

"And grass on a mate? Are yous serious?"

Duncan exhaled, shaking his head. "What did she take off you?"

Charlie didn't seem happy to provide information, but he still did. "A roofie... nothing heavy."

"Rohypnol?" Duncan asked and Charlie nodded. "Why would Niamh want a date-rape drug?"

"I have no idea, Detective Inspector," Charlie said. "Maybe she was tired of Alex's advances and wanted a night off... maybe he won't let her have the remote for the telly..." He shrugged. "I've no idea, but... she asked, and I could help." He folded his arms across his chest, his demeanour much brighter now he'd shared his secret perhaps. "What she was up to, I don't know." He smiled. "Can I go home now?"

"No. What did Alex want when you met him this morning?"

"Same as you," he replied. "Answers."

"To why you gave her drugs?"

Charlie shook his head. "No, he wanted to know why she wanted them. And I'll tell you exactly what I was trying to tell him earlier... I don't know."

Duncan studied him, trying to gauge his honesty. It was true you couldn't trust a junkie like Charlie as far as you could throw him, but in this case, he seemed very much like he was on the level. "I believe you. Thanks, Charlie."

"Can I please go home now?" Charlie asked as two men began singing as they were led past the door to be put in the cell adjacent to Charlie's. "Please!" he implored Duncan, grimacing as the singing, which was dreadful, went up several octaves.

"No," Duncan said, stepping out and closing the door behind him. A moment later he heard Charlie throw himself against the cast iron door, hammering on it with his fists.

"Let me out! I can't stay in here any longer!"

Duncan opened the viewing slot as he handed the keys off to the constable beside him. Charlie looked utterly dejected, glaring at him.

"Sit tight, Charlie," Duncan said. "I'll phone in a pizza for you." He closed the flap and turned to the constable beside him. "Get him a cup of tea and a bag of crisps, would you?"

"Will do, sir," the constable said with a smile.

Duncan left the custody suite, taking out his mobile as he walked. The booking desk was still occupied but the number of people waiting to be processed had already halved, but it was still noisy. In the corridor, Duncan called Dr Dunbar. He answered swiftly.

"Duncan! What can I do for you?"

"Have you got a moment?" Duncan asked.

"Of course," Dunbar said. "I'm just in the off licence selecting a bottle of red... but ask away."

"Rohypnol," Duncan said. "If you take it... you become drowsy, slip into unconsciousness..."

"Once ingested the effects are almost immediate. The drug quickly crosses from the blood and binds to specific receptors in the brain. The individual under the influence is likely to experience sensations of intense drowsiness, impaired motor skills... and memory loss, of course."

"Would you detect that in a toxicology screening?"

"In the Phelps case?"

"Aye," Duncan said. "Is it possible?"

"Well... yes, it would show in the test results if it were searched for. But I didn't run that test. There were no signs on his body of him being victim to a male rape, so..."

"I understand. Could you check?"

"No can do, I'm afraid. The reason it's such a popular sedative in so-called date rapes, is because it doesn't last long in the victim's system."

"How long?"

"Hard to say with any degree of accuracy. Sixty to seventy hours... perhaps more or less, depending on the person's physiology, and how much they ingest—"

"I'm thinking it couldn't be a lot, because it's Steven Phelps we are talking about, and he was a big guy."

"Yes," Dr Dunbar said, "I agree. If you were to knock him out then he'd stay where he fell... a small dose, however, would make him pliable and, I dare say, more amenable to whatever you wanted him to do."

"Which would explain how he could be overcome without being physically subdued," Duncan said.

"Indeed," Dunbar said.

"Could he still be able to move under his own steam, so to

speak? I mean, if someone drugged him but also needed him to walk, for instance."

"I dare say so, yes. If the dosage was enough to make him amenable without completely subduing his consciousness. It would be a delicate balance. But who would want to do such a thing?"

"That's the question," Duncan said, "along with why."

"I do apologise," Dr Dunbar said. "If I missed something significant."

"Don't worry, Craig," Duncan told him. "It's the last direction I anticipated this case to take as well, but it's only a theory at this point."

"Dear me..." Dr Dunbar said quietly, sounding deflated as Duncan hung up. Duncan quickened his pace, mounting the stairs up to the ops room, taking them two at a time.

CHAPTER THIRTY-FOUR

DUNCAN ENTERED the ops room to be met by Alistair who was leaning over Russell's shoulder, looking at something on his monitor. "Here's the man himself," Alistair said. "We're just going through the files the Ministry of Defence have finally bothered to send across to us."

"Caulfield?" Duncan asked, moving to join them.

"That's right," Russell said. "It's *really* interesting!"

"Give me the abridged version because I've got something else to tell you about," Duncan said. Alistair arched one eyebrow and then patted Russell's shoulder.

"Come on, out with it." He gestured to Duncan. "This man looks ready to burst with whatever he's sitting on."

"Well, the newspapers are full of it," Russell said. "I'd read around Caulfield's suicide, as you know, but the papers got it wrong. She was based at Leconfield, but when she died, she'd been on a training course elsewhere for the previous few months. And it was this camp where the suicides and suspicious deaths took place."

"Where?" Duncan asked.

"That's the interesting part, sir," Russell said. "She was participating in the *P Company* course at—"

"Catterick," Duncan said, folding his arms across his chest.

"Aye, Catterick. The same place where Steven Phelps was an instructor."

"There's the link between those two," Duncan said. "I thought Caulfield was the Royal Logistics Corps?"

"Aye," Alistair said. "But you can join the Paras on attachment from other regiments. Prospective candidates need to complete some aspects of the paratrooper training elements, but not all of them."

Duncan moved to stand beside Russell, also looking over his shoulder. "Have you got a list of the soldiers stationed there at the time, either on... what was it you called it?"

"Attachment," Alistair said.

"Yes, I do," Russell said, glancing up at Duncan.

"Brennan. Check his name, will you?"

"Hang on," Russell said, typing his name into the search bar and hitting return. Russell shook his head. "No, no Brennans on the list."

Duncan sighed. He looked sideways at Alistair. "You said your other half worked with Niamh when she came back to the island."

"Aye," Alistair said, "so what?"

"Where had Niamh been?"

Alistair shrugged. "I don't know. I don't remember her ever talking about her past very much."

"What was her maiden name?"

Alistair's brow furrowed. "Um... Morrison... no... Murray. That was it, Murray."

Duncan patted Russell on the shoulder and pointed at the screen. Russell typed in the name and tapped return. "Well... I'll be damned," Russell said. "Niamh Murray, Lance Corporal..." He sat back in his seat, staring at the screen. "I didn't see that coming."

Duncan took a step back, a hand across his mouth absently stroking his chin with his palm. "Niamh," he said quietly. Alistair glanced at him.

"You think?"

"It was Niamh who Fraser saw with Charlie Lumsden that night. The two of them go way back. She was driving her husband's Toyota. Charlie just told me downstairs." Alistair was about to protest, much as Duncan had done, he suspected. "We assumed it was Alex... but it was her."

"Then... Niamh probably knows Phelps," Alistair said.

"Not only... she was the sentry who discovered Caulfield's body... and," Russell said, "she made an allegation against Phelps in the weeks post Caulfield's suicide." He pointed to a copy of a document he'd brought up on the screen. "Although the investigations concluded there was a culture of bullying and misogynistic behaviour at the Catterick camp, and significant failures within the leadership team at all levels... it was concluded that the privates took their own lives for *undetermined reasons*," Russell said.

"What was the nature of Niamh's complaint?" Duncan asked.

Russell frowned. "Bullying, psychological and physical intimidation... and..." he looked round at Duncan, "and rape." Russell looked back at his screen. "The allegations were investigated, but no hard evidence was found, and they were discounted." Russell was reading through the summary of the report's conclusions. "A culture within the training camp had been allowed to fester in preceding months where instructors with — this is interesting — *known disciplinary and attitude deficits*, had been assembled in a training facility in order to minimise negative tendencies in the wider field of operations..." Russell arched his eyebrows.

Alistair snorted. "They dumped all the degenerates into one place to keep them under control."

"And it had the exact opposite result," Duncan said. "When did Niamh leave the army?"

Russell accessed the information they had on her in the files. "Four months after this report was published," he said. "She was pensioned off on a medical discharge."

"She had a breakdown," Duncan said.

"And then, years later, Steven Phelps rolls into town," Alistair said.

"Russell, can you bring up that CCTV footage we have from the estate. You know, where Tony Sinclair's stag party are out after hours?"

"Aye. Hang on a second."

"What is your thinking?" Alistair asked Duncan.

"You remember that TV series, back when we were kids, Duncan Dares?"

"After my time, I should imagine," Alistair said. "Why?"

"They dared each other to break into the laird's house and see who could steal the most valuable item."

Alistair raised his eyebrows. "Did they now? Who won?"

Duncan shook his head. "No idea." He pointed at the footage as Russell opened the folder on his computer. "We saw them all heading off through the woods, right? From their direction of travel, I reckon they were going towards the main house, but Steven Phelps... he goes in a different direction."

Russell brought up that video file and they watched as Steven Phelps doesn't follow the same route as the others.

"Which way does he go?" Duncan asked as the three men watched. "Anyone have their bearings?"

Alistair nodded. "He's going towards the Brennans'."

"The Brennans'," Duncan said. "Why do you think he would do that?"

"He recognised her," Alistair said. "He recognised her and... went to... what? Get his revenge?"

"Attack her again?" Russell suggested. "Although, her allegation in the report doesn't name who the victims of the rapes were nor who carried them out."

Duncan met Alistair's eye and he must have seen something in Duncan's expression that concerned him. "What is it?"

"No one has seen Niamh since this morning as far as I know. I found her mobile and house keys in the car, unlocked."

"And the dog..." Alistair said, leaving the thought unfinished.

"What dog?" Russell asked.

"Get that list back up, would you please, Russell?" Duncan asked. The detective constable did as requested. "Name check, Ryan Masters."

Russell typed in the name and hit return. Ryan's name came up. "He was an instructor there as well. At the same time." Russell laughed. "Can you believe that?"

"Aye," Duncan said quietly. "What a coincidence."

Alistair smiled at Duncan, his eyes gleaming. "You think Niamh did for Steven Phelps? You cannot be serious?"

"Charlie Lumsden supplied her with a date-rape drug," Duncan said. "We know that Niamh... has issues around intimacy with her husband which is one reason he went elsewhere."

"That and he's an arsehole," Alistair said.

"I'm not arguing, but their marriage is in tatters. They're sleeping in separate rooms, Alex is straying... and now we have this," Duncan said, gesturing to the screen. "And now she's also missing... and Ryan hasn't checked out of the accommodation today along with his friends. The clothing stashed outside the Brennans' house, the gloves... if Niamh had returned in the early hours, maybe just before her husband got back from his night away at Kara's place—"

"She wouldn't have had time to get rid of it, and so she stashed it wherever she could," Alistair said. "She couldn't throw it in the water and risk it washing up on the estate an hour later."

"And Alex didn't know," Duncan reasoned, "and so when we asked for his alibi, Niamh was more than happy to give him one because it was *also* her alibi. Alex Brennan put her on the other side of the headland, away from where she really was, killing Steven Phelps. You have to admit, it's very clever. If asked, Alex would swear she was with him all night, because he didn't know any better."

"But how did she get Phelps out to the Cuillins?"

"The Brennans have a boat," Duncan said, "but we only saw the trailer in the barn they use as a garage and storage unit. Remember? If you're even barely competent then you'd be able to pilot a rib from Culnamean across Loch Brittle and around the headland to Coruisk, even in the dark. You just keep the land mass on your left and you can't miss it. She would never even have to set foot on land until she reached the jetty at Coruisk, using the memorial hut as a landmark. It's painted white. It's pretty much a lighthouse at close quarters. No one would have seen you or heard you. Pretty much perfect."

"How do the gloves play into this?"

Duncan wasn't sure. "Were they the gloves she was wearing when she found her friend, Sharon? Poetic justice, or something similar? I've no idea."

"And Phelps wouldn't have something to say about this?" Alistair asked.

"Rohypnol is a date-rape drug for good reason," Duncan said. "In small doses it can leave you open to suggestion, at the very least. You don't have to be out cold."

"Well... if Phelps recognised her, then Ryan would be likely to as well, right?" Alistair asked.

"And if we've put it together, then..." Duncan left the comment unfinished. "Where would he take her, do you think?"

Alistair went to stand in front of the information boards where a map of the area was on display, coloured pins indicating where Phelps's body was found along with every other point of note in the investigation. "Well, let's be logical and pragmatic, much like a military mind would be."

Duncan came to stand alongside him. "If he's abducted her..."

"Or she, him," Alistair said. "She got away with it once."

"Or she, him," Duncan repeated, staring at the map. "They would be facing the same problems as Niamh potentially did with Steven Phelps previously. How do they get away from the estate unseen? And to a place where they could dispose of a body where it wouldn't be found for some time—"

"Giving them the opportunity to get away," Alistair said.

Duncan snorted. "You'd do the same thing again, wouldn't you?" he asked, checking his watch. "The same parameters exist. You don't want witnesses, and there's no one around on the headland at this time to see you. The last boat trips would have collected the visitors from the foothills of the mountains by now and anyone hiking around the bay would be long gone."

"And no one will return to Coruisk until first thing tomorrow morning," Alistair said.

"By boat, to the Cuillins," Duncan said confidently.

"Aye," Alistair said, tapping the map with his forefinger. "The Cuillins."

CHAPTER THIRTY-FIVE

"ARE you sure this is a good idea?" Duncan briefly looked sideways at Alistair, smiled and cracked the door open. The wind hit him as soon as he got out of Alistair's pick-up and he drew his coat around him, fastening it tightly. Roddy Mcintyre's boat bobbed in the swell of the tidal loch despite being securely moored at the jetty. Duncan could see Roddy at the helm, waiting for them.

The police presence and the manner of their arrival had been deliberately low key, three cars including as many uniformed officers as could be spared had accompanied his CID team. There were no lights and no sirens. This scenario required stealth. Back in Glasgow, Duncan would have requested aerial cover, but they had no chance of raising a police support helicopter for the islands, and private operators had no licence to fly in after dark.

Duncan felt the first few spots of rain on his face. Turning towards the mighty Cuillin range, he could see what was left of the sunset, a faint glow framing the mountains to the west of them across the water. This side of the Cuillins was already in darkness and by the time they made landfall at Coruisk, night would have truly fallen.

"Come on," he said to Alistair and his DS beckoned for the small party to make their way along the quayside to board Roddy's boat. The young skipper met them as they climbed over the gunwale, nodding curtly to Duncan as he boarded the vessel, followed by Alistair, Angus, Caitlyn and the uniformed officers, Ronnie Macdonald being the most senior.

"The weather is closing in on us," Roddy said to Duncan, taking him aside. "It'll make for a rough crossing."

Duncan looked out across the water towards the headland, peering into the darkness. The clouds were already starting to black out what was left of the glow he'd admired only moments previously. "How quickly can you get us across?"

"Three quarters of an hour," Roddy said, inclining his head. "If I push it, maybe a bit less. It might be better to wait until the morning though."

Duncan met Roddy's eye. "By tomorrow morning, someone will be dead."

Roddy nodded. "It's your call." He returned to the helm, signalling to his crew waiting at the bow and stern to cast off. Soon enough, the idling engines roared into life and the boat pulled away from the quay. Duncan was standing close to the wheelhouse, both hands holding tightly to anything solid.

No one spoke as they made their way out into the loch, and Roddy was right about the swell. Judging by the faces around him, Duncan could see no one was enjoying this trip. Alistair clung to the boat's superstructure, the whites of his knuckles visible, his expression fixed. Sea spray blew across them and Alistair leaned in towards Duncan, raising his voice to be heard above the sound of the engines and the water crashing around them. "Are you sure this is a good idea?"

Duncan smiled, Alistair returning it with a rueful grin of his own. "You'll find your sea legs soon enough!"

"Aye, I'm more worried about getting wet feet!" Alistair said as the boat lurched to the left and several people groaned or murmured their displeasure. "Any chance I can stamp my card early?"

"You?" Duncan asked. "Retire? You'd be bored witless in a matter of days."

"Aye, but I'll not drown, will I?" Alistair smiled, but it was forced. He wasn't enjoying the ride any more than the others. Angus, in particular, looked distinctly queasy and his colleagues had shifted away from him just in case he brought up the contents of his stomach. "And I reckon Kermit there will say the same," Alistair said, nodding towards the DC.

Further conversation didn't happen until they approached Coruisk and the shallower waters around the landing jetty eased the aggression of the waves. Duncan mounted the ladder to the wheelhouse, Alistair joining him beside Roddy.

"Well, we're not the only ones here," Roddy said, glancing at Duncan. A rigid inflatable boat was moored at the jetty. Roddy expertly brought them alongside and Duncan hung out of the wheelhouse, looking down on the vessel. Slightly more than twenty feet long, it was jet black, with four visible upright seats and powered by two mercury outboard engines.

One of Roddy's crew climbed onto the jetty and secured the bow of the boat in place, while Caitlyn nimbly stepped across onto the RIB. She made a quick sweep of the vessel but there was no one aboard. Something caught her attention and she knelt at this point, using a torch to illuminate the area.

"What is it?" Duncan asked.

She held up her hand, visible in the light of the torch. "I think... it's blood."

Duncan exchanged a quick look with Alistair and the latter

climbed down, then stepped across to join Caitlyn on the RIB. It took him only a moment for him to draw the same conclusion. Duncan ordered his team to disembark and then he approached Roddy. "I don't want you staying here." Roddy didn't argue. Clearly, he wasn't keen to hang around if there was a potential killer lurking nearby. "I know it's rough, but can you drop anchor out in the bay, and I'll call you when we're ready to be picked up?"

Roddy angled his head, looking out into the inky blackness. "I can... but there's no mobile signal out here." He tore a sheet of paper from a notebook, scribbling some numbers on it before handing it to Duncan. "This is the radio frequency we use on the boat. You can use your police radios to contact me."

"Okay, thanks."

Duncan turned to leave but Roddy tapped his arm, stopping him. He opened the lid of a storage compartment to the right of the wheel, taking out a flare gun and a couple of flares. "Worst case scenario, pop one of these up and I'll bring the boat back in."

He passed them to Duncan, who nodded appreciatively. He'd never been a fan of handguns, in any form, and once he was clear of the boat, he handed the flares and the gun off to Alistair. His DS had no such concerns, pocketing the flares and slipping the gun inside his coat. The crewman cast off the guide rope and leapt back onto the boat as Roddy applied power to the engines, guiding the boat away from its mooring.

"And there goes our ride," Alistair said quietly, waving to Roddy as the boat slipped away. He turned and looked up at the mountain towering above them, dark and foreboding. "We should have waited for Willie and his team."

Alistair was referring to his friend, Willie Maciver, who led the mountain search and rescue team for the island.

"Well, we're here now," Duncan said, "and we'll have to

make do. Unless you think we should leave it to our man's sense of right and wrong when it comes to Niamh?"

"I'm just saying," Alistair said. "Running around the mountain in the dark is asking for trouble."

"We'll split into three teams and take the established paths," Duncan said. "Take it slow and steady... if anyone runs into any drama, we'll converge on that point and deal with it."

"I'm on board, don't worry about that," Alistair said. "I was just saying."

The team assembled a short distance away from the sound of crashing waves but the salty spray, thrown up onto the breeze, still drove across them. Duncan split the group up. Angus would take two uniformed constables on the walking route around the loch. A full circuit, roughly four miles, would take three to four hours in daylight. A second team of officers, led by Caitlyn, would make their way up towards Sgùrr Alasdair, while Duncan and Alistair would go as a pair to climb the nearest, and most accessible peak, Sgùrr nan Eag.

Duncan figured this would be the most likely candidate if they had indeed gone towards higher ground. On a normal hike, they would ascend Coire a Ghrunnda first and then walk along the ridge to Sgùrr nan Eag, but Duncan figured making this extra climb was unnecessary, bearing in mind what little time he felt they had available to them. The route they would take tonight would be more arduous – dangerous even – but it made sense to him.

Sgùrr Alasdair was the highest peak of the Black Cuillin range, and to force march someone up it, especially at night, would be difficult to say the least. To Duncan's mind, if the idea was to replicate the fate of Steven Phelps, then Sgùrr nan Eag was their best bet.

Everyone was given strict instructions not to engage unless they considered it absolutely necessary, but rather they should contact the other teams and take the suspect down together. Duncan was very clear that they didn't know what they were walking into, and everyone should keep an open mind. It was possible Niamh Brennan was the antagonist on this occasion.

Each team was equipped with a radio and head torches to enable them to see the terrain they had to cross. To do so blind would be foolhardy, although the trade-off was lack of concealment. Whatever they were walking into, it was likely that they would be seen coming, and from quite some distance.

"Remember, open communications and check in every thirty minutes," Duncan said as they all made ready to depart. The peaks of the surrounding mountains were shrouded in low cloud now, and a sea mist was drifting across the loch reducing visibility even further.

"As if things couldn't get any creepier," Alistair said once he and Duncan were alone, beginning their ascent.

He was right. There was something about this part of the island. Once clear of the water, the never-ending quiet and stillness was only punctuated by the ripple of streams passing through the rocky landscape nearby, heard but not seen in the gloom. There was a wild, eternal and inhuman feeling to the landscape which was almost palpable.

"Do you know why so many stories and songs are written about this place?" Alistair asked, as they climbed.

"Why's that?" Duncan asked, finding the going tough and breathing heavily. The mountain range was formed from gabbro, jagged peaks and loose scree making up the slopes on either side of a ridge stretching for miles.

"They say there's a kelpie in the loch," Alistair said, referring to a mythical water-bound creature, similar to a horse, of Scottish folklore.

"Is that right?"

"Aye," Alistair said, pausing to catch his breath. "It lures people close to the banks and then hauls them down into the murky depths... to live forever at the bottom of the loch."

Duncan pulled up next to him, grimacing with the exertion of the climb. They'd been climbing for almost an hour at this point, and he was feeling the strain. "And here was me thinking I liked horses," he said, wincing. "Better check in." Slipping his small backpack off his shoulders, he moved it around in front of him and reached inside for the radio. Just then, a scream tore through the glen, deadened by the mist hanging in the air around them, the tortured howl seemed to linger before an eerie silence resumed.

Both Alistair and Duncan stared ahead of them, up the trail, seeking a reference point. However, pinpointing the direction of where it had originated was nigh on impossible. The beams from their head torches reflected back at them, perversely reducing their visibility rather than helping them to see farther ahead. They listened keenly but no further sound carried to them.

"Well," Alistair whispered, angling his head down to minimise the risk of giving away their exact position, "I think it safe to say we're probably on the right track... Do we call it in?"

Duncan crouched low, turning off his torch and Alistair did the same. He had no way to determine how close they were to their quarry or if their approach had been seen. The cloud line had dropped towards them and that, coupled with the dense mist, meant visibility had been cut to barely thirty feet in every direction, sometimes more and at others, less, as the mist swirled around them.

The slope was steep at this point and would remain so until they approached the summit or intercepted the ridge line above. There were plenty of natural obstacles to mask their approach, but that advantage worked for their adversary too. Duncan considered their next move. If he called the other two teams towards them, it could be close to two hours before they would regroup, and likely longer as the teams were on their own routes.

The chances of missing one another, probable in these conditions, could see several officers blundering around on the mountain, falling foul of the treacherous terrain. Not least, active communication would give away their position and Duncan didn't know where the threat originated from. Alistair may have been right with his earlier reservations.

"We wait," Duncan said quietly. "Go on alone, for now."

"So," Alistair said, "it's just you and me."

"Aye."

"Did I mention that I thought this was a bad idea?"

Duncan smiled, knowing Alistair would see it regardless of the all-encompassing darkness. "Perhaps you did, once or twice."

"Thought so." Alistair grinned, his teeth visible despite the gloom. "Just checking."

Duncan gestured for them to proceed, and Alistair took the lead, guiding them higher into the dense mist swirling all around them.

CHAPTER THIRTY-SIX

THEY'D BEEN WALKING for a further ten minutes when Alistair signalled for them to stop, dropping to his haunches as he stared into the gloom ahead. Duncan eased himself alongside Alistair, crouched over to make himself as small as possible. "What is it?" he whispered.

"Something ahead," Alistair said, keeping his voice low. "The mist parted, and I saw them. I think."

"You think? Now's not the time for hallucinating."

Alistair smiled. "They're there," he said, pointing ahead and to their right. There's an outcrop... it's flat... ish. I figure it's about two metres, projecting out, a bit like the *Bad Step*."

Alistair was referring to an outcrop that hikers had to scramble over in order to get around the bay if they were to hike back from Coruisk to Elgol. The rock there was sloping and, if wet, could prove risky to manoeuvre across for some. Duncan looked at the rock all around them, cold and damp to the touch.

A gust of wind blew across them and the mist cleared momentarily, revealing two figures. The imposing frame of

Ryan Masters was clear to see and another, slight figure, on her knees, head slumped forward, chin resting against her chest, was Niamh Brennan. Duncan tried to determine her physical state because she seemed pained, but they were rapidly shrouded in vapour seconds later.

The breeze altered direction, so much so that the smell of the two, Ryan and Niamh, carried to Duncan. Thankfully, it wasn't the other direction because it struck Duncan that Ryan wasn't aware of their presence. If he was, then he was remarkably calm. The change of the wind direction also made them easier to hear, and masked any sound Duncan or Alistair might inadvertently make.

"He deserved it!" Niamh shouted, blood running from a cut to the side of her head. Her bottom lip was also cut, although the blood appeared to have dried. The mist partially shrouded them before clearing again a moment later, and Ryan lunged forward, gripping Niamh by the throat and hauling her upright. She struggled to stand, and the sound of her choking caused panic to flare in Duncan. Niamh was on her tiptoes, Ryan face to face with her, barely inches from one another. Her hands were bound in front of her, but Duncan couldn't see any rope or the telltale chink of metal handcuffs. She was probably secured with cable ties.

"You think so, do yer?" Ryan said, tightening his grip. Niamh, struggling to breathe, lashed out with her hands clasped together, desperately forming a closed ball with her hands. She didn't inflict any damage, pain or discomfort on her captor though. He simply grinned at her and shoved her away from him. She hit the rock beneath her hard, the back of her head making a sickening thump as she landed.

Fearful that she was about to pitch over the edge, she managed to roll and scramble back, away from the edge but that only brought her close to her tormentor, who kicked her in the stomach. Niamh screamed and doubled over, reflexively bringing her knees to her chest.

"Bitch," Ryan said. He moved to stand over her. Reaching down, he grasped a handful of hair and just as he pulled, she kicked out with her foot, striking him in the side of his knee. Ryan's leg buckled beneath his weight, and he toppled sideways. As he fell, Niamh attempted to roll away from him, but Ryan must have anticipated the action because he drove his elbow down into the small of her back. She screamed, her escape thwarted, and Ryan rolled on top of her, crushing her beneath his weight.

Duncan and Alistair were roughly forty feet away, but they were below them and to cover that ground at speed would be nigh on impossible to do without giving Ryan ample time to prepare himself. If he chose to seriously harm Niamh, he could easily do so before they were able to apprehend him. That is, *if* they could apprehend him.

Ryan got to his feet, hauling Niamh up onto her knees before backhanding his captive across the face and sending her sprawling back to the rock. She appeared to look directly at Duncan and he was certain their eyes met but she didn't acknowledge him, cry out or call for help. Ryan stood over her, snapping her head back by pulling her by the hair.

Niamh screamed as he hauled her to her feet. Alistair looked at Duncan and he must have been thinking the same, judging by his stern expression. They had to act. Alistair leaned in closer, although Duncan was confident Ryan wouldn't hear them. "I'm going to go up," Alistair said, pointing away to their left. "I'll circle back and come at him from the other side. When you give the signal, I'll come at him from above and we'll meet in the middle. Sound good?"

It was a decent plan, and Duncan looked up at the rocks above them. How Alistair was going to traverse those boulders without being seen or plummeting to his death, he didn't know but if he was confident then Duncan would let him. Alistair made to move away, peering at the rocks above and formulating his route.

"What should I use as a signal?" Duncan hissed at him. He turned back.

"How should I know?" Alistair said. "You'll think of something. Duncan wished he had the same confidence. He was also too far away to make an attempt at detaining Ryan. So, just as Alistair disappeared into the darkness, his movements becoming one with the surrounding terrain, Duncan also crept forward using any aspect of the landscape to mask his approach.

It took several minutes before Duncan felt he was in a good spot, crouched behind a jagged boulder but with a clear line of sight to where Ryan had Niamh. She was on her feet now and he had her by the collar of her jumper. She was shaking, but whether that was through fear or exposure – she was dressed in a jumper and jeans – or a combination of both, Duncan was unsure.

The mist cleared, the clouds parting at the same time revealing a crescent moon overhead. Duncan checked his watch, but he had no idea of knowing whether Alistair was in position. Ryan shoved Niamh forward and she half stumbled, righting herself at the last moment just before falling off the ledge. She gasped in fright and Ryan laughed, roughly turning her to face him.

"Is this what Steve looked like? Before you pushed him to his death?" Ryan said to her, his eyes gleaming in the reflected moonlight. He reached for her and she attempted to bat his hand away but he brushed her defence aside, taking hold of her front and dragging her towards him. He sidestepped to his left, rotating her so she was side on to the drop, pushing her over the edge but holding on just enough so she could see the drop below. "Nice, huh?" he barked, grinning.

Duncan knew he was about to throw her over the edge and, although she struggled, he had a significant weight advantage. She would never be able to overpower or resist him. That was something that only ever happened in films or television, the slight individual overcoming someone two to three times their size. In reality, the smaller individual was brutally crushed... every time.

If he was going to do anything, then it had to be now. He rose and stepped out from the shadows. "Ryan!" he yelled. Ryan, caught unawares, spun and dragged Niamh in front of him, putting her between himself and Duncan. "Let her go!" Duncan instructed. He saw Ryan look to his left and right, but seeing no one, his confidence grew.

"Why would I do that?" he asked, manhandling Niamh closer to the lip of the ledge. She gasped, sensing the imminent danger.

Duncan edged closer, extending a hand towards Ryan, palm up. "No one else has to be hurt, Ryan. Everyone can walk away from this." He felt vulnerable, his position precarious. Because, as much as he knew Niamh couldn't overcome Ryan, Duncan didn't rate his own chances much higher.

Ryan extended his arm, pushing Niamh closer to the edge, jostling her slightly. Off balance, and unable to extend her arms to distribute her weight more evenly, Niamh gasped, on the verge of panic. "Ryan!" Duncan shouted, fearing he was about to release her or push her off the ledge.

Duncan heard a thud, followed by a whoosh and a red flash shot through the air. Instinctively, Duncan ducked, but the projectile was nowhere near him. The flare struck Ryan square in the chest and he threw his arms in the air in a belated attempt to shield himself. Niamh took her opportunity and lurched away from his grasp, but lost her footing on the damp, rocky surface and pitched forward. She rolled on her shoulder and came upright, turning in time to see Ryan flapping away at the flare compounds, caught in a haze of red smoke, his clothing ignited by the elements.

"Niamh! Come to me!" Duncan yelled, but she stared at him and again, their eyes met. She didn't move, still on her knees. "Niamh!" Duncan barked, holding out his hand to her.

Ryan had patted down the smouldering points on his coat and was now focusing on Niamh. Duncan moved to intercept him as he advanced on her. Niamh, realising she was back in grave danger, went to stand but just as she did so, from the left, Duncan saw Alistair appear out of the shadows, also advancing on Ryan, who hesitated.

"Niamh!" Duncan shouted again, running towards her now. Seeing Duncan's approach, instead of moving in his direction she turned, facing Ryan. The former paratrooper seemed just as surprised by this as Duncan, and remained rooted to the spot, his eyes darting from Duncan to Alistair and back at Niamh.

Then, Niamh propelled herself forward at a run, closing the ground between her and Ryan in moments, screaming a guttural cry as she did so. Duncan opened his mouth to shout but before he could speak, she collided with Ryan and the bigger man stumbled backwards, off balance. He lost his footing and the momentum Niamh had in her assault saw both of them stumble precariously close to the edge. Ryan, eyes wide, his feet slipping on the wet stone, cast his arms out, seeking anything to hold onto. All that he found was Niamh, and she allowed him to take hold of her.

The wind dropped and an eerie silence prevailed. Duncan,

almost upon them now, Alistair descending the trail to his left, also only seconds away, came within six feet. He was close enough to hear Niamh's words... delivered with ice-cold vengeance.

"I win," she said, leaping forward, Ryan's coat firmly in her grasp, and both her and Ryan vanished from sight in the blink of an eye. Ryan cried out but the sound faded and abruptly ceased. Duncan pulled up, his shoes slipping on the surface and his legs went out from beneath him. He hit the rocky ground hard, on his backside, sliding for a couple of feet before coming to a stop, his eyes staring at the place where Niamh and Ryan had been standing only a moment ago.

Now, all he could hear was the whistling of the wind as it tore across him. Seconds before there had been nothing but silence. It was as if the mountain itself had held its breath, then exhaled as it plucked them from the ledge and hurled them both to their deaths. Alistair arrived, kneeling by his side. "Are you all right?" he asked. Duncan nodded and his colleague patted his shoulder, then hurried to the ledge.

Raising his arm, Alistair launched another flare into the sky. The glow illuminated the jagged scree slope around them, and Duncan quickly crawled over to the edge, peering down the mountainside as the flare flickered overhead, dancing in the wind.

Beneath them, he could make out two figures lying prostrate on the rocks. They were some distance apart having tumbled in different directions before being caught on the rocks that eventually broke their falls. Neither of them showed signs of life, their bodies twisted at unnatural angles, figurines reminiscent of a child's rag doll. Duncan's heart sank and he rolled onto his back, staring up into the sky as the glow from the flare flickered into nothingness.

Alistair exhaled heavily as he sank down. "I told you this wasn't a good idea."

"Aye... next time I'll listen."

Alistair snorted, shaking his head as he laid the flare gun on the rock beside him. "No, you won't."

Duncan rubbed his face with his palms. "No, you're right. I won't."

CHAPTER THIRTY-SEVEN

DUNCAN OPENED the door to his croft house, finding Grace waiting there for him. He ushered her inside out of the rain. The storm front had gathered pace and the rain had been lashing down for much of the night. "Since when have you waited outside?" Duncan asked as they walked into the open-plan kitchen.

"Well," she said looking sheepish, "I didn't really know... you know?"

He smiled. "Yeah, I know."

"You look awful!"

Duncan laughed, glancing at the clock on the wall. "Thanks. I've only had a couple of hours sleep."

"No, it's more than that," she said, her eyes narrowing as she studied him. He winced, nodding and passing a hand through his hair, allowing it to rest at the nape of his neck where he absently scratched the back of his head, stifling a yawn. "You want to tell me about it?"

"I saw two people die last night."

Grace's mouth fell open. "That's terrible. What happened?"

He gestured for her to sit down and she pulled out a chair

at the dining table. Duncan made her a cup of coffee, setting it down in front of her and taking a seat opposite. His eyelids felt heavy, his eyes grainy and he rubbed his face to refresh his appearance.

"A woman... living here on Skye was kidnapped by a man who we believe was *one of* her abusers while she served in the army, years back," Duncan said, not wanting to go into too much detail.

"Was this something to do with what's been all over the news this morning... two more deaths out on the Cuillins?"

"Aye, that's it."

"And he..."

Duncan frowned, shaking his head. "No, we got to them in time... but she chose to end it her way. For the pair of them."

"You mean, she killed him?"

"Along with herself, aye." Duncan stared straight ahead, seeing the two of them in his mind falling from the ledge as he watched, helpless.

"She... what? Planned it?"

"No," Duncan said. "I think he planned to kill her... and she took an opportunity for revenge. She was... troubled, for want of a better word."

Duncan didn't want to explain everything to Grace, how Niamh had managed to lure Steven Phelps out to Loch Coruisk with, what Duncan believed, a plan to exact her revenge on him for what he'd done to her and her friends whilst serving in the army. Dr Dunbar was confident that Phelps had been struck on the head with a hammer prior to falling to his death, but whether the fall happened immediately after the blow or he fell during an attempt to escape from her was unclear. Either way, the truth of what happened out there that night or how Phelps met his untimely death would remain a matter for speculation. Those who knew for certain were dead, and there would be no definitive conclusions to be drawn.

"Awful," Grace said. "And you witnessed this?"

He nodded. "And I had to arrest a man who murdered his best friend for sleeping with his wife."

"Sheesh! There are some *horrible people* on this island!"

Duncan smiled grimly. "A few, but thankfully, in the main, we have good people here. Mind you, it could have been worse."

Grace snorted. "How could it possibly be worse?"

"Well," Duncan said, drawing a deep breath, "I had to go to the hospital to tell another man that his wife was dead... but he'd passed himself only an hour before, so I was spared that." He arched his eyebrows, thinking of Alex Brennan. "As was he, obviously."

Grace sat open mouthed. "You're right, that would have been worse."

"So... all in all, I've had a hell of a night," Duncan said flatly, rubbing his cheeks with his palms. "And I still have to write it all up. I'm looking forward to that, as I'm sure you can imagine."

"That's one hell of a job you have there, Duncan," Grace said. He couldn't disagree. Before she could speak, he sat forward and reached across the table, taking her hands in his. She fixed him with a sceptical eye. This wasn't how he tended to behave... ever. "Duncan?"

He smiled. "Listen, I've been thinking—"

"So have I," Grace said. Duncan squeezed her hands, getting her attention. She relented. "Sorry, go on. You've been thinking..."

"Someone said something to me," Duncan paused, assembling his thoughts into a coherent pattern. He'd had this tumbling around in his head ever since they'd hiked back down the mountain during the night. His two hours of sleep had been punctuated by these thoughts but even now, he was still struggling to articulate them in his own head let alone convey them to Grace.

She leaned forward, encouraging him with an affectionate smile. "What did they say?"

"That... if you are going to commit yourself to another, then you need to be open with them," Duncan said, pensively. "That they need to see you for everything that you are. Otherwise..." he shook his head. "I think he was saying you're starting off on a lie... or as good as anyway."

"Right," Grace said, her eyes narrowing.

"I don't want you to leave for the borders," Duncan said. Grace made to speak but Duncan held up his hand and again, she held her counsel. "I'll miss you too much if you go." His brow creased in thought. "You see, I'm not afraid of committing to someone, you or anyone else—"

"Really?" she asked, arching her eyebrows. "Me *or anyone else.*"

Duncan winced. "I didn't mean that the way it sounded. I mean..." he sighed. "I don't know what I mean. Anyway, can I..."

"Please," Grace said, smiling warmly. He sensed she was enjoying this, at least a little bit.

"The other night, when you called me to the bar... because—"

"Because of Callum, the Mcinnes boy, aye."

"Yes, Callum... you did that," Duncan fixed her with a stern look, "because you were testing me. You wanted to see how I'd react around Becky and—"

"I did, and I shouldn't have. That was unfair."

Duncan waved away her comment. "I get it. You see me... and her... and you know our history – or some of it at least –

and you think I'm holding back with you, because of her. Right?"

Grace nodded. "That's very perceptive of you, Duncan. Gold star for you!"

She wasn't mocking him. Grace always tried to make light of serious situations, to deflect from her own emotional reaction. He often did the same.

"But... you don't understand why... I am the way I am, around the family," Duncan said, hesitating. Grace waited, watching him intently. "I do have a history with Becky, but I promise you that's in the past but... Callum, her son... is..."

"Is?" Grace asked, tilting her head to one side expectantly.

"Is... my son," Duncan said, lifting his eyes to meet hers. She held his gaze, her lips parting slightly. "Callum Mcinnes is my son," Duncan repeated.

Grace bit her bottom lip. "Yours? Not Davey's."

"Not Davey's, no."

Grace sat back. "Huh... well, just when I think you can't surprise me anymore, you go and do exactly that. And... Callum..."

"Doesn't know, but I suspect he's got an inkling something isn't right," Duncan said. He stood up and came around to Grace, dropping to his haunches before her.

"I do hope you're not about to propose to me, Duncan, because if you do..." her eyes flitted to the door, "I'll be out of here quick smart!"

He shook his head. "No, no, I'm not. I just want you to know I... really care about you. I want to see where this might go, but I can't promise you I'll not mess everything up at some point in the future." He smiled ruefully. "It's what I tend to do."

"Yeah, tell me about that side of you, Duncan. What's all the self-sabotage about?"

He took a deep breath. *Warts and all,* he thought to himself. "I don't ever want to be that guy who spends his entire life blaming his failings on his folks, you know?"

"Go on," Grace said, watching him.

"I grew up, me and Ros, with a ring-side seat on the car crash of a marriage that my parents endured. My old man... he liked a drink. I mean, everyone on the island likes a drink... but he took it to the next bloody level! He was a superstar when it came to the drink. And," Duncan averted his eyes from hers momentarily, "when he had a drink, he got a bit handy with his fists."

"Also, not uncommon," Grace said softly.

"Aye, and my mum used to get in between us and him, as best she could. At least, for a while she did." Grace angled her head, trying to understand just what he wasn't saying. Duncan spelled it out. "One day... she stopped getting in the way." He shrugged. "I guess it all became too much for her. I think she was so sick of it, so sick of the almost daily beating, and like the victim of a bully in the playground, she was grateful for the respite when he took it out on someone else."

Duncan swallowed hard and lifted his eyes to meet Grace's. She had tears in her eyes, her lips pursed. "He started on you?"

"And Roslyn, too," Duncan said grimly. "One thing there was going for the guy, he didn't discriminate. He'd kick the daylights out of anyone, male, female, young or old. Not anyone who could fight back, obviously. He was a coward, after all. Outside the house, away from the croft, he was everyone's pal... *the great guy who had the messed up weans,*" Duncan said, bitterly. "And so... when I was old enough... I took off. And I had no intention of coming back."

"Why did you?"

He wrinkled his nose. "Why did I? Good question."

"Do you have an answer?"

Duncan pursed his lips. "I thought I could run away from my past, but... it's not the island that's the problem. It's in my head," he said, tapping his temple with his forefinger. "And that, I take with me, everywhere I go." He met her eye. "I'm not afraid to commit... I'm afraid of what will happen if I do."

"You're not your father, Duncan."

"And yet, it's his face I see in the mirror every day."

She reached out, taking his hands in hers and squeezing them gently. "You, Duncan McAdam, are much greater than the sum of your..." she shook her head, searching for the right words, "your... DNA. I love everything that you are... and everything that you will become, good and bad."

He smiled. "Can I get that in writing? Just for future reference, you understand." She smiled back at him. "Will you stay? Turn down that job offer... and stay here with me, on the island?"

Grace sucked her bottom lip, meeting his eye. "Duncan... I—"

"Please, stay," he said. "I'll make it worth your while, somehow. We can get you a studio here on the island... we can come up with something—"

"Duncan!" she said, interrupting him. "I turned the job down this morning, before I came over here."

Duncan stood up and hauled her out of her seat, and she threw her arms around him. Duncan lifted her off the ground and spun her in the air. He set her down, keeping his hands on her waist. "Really?" he asked, and she nodded. "And you let me say all that anyway?"

She shrugged. "I tried to tell you, but... you had to keep on waffling, didn't you?"

Duncan laughed, and somehow in that moment he knew everything had changed. For the better.

FREE BOOK GIVEAWAY

Visit the author's website at **www.jmdalgliesh.com** and sign up to the VIP Club and be the first to receive news and previews of forthcoming works.

Here you can download a FREE eBook novella exclusive to club members;

Life & Death - A Hidden Norfolk novella

Never miss a new release.

No spam, ever, guaranteed. You can unsubscribe at any time.

Enjoy this book? You could make a real difference.

Because reviews are critical to the success of an author's career, if you have enjoyed this novel, please do me a massive favour by entering one onto Amazon.

Type the following link into your internet search bar to go to the Amazon page and leave a review;

http://mybook.to/JMD-skye4

If you prefer not to follow the link please visit the sales page where you purchased the title in order to leave a review.

Reviews increase visibility. Your help in leaving one would make a massive difference to this author and I would be very grateful.

A DEAD MAN ON STAFFIN BEACH

THE MISTY ISLE - BOOK 5

Publishing 2025

ALSO BY THE AUTHOR

In the Misty Isle Series
A Long Time Dead
The Dead Man of Storr
The Talisker Dead
The Cuillin Dead

In the Hidden Norfolk Series
One Lost Soul
Bury Your Past
Bury Your Past
Kill Our Sins
Tell No Tales
Hear No Evil
The Dead Call
Kill Them Cold
A Dark Sin
To Die For
Fool Me Twice
The Raven Song
Angel of Death
Dead To Me
Blood Runs Cold
Life and Death**

**FREE EBOOK - VISIT jmdalgliesh.com

ALSO BY THE AUTHOR

In the Dark Yorkshire Series

Divided House
Blacklight
The Dogs in the Street
Blood Money
Fear the Past
The Sixth Precept

Psychological Thrillers

Homewrecker

AUDIOBOOKS

In the Misty Isle Series
Read by Angus King

A Long Time Dead
The Dead Man of Storr
The Talisker Dead
The Cuillin Dead

In the Hidden Norfolk Series
Read by Greg Patmore

One Lost Soul
Bury Your Past
Kill Our Sins
Tell No Tales
Hear No Evil
The Dead Call
Kill Them Cold
A Dark Sin
To Die For
Fool Me Twice
The Raven Song
Angel of Death
Dead To Me
Blood Runs Cold

Hidden Norfolk Books 1-3

AUDIOBOOKS

In the Dark Yorkshire Series
Read by Greg Patmore

Divided House
Blacklight
The Dogs in the Street
Blood Money
Fear the Past
The Sixth Precept

Dark Yorkshire Books 1-3
Dark Yorkshire Books 4-6